GW00674552

Meeting Him

Ella Jane: Book One

Edward Green

Cover Designed by Edward Green

Paperback ISBN-13: 978-1-916638-00-6

eBook ISBN-13: 978-1-916638-01-3

Also By

Continue to follow Ella Jane's explorations in **Ella Jane Book Two: Exploring with Him**

Having moved into his hotel suite, Ella Jane stays with him for the holiday part of his time in New York, and begins to appreciate the implications of his wealth and power. She encounters more of the people in his world, and they each discover more of the other's deliciously wicked ways.

While they get to know one another, and begin to face the possibility of a longer dalliance, others manoeuvre to push them together or apart for their own ends. Be sure to pick up your copy now.

Get it here: https://mybook.to/ExploringWithHim

If you enjoyed reading about Ella Jane, you may enjoy **Meredith's Journey Begins**

Meredith Webb has built herself a pleasant, though unchallenging life, with a decent job she doesn't strive too hard at. Oh, and she has two cats she loves very much.

William Farrow on the other hand, knows there's something missing from his.

Reader Comments:

"A richly crafted journey into passion"

"Tantalisingly teasing"

"Stylish, smart and captivating! Sprinkled with moments of spine tingling awkwardness and evocativeness."

Get it here: https://mybook.to/MeredithsJourneyBegins

Trigger Warnings

This book contains:

Descriptions of sexual acts including consensual sexual violence

Forthright defences of freedom of speech and human bodily autonomy

Moderate alcohol consumption

Consumption and enjoyment of bacon, cheese and other delicacies

Exercise

Firearms possession use

People enjoying themselves in New York

New Yorkers behaving with consideration and humour

British people who've never enslaved anyone (other than consensually and with safe words in play)

A person who travels by private jet but doesn't object to others travelling by car

Contents

1. Hello, New York!   1

2. Her Dinner Companion   11

3. His room   35

4. Her Choice   65

5. His Breakfast   97

6. Their First Panel   115

7. Her Seductive Surprise   129

8. He Grants Her Wish   161

9. Her Quandary   179

10. His Diversion   187

11. Their Gifts   201

12. Her Surprise   209

13. His Invitation   223

14. Her Final Statement   229

15. Her Satisfaction   233

16. His Teasing   249

17. Her Fancy and His Fun   257

18. Her Musical Pleasure   273

19. His Question   283

20. Her Secret Reveals   289

21. Her Reward   293

22. Her Sweet Punishment   305

23. His Forgiveness   311

Credits   313

Also By   314

About Author   317

Hello, New York!

H^{ER} Ella Jane is nervous as the plane takes off. It's not the conference. It's meeting Him that concerns her, but now she's in the air and on the way to see him. He's a delegate at the conference too, so she can hardly back out of their dinner date knowing she's going to see him tomorrow anyway. She swallows, puts her head back and closes her eyes, but all that does is conjure up things he's told her he wants to do to her, and the images of favourite toys and restraints they've exchanged.

When Ella Jane's flight lands at Laguardia, she joins the line at baggage collection, waits until she sees her suitcase, then curses silently at how awkward it is for someone of her stature to lift it from the moving carousel. Having wrestled her case free, she makes her way through the airport and between those waiting for friends or staring at the phones watching their Ubers progress, to join the arm waving mob trying to match up with the legion of waiting taxis. The crowd moves quickly, and so does the wide river of bright yellow New York Cabs.

The driver's eyebrows rise when she gives her destination as the St Regis, but she's the fare. Time is money, so he says nothing, though he also makes no move to help her with her bags.

When the cab arrives, she stands on the sidewalk taking her bearings. The hotel is near the corner of Fifth Avenue and East Fifty Fifth that remains a little patch of pre-skyscraper New York, with another hotel and a huge church. Having resolved to look around after checking in, she carries her things up the steps and past doorman's strange combination of dubious expression and exquisite manners.

She drags her bag across the lobby wincing at the sound of its wheels and formulates, but doesn't verbalise, a curse when she has to manoeuvre around two businessmen in her way. One of them manages to double her irritation by giving her the eye having failed to notice her until it was too late to be useful. So she gives him a 'not if you were the last man on earth and had pizza' look in lieu of a richly deserved earful before moving on with her heavy bag.

After a moment waiting at the reception desk, she clears her throat and a moment later an employee looks up from the screen he had been browsing. "Can I help you?"

"Yes, I have a room reserved. Ella Jane Tyler."

He looks up her details, gives her the key, and directions to her room. Then he wishes her a good day and goes back to whatever had been more important than a customer thirty seconds beforehand.

The room is plush. Not just plush compared to her student accommodation or her room at her parents' house, but brochure plush. So much so that, having unpacked and hung her suit and her two good dresses, she tucks her suitcase out of sight at the bottom of the wardrobe to stop it spoiling the look. She then snaps half a dozen pictures before she checks the prices on the room-service menu and, suitably chastened, takes the elevator back down in search of something light to eat. It only needs to be better than airline food and cheaper than that offered by her otherwise delightful hotel. A quick check of her phone as she stands outside the entrance sends her walking in the direction of Third Avenue as a large black BMW slows in front of the entrance.

HIM

The Gulfstream is as comfortable as always, even it if it is whisking him away from his beloved home. It will be the longest trip since he found his place and used a fraction of his fortune to save it from ruin. This flight is taking him to a conference. He doesn't do events, not anymore. His publisher and agent handle publicity, and so does the world's media, though they all plead for him to *do his bit*. There have been *other things* that have been more important.

There's a reason though, a connection, or what he senses to be one. The young American whose writing showed so much promise that he mailed her a critique, and he sent his agent a missive suggesting they seriously consider her, if she were to send them a manuscript.

He chuckles to himself and checks the time, then makes his way to the plane's space age cockpit. "We aren't expecting any turbulence are we?"

"No Sir."

"Good stuff. Fancy a bite? I'm doing myself an omelette."

3

"You don't have to Sir, but that'd be great."

"Cheese, ham and mushroom okay?"

"Sure."

He hums to himself as he cooks. I It's a simple pleasure, and he knows he's so very good at simple pleasures, maybe even as good as he is as sinful ones. With that thought he plates up, carries the pilot's through and returns to take his own into the comfortable cabin. Cutting into the omelette releases the rich aromas of vintage cheddar and fresh herbs. He'd put just enough cheese in that the crisp golden shell opens to soft, slightly gooey interior.

He tastes. It's divine, but then it always is, and as always, he eats his generous meal with a relish. When he finishes, he leans back, closes his eyes and thinks ahead. He laughs to himself. She may not even show up.

He finishes his meal and loads the dishwasher before the plane starts its descent. Then he changes and returns to the cabin to enjoy the view and handle a couple of emails.

There are two cars waiting when the Gulfstream lands at Teterboro. The suited driver of the first vehicle emerges as the plane's steps fold down. He's more mountain than man, but his craggy face breaks into a grin as he strides towards the plane. "Welcome back to land of the free, Sir." There's a sincerity in the way he speaks the words.

"Glad to be back. It's been a while since I've been over the pond." His hand is already out to shake, and the giant seizes it.

"Certainly has, unless you've been sneaking across to see other drivers."

"I wouldn't use another company, and I doubt yours would dare assign me anyone else."

He climbs into the seven series, with just his laptop bag, leaving the ground crew, customs officer, driver, and other car's driver to deal with his luggage.

"Damn right, Sir. Straight to the hotel?"

"Yes, thanks. I ate on the flight; it's the St Regis this trip."

"Route's already set. Is everything to your liking?" The big man says it more as observation than question. It would have been for the least of his clients.

There's a bottle of iced water and a double espresso waiting for him in the car and he lifts the cup in a salute.

"If I hadn't remembered the system would."

Once they get to Manhattan, and he and his driver are more certain of their arrival time, he calls ahead to fix his meeting.

A doorman is on the way down the front steps before the limousine comes to a halt, and seeing him on the way, he exchanges a smile and a final pleasantry with his driver. "It makes me feel like an old man when they open doors for me."

"But you're too damned English not to let them do it?"

"That's right. See you soon."

"Hope so Sir."

He gets out with a nod of thanks.

"Any luggage, Sir?"

"No, thanks, just this." He raises his laptop bag and strides up the steps with the merest glance at the surroundings. The doorman looks disappointed, but does his best to escort him up steps and see him through the doors, then smiles his appreciation when he receives a bill for his attempted act of service anyway.

The lobby has just enough people to risk someone stepping into his way, so he alters the way he sets his heels down. He exchanges his habitually silent footfalls for a polite tap as he strides across the intricately patterned marble floor. A group of suited strangers turn towards him and move aside with a nod from the man he presumes is the leader. He returns it as he sweeps past on his way to the desk.

When he gets to reception there's already a member of staff waiting expectantly for him to begin speaking.

"Good afternoon. You have a reservation for Falchion?" He uses one of his 'extra-English' voices, filled with vanilla and honey and the centuries of breeding, privilege and habits of command that, so far as he's aware, not one of his ancestors got to enjoy.

"Yes, Sir…" the woman's eyes don't leave him as she taps briefly at her keyboard, only flicking away briefly after her final and loudest 'enter' click to check the booking. "The Presidential Suite."

The way she gushes shows he's got the look and the voice just right. "Excellent, I hadn't been sure it'd be free." He thanks her warmly before making his way to the lifts. When the car arrives, he presses the top button and then touches his keycard to the security check. The button lights up, and the doors close.

There's a knock at the door shortly after he lets himself in, so he opens it. There's someone from butler service there. "Welcome to the St Regis Sir. Can I help you get settled?"

Ten minutes later he's been shown where his pre-delivered things are, learned the layout of the suite and how to operate the kitchen, baths and showers. He has a pot of tea on the way too and is expectant that it's been made with the blend his office sent and to the instructions that had accompanied it.

"I'm expecting someone. Could you show him into the lounge while I shower, then do the tea before you head off?"

"Very good, Sir."

He nods his appreciation and continues leaving the professional to take care of greeting and refreshments.

His guest is just settling into an armchair when he enters, now dressed in jeans and a casual shirt.

The man, who has made himself quite at home, looks up and observes, "Slumming it I see old boy." Then casts his eyes appreciatively around the sumptuous room.

"Good to see you too Roger. You know me, couldn't let the facade slip just because I'm traveling. Thanks for popping up."

"Humph, seeing as how you made this the most convenient location," he complains, "I don't see why we couldn't do this at home."

The butler re-enters from the kitchen, sets down his tray and begins serving, using his eyes and hands to communicate expertly, doing his job immaculately without interrupting their conversation.

"I wasn't going to London."

"Or your place."

"The decorators were due to move in about an hour after I left. You're welcome to fly back there and smell paint while we do this over Zoom."

"You have an explanation for everything, as always."

He signals his thanks to the butler and dismisses him. "What's the matter? Didn't they let you wangle a room here even once they knew I wasn't staying at the conference hotel?"

"I wasn't going to get your young lady bumped over here and not pull the same stunt for myself, was I?"

His lips twitch as he snaps a biscuit. "Ah, the hardships! Now what do you have for me?"

There's cover art and back blurb for a film adaptation edition, and a proposal from Netflix to adapt one of his series that's teetering over the question of editorial control.

"They do know I can just not let them base anything on the bloody books, don't they?" he grumbles.

"They want to make the story more relatable."

"To people who aren't interested in my books?"

"That's how I said you would see it," his guest agrees.

"Tell them they can make changes without my sign-off for twenty percent over what they're worth. What's their market capitalisation?"

"Netflix or the production company?"

"Netflix."

"Quite a lot, I'm sure you know it better than I do."

He googles it. Then confirms for his guest. "If they haggle, they can do it for plus eighteen."

"You might want to consider a move into the production business if you feel that strongly. That would give you complete control."

"I'm pretty sure there are people who'd be a bit unhappy if I got another a new hobby." He gives his friend a sidelong look. "You might even be one of them."

"You *could* arm's length it?" his friend suggests.

"If I could let myself do that. Can I take it you have some form of ulterior motive here?" He knows his friend well enough to tell when there's a deeper motivation.

"There are those who might be interested."

"Hmm, keep your secrets, old man. You have my blessing to put whomever you're scheming with in touch with Mr. Walters, but you won't get my signature without his approval *and* full disclosure."

Business concluded, his agent concedes, "Very well. You can't blame an old man for trying though."

"I don't blame anyone for anything."

"No, you just manage people and situations, or get someone else to it," his agent points out sardonically.

"You make me sound positively Machiavellian."

His agent grins. "I'm never quite sure whether it's some of your characters rubbing off on you or the other way around." He escorts him to the door. As a parting reminder that more than one person can do favours his visitor notes, "Oh, and your friend has checked in." Then he bids farewell, and they part ways.

With official matters handled for the minute he takes a minute to send a message.

I've landed stateside. You still good for dinner?

Her Dinner Companion

Having talked so long before meeting is a first for her. As is the way they've talked. Everything about him is new, but he knows every twisted fantasy that has crept into her mind from reading, watching or the darkest recesses of her soul. Not only that, she knows his and has come to him anyway. As result, the lead up to dinner is tense.

They'd originally arranged to meet before she'd known who he was too, and then the name could still have been a coincidence. They'd only exchanged pictures the day before. What does a girl think, do, and say when her online flirting partner turns out to be famous? It's one thing to fantasise online with a stranger about being abducted by him to his dream castle or private island, but another to find out he's so successful he could conceivably own both and to be going to meet him in the flesh!

At least they're eating in the hotel's restaurant, so she can run away back to her room.

Ella Jane takes a deep breath before she leaves. She thinks about the things she herself has brought to the hotel. Things that are now secreted in the little zip compartment at the bottom of her suitcase. She has matching nose and anal hooks, a ring gag and connecting straps she saw, loved, and bought.

Until now, she's never worn the whole set together with anyone, just tried it out on her own. Bringing them had been her decision rather than His. She hadn't told him. Having them there gives her the freedom to decide whether to let Him to subject her to them. If they hit it off in the real world as well as they did in the virtual world, and if their play lives up to her fantasies of it, and her masturbation about it...

The thought of herself bound in that way, unable to move her head without pulling on the tight muscular rings of her ass, and on her nostrils, with her mouth held open and drooling, unable to speak but available.

She'd sent him pictures of them, but never of herself wearing them. Or should that be, *fitted* with them? He'd liked the idea and said he'd never used a nose hook on a girl before. Then he'd replied with a photo of what he referred to as *some of his anal hooks*. That had been hot, with the variety of sizes and fittings. She'd imagined herself being measured and waiting for him to decide whether to bind her hook to a belt or collar, or to a leather thong plaited into her long hair.

Her body likes the idea, and warms in response, liking it even as she asks herself whether she wants to go that far more than just whether she will with Him.

She takes a quick glance at the time on her phone and another at the case hiding its deliciously guilty contents and a final deep breath. Then she makes for the door. It would never do to be late, and it would be worse still to turn up late with her skin glowing with the after-effects of private onanism. So she goes to the door, and with only the briefest of backward glances and wistful thoughts, she makes her way down to the restaurant to find her surprise date.

Just as with when she'd stepped into her room, Ella Jane stops at the entrance to the hotel's Astor Court restaurant. She looks around so wide eyed that it takes her a moment to register that the Maitre D has spoken to her. "Er sorry?"

"Does madam have a reservation?"

"Er, yes, um." He'd given her a strange name to say, and the room has jarred it from her mind. "Falchion! I'm meeting Mr. Falchion."

"Ah, this way please." He stands as they approach his table, tall, broad, with salt and pepper hair. He's the man she's told her every fantasy and borrowed others more exotic just in order to drag out their conversations and have him continue to expand on the seemingly infinite ways in which he wishes to enjoy her.

"H-hi."

"Good evening, Ella Jane, so good to see you in the flesh."

He moves around the table, takes her lightly by the shoulders and touches his lips to each of her cheeks and then to her own. His lips he's described bringing her to ecstasy with a dozen times, and hers that she's written of being stretched around a ring gag and around him.

Ella Jane looks up into his eyes and their gazes lock, letting those stories and fantasies flow freely through the electrified air.

Her ears tell her someone's speaking, and she drags her attention away.

"Can I get madam a drink?"

"Ah, er, sparkling water please."

"Very good ma'am we have..." her attention is back on her dinner date. "Very well ma'am."

He draws out her chair, and she lets him seat her.

"So."

"Yes?"

They both begin at once. "How was your flight?" and then stumble over one another's variations on *Fine, it was just a flight.*

The humour of that breaks the awkwardness, and after an exchange of smiles he rumbles, "It's so good to finally meet." Then lifts his wine bottle and offers.

His eyes lock with hers again and speak of all the fantasies she wrote him from the safety of her bed. Then they flow down to her chest, lingering there until she glows with awareness before returning to the windows of her soul.

"It is." She smiles automatically and nods.

He asks, "Are you hungry?" as he pours, and when she moistens her lips and nods again, he continues, "Then let's eat before we..." His eyes complete the question and read her body's answer.

Her mouth says, "You can't say that." But her eyes have already agreed with him. It's why she's here in her best dress and her best underwear, and unless he does something to break the spell then yes, this is a *before* date, not a *whether* one.

The menu is blessedly short, and the food is as fine as their surroundings had led her to hope, but neither the food nor the spectacular room draw her away from the situation. The man she's been talking to since before she got her deal, before she even finished her book is sitting across from her. He's the one she's been confiding in and fantasising about since before she could be sure he was a man.

Ella Jane looks up from her menu having almost decided. "So what happened to your other businesses that you became free to come?"

"I managed to line up a couple of side trips in the states, so this is pretty much leg one of a tour."

She tilts her head. "You're a big enough writer to have a tour without side trips aren't you?"

"I've got a couple of signings lined up, too, to keep my agent and publisher happyish."

"Really, I've never done a signing. Do you get nervous?"

"Not really, not anymore anyway. It's nice meeting people who like what you write. I don't know about you, but I sometimes find myself hacking away for a hundred thousand words more or less in isolation."

"Long lonely evenings, yes. Though lately," she confides, "some of them have been improved by the virtual company of a very bad Englishman."

"The cad!" He gives her his best rakish look. "Doubtless he's the sort of fellow who frequents swanky New York hotels hoping to pick up beautiful young women and do unspeakable things to them."

"This is certainly that sort of place, I can imagine..." she looks up at the ornate ceiling and takes it in again. "I thought it was a shame we weren't in the main conference hotel till I saw this place. I didn't realise it'd be *this* nice."

"Quite something isn't it? The hotels and restaurants from the early twentieth century are the true highlights of New York's architecture." He sips. "Didn't you look it up online when you got your booking?"

"No! I wanted to experience is with new eyes." Her eyes dance with excitement. "It was worth it. They only put me in a standard room, but it's so beautiful, I laughed when I stepped in. Now this!" She gestures at the space around them. "If I'd known, I'd have dressed up to arrive!" and leans forward to whisper, "I was worried they'd think I was in the wrong place when I checked in."

"You don't have to worry, just look comfortable. The wealthy and those who work for the kinds of companies that put their staff here don't always bother dressing up."

"Thank you for that. I don't know any –" she grins awkwardly at possibly the first wealthy person she's met. "Many wealthy people. I was worried what they'd think I was here for."

"You've watched too many films."

"Don't you think I could pull off hooker?"

"This is one of those open holes in the ground conversation points, and I'm not stepping into it. You're lovely, bright and have a filthy imagination. I'm sure you'd make a wonderful, um, undercover reporter."

"But not –"

He blinks false innocence. "Still not going there." Then takes up the wine bottle and tops up each of their glasses. "But you are heading rapidly in the direction of becoming a spankee for the night." The corners of his eyes crease and those of his mouth turn upwards, and he returns to their original topic. "The St Regis is a lot more comfortable, but it's the architecture and service that make the place. It's only a mile from the conference hotel anyway."

"That'd be half-way across my home town."

"It's just round the corner here or in London."

"It was lucky they put us in the same place."

"Lucky for me they put you here. I'd always have been up here near Central Park. It's my favourite part of Manhattan."

"Lucky me then, that it's the only one I've ever been to."

"Really?"

"Yup, I'm a New York newbie."

"Then I shall have to show you around, so long as it doesn't turn out that we hate one another."

The waiter arrives with the sparkling water and pours Ella Jane a glass, looks at him, and pours him one too, almost overfilling it as he does. He stumbles out the beginnings of an apology before taking their orders.

She sips and tastes. "What's it like having a film made of one of your books?"

"It varies. With the Dark stories, it's usually like watching someone try to kidnap one of my children."

"Really?"

"Uh-huh some companies want to borrow a title and rewrite the story or characters. On the bright side, With the Smith's series, it's like watching one marry someone I like."

"What happened?"

"I'd been reluctant to allow anyone to touch the story. They're a friend's children's favourites, so I was reluctant to let anyone break it. It wasn't until I got approached at an event and was told the guy who'd been lined up to direct them is a fan, that I considered it. We met and got on, and he brought in a production company willing to give us the control of casting and locations we wanted."

"Do the kids like the films?"

"They do, though the girl was a bit upset that she didn't get to play a starring role."

"That's sweet." The unexpected thought of her mysterious twisted online playmate as taking such care over someone else's children jars Ella Jane from her train of thought, and she asks, "How did you get the idea for the infusers?" grasping the idea from their online conversation when she'd first asked what he did.

"Those? I was background thinking for Magnate. I dreamed them up as an idea for how he got started, then I looked them up and found out nobody made one, so I couldn't try it out." He rolls his eyes theatrically. "I was still curious, so I got two regular ones and put them on timers, and it worked. Then I was looking for a way to invest some royalties and I thought, *fuck it, why not*? And that was the first. The rest is history. Oh, and we make a range of clitoral vibrator heads for various electric toothbrushes."

"You're kidding. Those are yours?"

"Yup. I never joke about the things we make. Well, not often, and when I do I make notes."

"Why?"

"So I can ask someone who knows more about the detail if we could really make those things."

She nods. "I suppose that makes sense. Do you make anything else yet?"

"This and that. We make air filters and purifiers for hospitals." He decides to hold off on telling her about the energy and arms companies or the hedge fund. "Nothing that exciting."

"That's impressive!"

"I told you, I'm an impressive chap," He takes a sip of wine. "Oh! And just to be a bit fashionable, I have an interest in a reuse and recycling business, and there's a small company trying to make money out of clearing plastic from the ocean."

She swirls her glass and waits to read his attitude to those, then, when she sees his lips twitch with amusement she observes, "How very green of you."

"One has to give the impression of trying to do one's bit so one can sneer at those who like to give the impression of doing their bit."

"Does that mean you're as wicked outside the bedroom as you claim to be inside it, rather than having a kind heart and pretending not to?"

Their starters arrive, and he switches to small talk and thanking the waiter until they're alone again.

"Possibly more so," he grins and sips. "If that's possible."

"You didn't tell me about your fake or real humanitarian side when you were trying to persuade me to meet you. You hardly told me anything about who you were when we were chatting online!"

"No, I didn't, we were a bit more focused on, um, other things." He gives her a look not unlike the ones she's imagined from him for months, but his physical presence, his voice and that accent... "Besides, I've always thought, '*I'm rich*' would come over as a pretty crass chat-up line." And he makes a face. "Too many ways for it to go wrong."

"Such as?"

"Well, there's attracting women who only want to have a relationship with my money for one thing." He raises a hand, "Not that money isn't sexy of course. I just don't really want to feel like a third wheel in my own bed." He winces and waits for her to raise her glass. "And there's the risk that it might come over as an indirect way of saying are you a prostitute, or asking would you be for the right price." Much to his relief it works, her sudden laugh almost makes her spit wine out. That smile, that hint of embarrassment. He can't help returning it before continuing, "And that sort of question might put off the right sort of woman."

His candour makes her feel brave. "And who is the right sort of woman?"

She begins her starter as he answers and is relieved that it's so good that with any luck it will make coming worthwhile, no matter what his answer is.

"Adventurous... clever, interesting, pretty," He smiles, tilts his glass in salute, and his eyes study her face noting her pleasure and a hint of shyness. "But not shallow..." and his eyes apologise. "Even if saying pretty inevitably makes me sound shallow myself. I just have this thing about beauty. He shrugs at his own self-deprecation, empties the last of the sparkling water into their glasses, then summons another with a raised finger.

When it arrives, he takes his eyes off her to thank the star-struck waiter and compliment his attentiveness.

His touch and his eyes have said all the things her imagination could have wished. He's said the *right* things so far, so she risks hinting at a shared passion they've discussed before they talked ever meeting in the flesh. "You didn't mention tied up?"

He leans forward, but stops himself, half smiles and says "I was rather thinking that between us, I could take that as read, or hopefully as any word other than red," in a bone tinglingly deep whisper. His eyes stay on her long enough for her to colour then he blinks and leans back. "Now, enough about me! Tell me a little about you."

"There's not much to say. I've only just finished my master's."

"Completing your master's and your first novel at the same time, then getting both accepted isn't *not much*. How long had you wanted to be a writer?"

"Since I was a child, my mom read to me, then I read, and then I made up stories of my own and started writing them down." She then turns the question back on him. "How about you?"

"Similar childish dreams, only it was my father, and he made up the stories he told me. Only once I got to school, the teachers didn't like the stories or my handwriting. To be fair, they had a point about the handwriting. Then mundane happened, and when it finally all went wrong, I found myself divorced and living in a crappy flat with a PC and a couple of ideas. I was reborn out of necessity."

"All of your books, films made from them, and businesses too! You've rebirthed yourself very successfully."

Their mains arrive. Thinking about the night ahead, Ella Jane does her best to graze lightly on her meal. Each item is delicious though, so much so that she eats more than she had initially intended.

"Thanks, I try." He stops and makes an effort to steer the conversation. "Can I ask what you like best about dominants?"

"You may." She gleefully appropriates his pickiness. "There's the confidence when they do what they're best at," and she smiles a saucy smile at the way his eyes soften with amusement then narrow and harden again, and how that hardness doesn't quite stretch to his twitching lips. "If they're good at it, that is." Before her eyes drift into the distance. "The big thing, though, is wanting someone I can trust completely, let go with...." When she draws her attention back into the room she feigns disinterest, "Why do you ask?"

"Oh, simple curiosity really," He shrugs, "I can't stand us myself. When anyone tries telling me what to do, it makes me want drop them off a cliff."

"I never quite know whether you're joking or being serious."

"There's an art to it. The trick is that I'm usually joking and being serious."

"How does that work out for you?"

He drains his glass. "Confuses me almost as much as it does everyone else."

They sit in silence for a moment, and when she pulls her vision back inside herself, she sips, thinks, and gives him an appraising look, then decides. "What is it you like best about submissives?"

While she grazes, he devours, both with his appetite and his eyes.

He muses and purrs in his basso voice, "That vulnerability earned and offered, the moment she offers her wrists to be bound..." His sight drifts first into the distance, then he shifts his focus to her hands, and suddenly, his eyes are on hers, and he leaves them there until every blood vessel below her hairline reacts. He'd spoken so softly in his cut-crystal upper crust English accent rumbling so she'd feel the words as much as hear them. "The gift of herself, rewarding her trust, holding her afterwards."

He asks for the dessert menu with an, "If you haven't had enough?" to Ella Jane. The words are spoken so softly in his rumbling voice that she feels the words as much as hears them despite his crisp actorish English enunciation. In the fine restaurant, this is so unlike a party or a scene, but the heat is as real as any furnace.

She gives him a pleading look across the table, manages a hissed, "Stop it!" as she glows under the weight of his gaze and his words.

He stays silent. Completely still. His eyes on her. In her.

She realises she's holding her breath, and that her mouth is open.

"Would you like to go upstairs?"

Ella Jane breathes his words in, murmurs, "Please." her voice thick with the weight of their months of conversation.

He smiles. "We can always have dessert sent up later."

The decision cuts through the tension in her and she's able to joke again. "Hmm, dessert." Her laugh tinkles in his ears. "In one way, I'm stuffed!" She isn't, but much more and she's sure she will be. "And in another, I haven't even seen the *dessert menu.*"

He tilts his head, only allowing the briefest moistening of his lips to betray his understanding. "Just espressos then?"

"Aren't you worried we won't be able to sleep?" She composes her face, or tries to, biting her lip to stop her smile spreading, but his vulpine grin in response sets her off.

"Do you want to sleep?" he takes a sip of wine while he's still smiling, then touches the tip of his tongue to the wetness on his upper lip. "I'm pretty sure I won't sleep anyway."

She bats her eyelids and bounces. "Why might that be?"

"Got this little redhead whose smile keeps playing on my mind. I'm hoping I'm in with a chance, but if not, I might just lie awake pining." He shakes his head as his eyes study her.

She colours in answer. "Should I be jealous?"

"Definitely. She's been sending me the filthiest ideas for months."

"Anything you found interesting?"

"Dozens of them."

Ella Jane basks in his words. "She sounds like an interesting girl. Maybe I will have that coffee, and you can tell me more about her."

He glances up towards a passing waiter who then detours in their direction. "I thought so. Talented writer, too."

She fishes, "I wish I were a talented writer."

"You *are* talented. I've seen your work."

While their eyes joust, the waiter arrives. "Sir?"

"Two double espressos please, and the dessert menus."

"Certainly, Sir."

Ella Jane's eyes narrow and she interjects, "I thought we were going upstairs *without* having dessert?"

"We're just going to play a what-would-I-have game."

"Tormentor."

"Funny, that little redhead said the same thing." He takes another sip, and gives another calculated smoulder. "But she said it was one of my best qualities."

"So, you like tormenting women?"

"The ones who find it exciting?" His voice and his eyes drift dreamily, "More than anything."

Ella Jane's teeth catch her lower lip. "You sound like a very bad man." She blinks at him. "And they sound like awful women."

"On the contrary." His eyes rove across her face and down her body like a confident caress, then back to her eyes. "They are by far the best women."

The espressos and menus arrive, and he says, "Thank you," and nods minutely, but does so without taking his eyes, or his attention away from her. He doesn't even break eye contact when he picks up his cup. "Are you ready to be tormented?"

"How do you know I'm one of those women?"

"Call it a lucky guess."

She lowers her eyes and smiles. "So arrogant."

He chuckles, "Funny you should say that."

"Oh, why's that?"

"She said that was another of my best qualities."

"Are you sure she wasn't just flattering you?"

"Why would she do that?"

"Maybe she wants to get hold of your money?"

"That's the funny thing. She didn't know who I was when we started talking."

"She seems a bit forward then."

"Not really. If she had been, I think she'd have mentioned how beautiful she is."

"Oh! So now she's beautiful, is she?" Her dark lashes flutter. "I'm not sure I can compete."

His eyes simmer and his voice flows like molasses, "Actually, you could pass for her identical twin."

Ella Jane colours and smiles at the flattery, but she's not ready to give up the game just yet. "Does that make this some part of a twisted threesome fantasy for you?"

"Hmm, perhaps, but we'd have to meet her in real life, and we'd all have to get along, and to fancy each other...."

"Our first date and you're already planning on bringing in another woman?"

"They only work for me if everyone wants to play with each other. Mind you, she seems lovely, almost as sweet as you do."

"So, I have some advantages over her?"

"Perhaps, I don't get to see her smile so much."

There's a brief silence and a lingering stillness, their hands in contact on the table. Ella Jane muses, plays the idea, wishes, but she has her likes, and it makes things simpler to be honest. She breaks eye contact and swirls her wine. "I'm going to be disappointment for you then." She sips. "I wish I did find other women attractive, but I just don't. I can see how lovely they are, but it just doesn't do anything for me in that way."

"Not disappointing at all." He leans forward. "Can I let you in on a little secret?"

"What is it?"

He leans forward, looks around and murmurs, "I feel much the same about men." In a conspiratorial tone.

Her laugh comes out louder than she intends, and she looks around too, though she does so genuinely worried that she might have attracted attention. Having checked the whole room isn't staring, she braves a challenge. "Not that you can't handle two women?"

The barb doesn't deflect or dissuade him in any way. "Two women?" His predator lips part, but he sips the hot coffee before answering, "I could handle two of most women, as easily as I'm sure you could two of most men."

It's her turn to make him smile with mock horror. "So now I'm some kind of hussy?"

"No, I simply get the impression that you're some kind of *more than just enough*." He takes another sip of wine. "Now, I think it's time to concentrate on this very fine menu?"

"Are you going to make me look?"

"Of course. At least, I shall if you don't say *red*." He takes her hand and guides it to her menu.

"Is dessert going to be my consolation prize?"

He grins again. "No, and I hope it isn't going to be mine either."

She swallows and shakes her head without speaking.

"Think of reading it as first torment of many."

Her pupils reply by dilating and her lips by parting, but her voice softly answers, "Promises, promises…" as she opens the menu and tries to hide behind it.

"Select something cold and something hot."

"So, I have to make two choices."

"It seems only fair. After all," his eyes make their way down and back up all that is visible of her behind the table with lecherous slowness. "I hope to make at least that many later."

Ella Jane gives him a long, slow look, but he remains shamelessly unrepentant, so she goes back to studying the menu rather than speaking in the hope that her cheeks won't flare brighter still. "So, naughty!"

He rises. "Are you going to make your safe call?"

"What do you mean?" she asks as she stands.

His devil eyes glitter, and his lips brush her neck just below the side of her jaw again, sending fresh tingles through her. "If we're going upstairs then," another feather soft kiss, "you should tell someone where you're going to be and why."

Ella Jane can't help laughing. "Is that necessary? I know exactly why I'm going."

"Of course not," he says smiling back at her, but he places a skilful fingertip under her chin. "But it is sensible." She can't help inclining her head to let him place the next kiss immediately below her ear any more than she can help the rush of sensation it elicits.

She takes a couple of pictures of him, but he pats the chair at the side of the table. "Works better if you're in the picture too." She slips from her own and onto it, leans up against him and takes a couple more while he his lips brush her neck just below the side of her jaw, sending tingles through her. Unsatisfied with her first efforts, she gives him a minxish look then plants a kiss on his bemused lips. Pleased with the results she adds 'It's really him!' as the caption and clicks send.

He whispers, "You are in so much trouble young lady," and she turns up to and into him.

This time, the kiss is melting and complete, not just minxish, and she has no idea how long it continues before she reluctantly breaks for air and answers, "I hope so," before catching her lower lip between her teeth and breathing, "Sir." A thought makes her break the thick silence. "What about you?"

"What about me?"

"Don't you have to make a safe call?"

He reaches under the table and bends towards her, kisses under her ear. "I have perhaps two thousand messages you've sent inviting me to do as many things to you, so long as you don't say *red*." Then he gives her another soft kiss, straightens and hardens his voice, "Now, the menu."

Ella Jane looks up enquiringly but can't read his expression, so she does as bidden. It isn't long, but it is tantalising. She dismisses the cheesecake tasting selection and others as too similar to things she might have somewhere else, though she does wonder what twists and creative additions there might be to justify their prices. Instead, her eyes are drawn to the chocolate and truffle trio. She looks up to speak, but he's watching her, and she doesn't want to cave in to his bossiness too quickly, so she goes on to read the descriptions of the hot choices.

While she reads, her stomach responds. They're appealing, but she wants to look her best, and not to feel overly full. Looking up, she sees he's still studying her. It draws a flush to her cheeks, and she tries to distract him, "Aren't you going to look?"

"I've already decided what I want." His voice deep and his eyes hungry.

"Are you going to tell me what it is?"

"Yes, but not until you choose yours."

She tightens her jaw. "Choose the gorgeous things I'm not going to get to have?"

The corners of his eyes crease with amusement. "That's right."

Her eyes narrow, but her lips smile, and she turns her attention back to the menu. There aren't many options, and they all look delicious, but having decided on one exotic choice she plumps for. "The chocolate pudding. If only to find out what could possibly make a chocolate pudding worth so much."

His eyes bore into her. "Given the right inspiration, a skilled craftsman can make the simplest thing special." He strokes his fingertips along the back of her hand.

"Then that simple thing," she breathes, and then continues, "and the truffle trio, so the chef can show me all of his skills if he has them." She draws out every word while her eyes appraise him.

"Can I tempt you to the tiniest taste of the chocolate pudding if I order myself a portion?"

She breathes again, and nods without speaking.

His raised eyebrow summons the star struck waiter, and he orders with a soft rumble and a gesture of his hand, and the waiter departs. Then they touch hands and glances and exchange words that allude to what they're both thinking but without speaking it aloud while they wait.

When it arrives there are two spoons, and two more coffees. She takes a spoon, and her eyes dare him. "How can I be sure I'm not taking too much?"

"I'll give you a choice. You can help yourself and risk a punishment or let me feed you."

His boldness! She looks around wondering what the other diners will think if she lets this older man feed her in this grand dining room, and what punishment might be in order for eating too much

29

of his dessert. "What kind of girl offers herself up to a strange man's judgement and gifts him the right to punish her?"

He pulls his lips back just far enough to reveal a trace of his teeth. "An adventurous one."

Ella Jane tilts her head, and her teeth take a hold of her lower lip. "And what kind lets him feed her in the fancy restaurant in their hotel?"

He smiles a smile that shines from the depths of his eyes. "A trusting one." and uses his spoon to carefully cut a morsel. He looks down at the spoon, then back to her, tilts his head, raises the spoon to a point midway between them and waits.

Her mouth responds to the pudding's rich aroma, and she swallows, and then takes her lip between her teeth again while she decides. She tries to pull his hand towards her, but fails, so she reluctantly opens her mouth.

He smiles a smile of victory, as he teasingly moves the spoon first towards his own lips and then between hers. The pudding's richness combined with their interplay is overwhelming, and her mouth responds with a flood of saliva and a reflexive laugh. She only barely contains both while he helps himself to a taste.

They eat the first half in silence as he shares with both scrupulous fairness and merciless teasing. "This is a *really* good chocolate pudding."

"Mmm," she agrees, "But..."

"But it's my dessert?"

Ella Jane shakes her head.

"But you want to go upstairs now?"

She nods. And he makes a great show of finishing it with a relish but without relinquishing either her hand or her eyes, only allowing her one more morsel while he does. Then he drains his cup. "Then we should adjourn, if you don't want to sample the cheeseboard."

It's what she's been more than hinting at, but she still plays the game back at him. "Adjourn to do what?"

"Oh, I don't know." He trails his fingers along her hand, "Whatever takes our fancy."

"Even though I haven't brought my mysterious, near identical twin with me?"

"If it makes you feel better about it, we could keep her with us in spirit by doing all of the terrible things I talked about with her to you."

"Hmm? And what would I get out of that?"

"I'm sure you'll find some interesting ideas among it all." He chuckles wickedly and leans close to murmur, "After all, she seems very creative."

He studies her, and she watches him, feels his attention, sees him reading signs she feels her body giving out without her speaking a word.

Ella Jane realises she's holding her breath again, and that her mouth is open. "Are you really as good as you say you are?"

"Slightly better actually." He winks. "But I'm modest too." And he smiles the smile he's taunted her with from time to time over dinner. "Would you like to go upstairs now that you've finished wasting time over desserts and coffee?"

Her eyes narrow, but she nods.

"Shall we go?" His voice is even deeper, even softer.

She doesn't answer, but when he rises and holds out his hand, she takes it and allows him to lead her from the restaurant.

As they move across the lobby, a thousand thoughts rush through her head. Thoughts of their conversations online, all the extreme fantasies, things she's dreamt and told him from the secure privacy of her own room. Thoughts and fantasies from before she thought they'd meet, before they were certain of each other's real names. Does he have one of those fantasies in mind, and does she want him to? Should she play the lover? The captive? The slave? The vixen? The ideas flood through her, ideas to write, to live, to send to her secret online playmate cum lover even though right now he's walking by her side.

Ella Jane steals a glance at him. He's more handsome than she'd expected, more imposing, and more physically real. Like a boss, but with a bodyguard body as his tailored suit betrays hints of athletic muscle beneath it. She leans into him and discovers a solid warmth there. His presence and confidence, and the way he switches from gentleman to bad boy to wicked man and back again without his focus drifting away from her entrances her.

Waiting for the elevator, she squeezes his hand, looks up at him, and then blinks her eyes downwards as she catches sight of the hungry wolf in his. As she looks down, his arm moves around her shoulders drawing her into his side. She registers that he, too, has had a physical response to their flirting.

He holds her and kisses the top of her head. She tries to ease around to face him, but he holds her where she is, staying more sideon than face on so as not to press his hardness against her yet. Even so, this feels sexual and not just peaceful like a moment ordained. A wild thought that he could just take her here strikes him. He senses that she's as ready as he is, and that this was meant, that the world would let them because this is meant.

They're still alone when the car arrives, and they stand aside while its occupant exits. Each has their own wicked thoughts as to the possibilities of having the car to themselves. They step inside, but a voice calls out, "Hold the lift!" as He's about to press the door close button. The two exchange a look of frustration, but he presses the door open button with a look of apology, and a darkening hint of playfulness.

The couple get in and thank him, and he acknowledges them with. "My pleasure. What floor can I get you?" in a thick Texan accent that causes Ella Jane to cover her mouth to hide her reaction.

He draws her to the rear of the elevator car as the other couple enter and holds her close. His hands tease behind her back, until the car stops and the couple get out.

"Why did you put an accent on?"

"I didn't want to be dragged into a conversation with a fellow countryman when I could be spending time with you."

"You say the nicest things." She places her hand at his waistband, then frowns. "Oh, you aren't wearing a belt."

"I didn't want to rush things, but..."

She nuzzles against his shoulder. "But you've brought one?"

"I've brought a selection."

"Mmm," and with the car to themselves she moves in front of him and leans against his strength. "Whatever for, you wicked man?"

"I can't remember. I'll have to check the two hundred messages you sent on the subject."

Her, "Don't!" is sudden, as is the way she tightens her arms around his firm waist. After holding him like this and receiving a squeeze from his encircling arms and a kiss to the top of her head she breathes, "Don't, but do." And presses her lips to his chest.

The car comes to a halt, and he leads her out and across the high-ceilinged lobby to the door to his room.

His room

He holds opens the door, flicks the light switch with a flourish, then stands back to allow her to enter first with a wave of his arm.

Ella Jane draws her lip between her teeth, doing so partly to avoid looking impressed at what lies beyond the threshold, and partly just because.

He shuts the door to the suite and puts a light hand on her shoulder. "Stand still."

Rather than just standing still, she, carefully places her bag down, sets her feet apart and raises her hands to the back of her head. "No one's ever tried to laugh me into bed before."

His hand traces the line of one upraised arm, and his chuckle is close enough that she can feel it on her skin. "I could ask how you like your eggs in the morning?"

She glances behind her, smiles, shakes her head, looks down and then blinks up. "I haven't got my toothbrush."

"I have a spare. If you don't like it, I can gallantly fetch yours from your room."

He goes in for a kiss which she evades with a downward glance. "But can I trust you not to go prying around in my room?"

"If you can't, then I'd advise you not to come to mine, and it's a bit late for that..." Rather than trying again, he just looks at her with a wolfish smile.

Ella Jane makes a show of looking around. "So, it is." And her eyes challenge his.

"Though I must confess..."

"What?"

"Now I'm curious what can be in your room that's more private than some of the fantasies you've shared with me."

"Ah, too bad." She turns and bats her eyelashes. "You'll only find out if I invite you, or I don't like your toothbrush."

"Then I'll have to do my best to make sure it makes a good impression." He places the palm of his hand on the curve of her bum, just where the best spanks land.

"Is that an innuendo, Sir?"

"It was certainly meant to be, but if you're not sure, I could go on about hard-to-reach places and making you feel all tingly and invigorated." He grins at her smile. "Glad you saw the funny side before I ran out of double-entendres."

This time she accepts the kiss and lingers in it. Though she still playfully enquires, "And that I didn't bristle?" when their lips part.

"Or foam at the mouth." He steps around her and his fingers brush across her lips. "So many better uses for a pretty mouth than making foam."

Ella Jane touches the tip of her tongue to that of his exploring forefinger, presses herself back into his solid form and allows him to sweep her long hair aside and kiss the back of her neck as his hand strokes tantalisingly close to the side of her breast.

Her body reacts. After the months of teasing and their long flirtation over dinner, she's ready for him, and she can feel he's ready for her too.

He lowers his lips to her ear and softly rumbles, "Bed?"

"Mhm." She allows him to lead her through the reception room into an equally grand bedroom and lets him undo her dress.

Despite the hunger in his eyes, he doesn't tear it from her, or throw it aside. Preferring to drape it along the glass top of the walnut cabinet along one wall, he then shrugs his jacket off and lays that out neatly, too. He does both without taking his eyes from her increasingly nervous and expectant form. At least she's wearing her best lingerie set of a little lacy black bra and matching small, but not too small, thong. They even go with her heels. When her fingers go to loosen his tie, his hands gently but firmly stop her, guiding her arms back to her sides as his eyes continue to inspect and admire her barely clad body.

Once she's positioned as he desires, he caresses and kisses. His hands tease around and past every part of her that eagerly seeks to press itself into their warm strength. When she mewls in complaint, he rumbles a chuckle and touches his lips to the side of her neck murmuring, "Patience is a virtue."

"I want you now!"

That chuckle comes again; he strokes his hands down slowly to cup her bum cheeks then lifts his right palm away. She holds her breath and braces for the expected spank, but it doesn't come. Instead, he wraps his grip lightly around the side of her neck and touches his lips to hers, before repeating, "Patience...is...a...virtue."

Her eyes offer defiance, but he holds firm and brushes his thumb over her cheek. Eventually she lowers them and allows him to continue. He deftly undoes and removes her bra, caresses the lines its straps have left on her skin, then moves so his hands come close enough to the swells of her breasts and their already achingly stiff buds for her to feel their warmth.

Ella Jane allows her eyes to scream, *Take Me!* but keeps her silence as, though his growl promises to do so, he keeps an iron grip on his needs and his strong hands continue their exploration, their claiming of her body.

He kneels, lowers her thong, touches his lips to her mons, and 'ahems' her into stepping out of them without stepping out of her heels. With her naked except for her shoes, he lifts her even though the bed is just a few steps away. He lifts her as though she were nothing more than a feather and sits her on the bed.

She allows him to lay her back and kiss his way down her leg on his way to easing the shoe from her foot. Once he's set it aside, he holds her foot in both hands and presses his thumbs into her sole with firm strokes that melt with their irresistible force. They continue until she lets out a sigh and he rumbles his amusement as he lays her leg down and repeats his actions on her other leg.

With her completely naked, he steps out of his shoes and lifts her fully onto the bed.

Her hands try to undress him again and he stops them again before slowly kissing and caressing the length of her body. This time, he uses his lips, as well as his hands, to brush the curves of her breasts and the swell of her mons. She adjusts her legs as he does, exposing her readiness to him, expecting him to try.

He continues to take his time though. She's mewling by the time he completes his next round of caresses and sighs as he uses a fingertip to draw her wetness to his lips.

She arches as his kisses circle her breasts, croons as his lips embrace and suckle their erect tips, lets out brief giggles as he blows cooling air over her freshly wetted buds and claws her hands on the luxurious covers in order to hold herself back from touching him.

He moves on. Downward. Takes a firm grip on each of her thighs. Parts them widely and sets his forearms between them so his thumbs can frame her mons.

She rarely allows a man to use his mouth on her. Never unless she's bound, but no matter how she tries her legs can't move his shoulders or even unsettle his fierce hold enough to force him to ease up. An effort to use her hands to push him away wins her nothing more than a stony look, one that part melts, and part quells.

He pries her vulva wide with his hands pressing the swollen flesh of her outer labia into her pubic bone as the pads of his thumbs work on her mons with electrifying effect.

When he pauses, Ella Jane looks down and sees him grinning cockily up at her. With her eyes on him, his tongue languidly makes its way up the length of her opening. He places the warm flat of a hand onto her mons, presses onto her pubic bone and upwards. The way his hand holds her opens out her folds and lifts her hood clear of the head of her clitoris allows the tip of his tongue to circle at its leisure, first one way and then the other.

With her petals spread, he settles into a lingering exploration of her. First his tongue makes it quite clear that it knows precisely where everything is, and his lips and teeth demonstrate equal knowledge of where to suck and where to nibble. That done however, he takes his time and reads her breathing and her body's responses, slowing or easing pressure as she nears her crescendo. He lifts away and slowly massages the bones and muscles of her V as she curses and calms, and then resumes his attentions. She bucks but his heavy shoulders turn to iron, clasps at his shoulders and his guttural growling sends her fingers to claw the sheets instead and eventually she howls.

When it comes to holding her still while driving through her reserve and taking her to orgasm, he uses his greater strength artfully. When she clings to him, her defences swept away by crashing waves of ecstasy, she gasps and clings to him as her insides pulsate and her muscles spasm against his mass and strength.

He drives her on until her cries turn to whimpers before he relents, releases the suction of his lips and withdraws the wickedness of his tongue's tip and groove. He then applies a kiss as light and tender as a blessing to her centre before moving up her body to face her.

Ella Jane blinks up to see him looking down, then scrunches her eyes closed and covers her face. Despite this she welcomes his kiss, and her taste, but she still doesn't open her eyes to face him.

When he eventually breaks the embrace, he asks, "What?"

In response, she clenches her eyes even more tightly closed. Other girls got laughed into bed, she knows that, and on an intellectual level she gets it, but she doesn't. She's drawn to seriousness, that stern, intimidating quality, yet here she is laughing and indisputably in bed in the arms of a man. In truth she didn't even fully realise he had a lighter side until they met in person today and perhaps the sheer physicality of him is enough to satisfy? She supposes the hundreds of emails had something to do with it. He was very clever with words in those emails, spinning webs of words and dreams that had meshed with her own dark fantasies. In her mind, He had become beast to her beauty, and now He is there, handsome, broad, powerful and with those hazel eyes deep inside her.

While she plays out her thoughts in the darkness behind her eyelids, he rolls off the bed and undresses. Ella Jane opens her eyes and watches, and he continues quite shamelessly, perhaps even adding a hint of showing off. There's certainly something worth showing off. Her older man has a body more like an older NFL quarterback. No wonder he'd been able to hold her down!

She looks at his shoulders and the heavy curves of his haunches; she'd had no idea about those. He's definitely a man of many layers she thinks, as she dares to brush her fingers along the striations in their heavy muscle. In her experience, a man usually wears fine clothes to hide the mess his body is in, not as an accent to the work of Michelangelo. She bites her lip as her fingers trail and her eyes drink. The wisps of silver in his hair accentuate his gravitas, and those golden hazel eyes, she, at least her body, decides she's ready again and notices that He is too.

Eventually the memory of one of his earliest boasts and how she'd scoffed at it rises in her mind and crashes into the realisation that it was no mere boast. She says, "Don't say it! Just don't say it!"

"Don't say what? I'm going to need a clue." His voice drips with insincerity as, now naked, he climbs back onto the bed.

She mimics his formal English accent, "See, you aren't just a masochist; you don't need pain."

The impression makes him chuckle. "Oh, that! I wasn't going to."

She squints up at him through narrowed eyes. "Really?"

"I was thinking about something else."

"What?"

"Well, if you aren't too tired," and his hand and eyes flow down the length of her body. "We could experiment with how much you like pain, or..."

"Or?" She angles her hips towards him in a poignant reminder that while the orgasm had been earth-shaking she has further needs.

"Or we could do something else..." He doesn't let her rest, not fully, instead he turns her slender body and runs an iron hard thumb and forefinger down the length of her spine with the same inexorable slowness with which his tongue had teased her through the build-up. It finds every place that she usually carries her tension and applies his melting pressure there. When it reaches the line of her hip, he slides away and presses her face down. Once in that position, his other hand joins in and he gives her buttocks and then her legs the same glacially slow infusion of lava heat.

By the time his thumbs sink into the soles of her feet again they're both breathing heavily, and Ella Jane is as languid as a sleeping cat.

His kisses still taste of her when he uses his strength and mass to ease her unresisting form onto her back again, as with her back and bum, his curious hands apply their skill to her shoulders and arms.

The way his hands sink into her muscles sets her arching in anticipation, an anticipation he takes an age to satisfy with the inexorable movement of his hands. She mewls as they come together over her stomach, and again as they part and flow down the length of her thighs.

Her arousal rises again as the heavy caress progresses, and her eyes appeal for him to hasten to the caress they both know is to come, but his hands are in no more of a rush than his mouth had been. He explores the lines of each bone and every millimetre of the curves of her breasts and neck.

At length she takes a hold of his cock to encourage him to go quicker and to fill the emptiness her readiness has created within her. This time his eyes accept her movement. He doesn't let her draw him to her entrance, but he does steer his hand that way, moving closer and eventually finding her centre.

He settles on his side to her right as his fingertips and thumb play with her folds. His hand is no less knowing, and no less patient even though she clutches at his shaft more tightly each time he edges her. And he edges her until she whimpers with need before setting her in flight. There's nothing in her that can match the force with which his vice-like grip takes a hold of her when her orgasm begins, and he uses that hold and a rocking of his arm to draw it out until she begs him to stop.

She curls against him and he wraps her in the covers, holds her until her hand resumes its stroking of his hardness, and tastes her from his fingers and offers them to her. An offer she accepts musing, "You remembered?" before welcoming her taste, and his warmth into her mouth.

"I did." He holds her close, rocks in her grip, and when she uses her hold on him to try to draw him into herself, he laughs and rolls over to her other side, then resumes his caressing, this time with his left hand.

"I want you!"

"You're going to have me."

She grips tighter and tries to force his caressing hand to her opening. "Yes, but I want you *now!*"

He's too strong though, and his eyes mock her urgency. "Patience is still a virtue."

His left hand takes its time too, though, whether it lacks the artistry of his right or her body is still so stimulated that he can't keep her on edge for so long, she cums more swiftly this time.

She lays back, rubs her head against the sheets and croons in her afterglow, but he's not done with her yet.

Rather than let her rest he rolls to the side of the bed, reaches into the cabinet there and draws out something she quickly recognises.

"Have you no pity?"

"Have you just said red?"

She covers her face with her hands. "No!"

"Well then."

This time he pauses at her opening and holds still from time to time between caresses and applications of the wand to various parts of her mons and vulva. By doing so, he reminds her of his own urgency, of this knowledge that she's ready for him and of the iron control he has over both of their needs.

He raises her legs over his shoulders and enters her before making her cum for the fourth time, doing so by finally, blessedly pressing the wand's tip over her hooded clit and holding it there on a steady, slow hum while the fingers of his free hand tease and lightly pull at the sides of the tip of her right breast. When the orgasm peaks he sets the wand aside and tastes her from his fingers again and stays inside her rocking his powerful hips in time with her body's convulsions.

He's nuzzling her as she emerges from her daze.

She looks up at Him sleepily through her thick lashes. "Well, that was different."

He tilts his head a little to one side. "Good different?" He asks it with a look in his eye. The arrogant bastard *knows* how good.

Her initial response is to stretch up against Him, but as she gathers her wits she complains. "Are you going to attack me again?"

"Not yet." And he presses his lips to the top of her head. "Was that okay for a first attempt?" He asks it with a *God, I'm good* look in his eyes.

Even exhausted as she is, Ella Jane can't help but give him an accusing look. "You know it was!"

"A few bells successfully rung then?" He takes her deepening colour as his answer, and slides his fingertips possessively between her folds then growls, "At least all the ones you know about?" softly into her ear.

The words, and the tone of his voice multiply the effect of his touch. She likes fire, and she'd already been certain. She knows from his words that he's fire and having felt his warmth, she is now waking to her need for his heat, the need that had brought her to him. She curls against Him. More of her previous lovers had beaten her and thrown her into bed than laughed her there, but none of those had rung so many bells as he's found in one ringing session.

"That's both hands *and* your mouth! You shouldn't be able to just *do* that."

"What?"

"Make me cum like it was nothing!"

"It's never nothing when a pretty girl cums." Then he smirks. "And don't forget the vibrator."

"No one's ever been able to do that to me before."

"What? Make you cum?"

"No, *just* make me cum, like it's nothing. I can't do that to me."

He glows with pride, and lowers his lips to hers. "It's a matter of practice, and attention, and picking the right woman, and the right time, and a matter of..." he breaks off and brushes his hands so lightly over her skin that she'd normally be complaining that it tickled, but somehow it just makes her want him to carry on. "Really wanting to, and of her making me really want to." He smiles a smile of joy discovered and touches his lips to hers. "It helps that you make me want to smile."

She ignores his reach for yet more praise and continues. "I can't do it just like that! I've never even had one orgasm without getting kinky before except on my own! You could teach classes." His eyes tense, and his impassive expression wavers. "Oh My God! You have, haven't you?"

He hedges, "Um, just a couple of salons."

Ella Jane pulls the duvet over her head. "This is so embarrassing!"

The pitch of his voice rises in puzzlement, "Why?"

"You're a professional!"

"I've taught classes. I've never turned tricks."

She folds the covers back down and stares at him. "I can't believe you said that!"

"What?"

"Here I am with an older man and-" She hides her face again. "This is so weird!"

"Oh." After the exclamation he waits, but Ella Jane doesn't emerge, so He nudges her through the covers. "If every generation hadn't discovered sex? Mine wasn't the first either." The joke fails to draw her out, so he lies back, and enquires, "Could you at least tell me if it's good weird?"

The duvet asks, "Why didn't you tell me?"

"It's not the sort of thing you mention. It'd sound like bragging." He then lets out a laugh. "Besides, I'd look a right tit if it turned out I couldn't satisfy you."

She peeks out from her hiding place with narrowed eyes. "Has that *ever* happened to you?"

"No, but there could always be a first time."

Ella Jane's eyes narrow further, and the tensing spreads down into her core, to muscles that have so recently received his *professional* attentions. In doing so, it causes a wave of sensation that flows back up her body.

His eyebrows shoot up and his voice rises defensively, "Well, it could!"

That doesn't entirely pacify her, but she lets it pass and touches her hand to his under the covers. "How did you come to teach classes?"

"A former playmate suggested it."

"Really?" The muscles around her eyes tighten again. "And why was that?"

"Um. I think she was surprised." He tries to leave it there, but her silence and continued attention draw him to continue, "She told a mutual friend who ran salons."

"You used to just do that to her too?" She closes her eyes and sucks her lip. "You just do that to everyone, don't you?"

"Not without consent. It'd cause chaos in public places, and it'd take me ages to get anywhere." Throughout the whole exchange, Ella Jane has made no effort to remove his hand from her, though he has withdrawn his fingers, setting them flat across her mons and no longer pressing into it. "If you'd like I could do this instead." With a slight shift, he presses the length of his thumb and the ball of his

47

hand into the upper edge of her pubic bone and pulsing firmly as he does.

The effect is immediate, warm rivulets flow from down into her centre with each application of force. "It doesn't normally result directly in orgasm, but it's rather nice. Or so I've been told."

She squirms and laughs under his touch. "Are you going to spend the whole night doing these things to me?"

He muses, "I can." He runs a growl down the length of her neck. "It depends."

"You spent the last few months telling me you were super kinky!" His eyes lock with Ella Jane's as she says this, and she almost loses her nerve, but after a breath and a silent prayer, she continues, "You aren't just a supreme vanilla lover are you? Do you do freaky in real? Or are you just the Häagan Dazs of vanillas?" And there it is, the grin. It's not that it's cruel, some Doms and lots of bullies have worked out how to do a cruel grin or were born with one. It's not like that at all. It's a grin that any courtesan would blanch and turn from, and in his case, she suspects even the devil would. It's a grin that reaches into the darkest shadows of her psyche and sets them ablaze.

"I did, and I'm not. I do, and there's no such thing as just Häagan Dazs." He ticks off each of her questions and accusations. "I merely started simple. You wouldn't trust anyone to try that stuff on you if you didn't know he could do the basics, would you?"

After spending a while searching his face for any sign of insincerity and finding none, her eyes widen. "You call those the basics?"

His eyes fill with wolfish delight. "Yes, just a bit of practice, some anatomy, a few massage techniques, spot of tantric training...." he lets his voice trail off while she dissolves in hysterics. "What?"

"The *basics*?"

"Yes, vanilla is the basics. There's electricity, wax, impact, heat, cold, bondage, chemical play, all the things we've talked about."

"I wasn't sure you actually did all the things we talked about, but now." She bites her lip and strokes his arm.

His lips curl. "Do you want me to demonstrate a little bit of advanced?"

"That's not fair!"

"What isn't?"

"Asking that!"

"Whyever not?"

"Because if I say yes, I'm giving you free rein, and I'm not sure I can handle that. If I say no, I'm telling you I'm a wuss!" Ella Jane then covers her face and starts laughing.

"What?"

"Not sure I can tell you," she carries on.

He rolls over on top of her, pinning her limbs with his. "Tell. Me!"

Despite her predicament Ella Jane carries on laughing louder and harder. "And..." another convulsion strikes and she breaks off. "And if I tell you," she moistens her lips and blinks away tears. "N-nobody could be as good as you are arrogant. I'm really in trouble." Then blinks up in delight at her own cleverness and uncertainty as to how much trouble she's just got herself into.

He makes an effort to keep his eyebrows from climbing his forehead, and then another to prevent his features from becoming infected by her mood. "Just remember, red, pineapple, safe word, or oh, fuck! Cramp."

"I will." She kisses him and lets out another giggle.

"What is it this time?" he asks her, and she laughs again. "I'm used to men snoring at about this stage, not asking for round two."

"Oh, really?"

"Not quite, I'm used to them doing that about four orgasms ago."

"Hmm, that's hardly gallant; you've only had the four orgasms so far." He allows a hand to begin idly caressing her skin again while his eyes and voice caress her from the inside. "For me, a woman's pleasure either comes first, or I withhold it for a good reason."

Ella Jane blinks and chews her lip. "Is that so?"

To which he declares, "It is," with a firmness that it would credit the solemnest of bible readings.

She can't help enquiring, "And what might be a good reason?"

"To make it greater when it finally comes." He kisses her and gives her a sly smile. "Or because I choose to withhold it."

"I had one Dom who liked doing that."

"Oh?" How good was he at *not* withholding it?"

"You want me to say not as good as you, don't you?"

He blinks mildly.

"Oh my God! You *know* not as good as you, don't you?"

"Even an old man has an ego you know." This time he's the one to laugh at himself. "Anyway, I think it's *my* turn to enjoy *your* luxury ice cream."

"Hmm." Her voice is unconvinced, but she smiles as he rolls over her, welcoming his kiss, and guiding him to her entrance with a hand. "I suppose that's only fair, even if you are an arrogant bastard."

"Don't think I'll forget that young lady."

She laughs, "Moi?" and clenches her hands on his buttocks and her body around him.

His body is no less artful that his hands or tongue and like them, it not only knows what it's doing but has the stamina of an athlete in his prime. He takes her with a range of tempos, reading her desires, teasing her with that knowledge and his ability to satisfy or deny her as he fulfils his own.

From time to time he withdraws and kisses his way down her body, then returns to resume and kisses the sweetness of their union onto her lips. When she playfully seeks to stop him by digging her fingernails into the heavy curves of his buttocks, he rolls her over, slips pillows under her hips, delivers a single resounding spank to her upturned bum and resumes.

With her lying face down, her mons is free.He takes advantage of the position, commanding her to touch herself, but not cum until he does. They're both bathed in sweat by the time he buries himself in her and lets out a guttural sound. As he does, she issues up a silent prayer of thanks and squeezes the tips of her ring and index fingers around her hood and presses her hand against her mons and her hips into his solidity and lets her voice join his.

He rolls away, but leaves his hand in contact with her. "Warm?"

Drenched in their mingled sweat as she is, the question is superfluous, so she smiles as she pants out, "Mmm, a bit, you?"

"A tad." He reaches a thick arm behind him and snags a bottle from the bedside, then offers it to her. "Water?"

"Please," she answers smiling at his English gentleman tone and choice of words and rolls his 'a tad' around in her mind, as she takes it and sips the icy liquid. "Chilly."

"I can leave some off the ice if you want?"

He hands it to her and grabs one of the thick, soft hotel towels he'd put by the bed. She draws a long draught while he starts to dry himself. When she returns the bottle, he looks at the towel and grins before giving her a fresh one.

"I wondered what these were for."

"Being prepared. I'd have felt a proper Charlie if it had turned out that we didn't fancy each other."

She clamps her legs together and lays her towel across her body covering her nudity. "So, you think I fancy you?"

He rubs one corner of his towel over his hair then kneels on the mattress, bends over her and uses a fresh corner to wipe the perspiration from her forehead. "I thought you used to."

He then drinks deeply himself; he lays back and laughs until the well-used muscles of his stomach complain. "Ow." Then he laughs again. This time she joins his laughter, and his complaint. After a further moment's rest, he rolls back towards her and starts using the dry end of his towel on her.

Having dried themselves and each other, they spoon under the covers exchanging small jokes from their long conversations over the months of their online dalliance, and doze.

He's hard against her when she stirs, and she's warm, toastily so. His firm body and the covers make a perfect cosy nest. She looks around the room and smiles to herself. A few short hours ago her own comparatively modest room had seemed palatial.

After a few moments she feels him stir and rubs her hips against him, then chuckles at his vocal appreciation. "Mmm, hey you."

"Hey." His enwrapping arm squeezes her to his chest. "You good?"

"Mhm. I'd ask you to pinch me if I didn't know you really would."

"Ha, of course. Why might you want me to pinch you, aside from the obvious?"

"I still can't believe this."

"What?"

"You, me, us, finally meeting, being here in this suite, that you're *you!*"

"Afraid so. My anonymity is only keyboard deep, and I don't do basic rooms."

"Or basic suites?" The words are out of her mouth even faster than she manages to shut her mouth after them, then she rapidly changes subjects. "You were sweet with the waiter."

"It doesn't hurt to be nice to a fan. They make us."

"I wouldn't know. I haven't really got fans, except my folks and my friends, and they pretty much get to see me when they want."

"Not even your sister?"

"We're close on good days."

After a while he asks, "Do you remember the desserts game?"

"Yes, you were mean."

During their online dalliance she could safely fantasise about him doing deliciously terrible things to her for the least criticism, but here really together, she's vulnerable to whatever response he might choose to make, and his answer is to idly take the bud at the tip of her right breast between his fingertips.

She bites her lip and waits for the pain, but it takes an age in coming. First he teases it to full erectness. Then he gently kneads and stretches it. It isn't until she starts to move in sympathy to his pulsing grip that he pinches hard, and he only does it long enough to draw a gasp from her lips.

"I was finding out what you might want to eat after...."

"Hmm?"

"If you've been a very good girl, the butler service fairy will have put something nice in the fridge in the kitchen for you."

"What if I've been a very bad girl?"

"Then there might be two things." He nuzzles the back of her neck and transfers his attentions to her other breast. "Fancy exploring?"

"Mmm." After their exertions, the idea of a rich sweet dessert is certainly appealing. "Is it good girls or bad girls who like exploring?"

He kisses the back of her neck again and then her shoulder. "The best girls like exploring."

True to his promise, there is not only a tidy little kitchen in the suite, but in its fridge, there are two elegant rectangular plates each with three tiny, beautiful chocolate creations on it.

Refreshed and further delighted Ella Jane steers the conversation. "These are wonderful, but they certainly aren't vanilla."

He takes a morsel from his own plate and eats it with a slow relish while his eyes do the same to her nakedness. "This is true. Vanilla can only take a person so far."

"And explorers are never truly satisfied if they only get to go so far."

His right eyebrow rises. "Are you saying that you aren't truly satisfied?"

"I am, but I spend all those long nights reading the guidebook. It promised even more, all those sexily frightening things I'd only fantasised or hadn't even dreamed of." She eats too, and sucks and licks the spoon clean so thoroughly that surely not one molecule of the exquisite dessert could be left behind.

"Oh, well, in that case." His eyes dance. "I'd better see what we can do to save you from disappointment."

She takes her lower lip between her teeth and ponders while her eyes study him. Then, either emboldened by their good humoured exchanges or made reckless by them, she decides to poke the bear. She sets her empty plate aside. "I thought you'd never ask."

"Are you sure you want to go there young lady."

"Yes," she grins and bites her lip again. "No." Then uses her index finger to make little circles on his chest. "They're very perky."

"So are yours."

"Mine aren't usually." She kisses one of his perky nipples. "Are they always like this?"

"I think so; I don't always pay much attention to mine."

"Oh." She suckles and then blows on it. "I like them."

"So do I, but I prefer yours." He reaches out, brushes his palms across the tips of her breasts, then down their outer swells.

She twists from side to side and bounces on her feet, making her breast bounce. "That's understandable. Mine are fantastic."

He asks, "Are they indeed?" as he strokes her soft curves and the firmness of her ribs and sides.

"Mhm. I can almost cum by touching them."

His eyes light up. "Can you?"

"I've tried a few times. It takes ages, and I've only got close, but it's nice."

"We shall have to have a go at that!"

"If we get time, yes." She kisses his bud again making it wet with her tongue, circles it with her fingertips and touches her hand to the back of his hand on her breast. "That feels nice." They stand companionably, him caressing her, her watching him do so, but she hasn't forgotten the bear is supposed to be a bear. "Did you bring a single tail?"

"I might have."

She lifts her eyes to his and licks her lips. "Might did, or might forgot?"

He raises an eyebrow. "Are you trying to provoke me young lady?"

She swallows, looks down then glances up searchingly, but fails to read him. "May-be..." His face remains impassive, and his eyes hard, so, after a while she hedges, "Yes?"

"Yes? Or Yes!?"

Another blink, and a brief tug of her teeth on her lower lip later she confesses, "Yes, yes!"

"Good girl." His expression and voice soften, "And were you trying to manipulate me into getting that single tail out and laying into you with it?"

"I might have been." His look hardens again, and Ella Jane concedes, "I was, yes."

He takes her hand and lifts it to his lips, kisses her knuckles. "Well, I may or may not have brought one, but either way I won't be using one on you in our first session. I shall, however, reward your eventual candour."

"Do I get to choose how?"

"Hmm, I don't think we know each other well enough to give you a blank cheque. Let me see." He frowns and his hands continue to enjoy her. "You can suggest, or you I'll give you a choice of three options."

She blinks quite deliberately and composes her face into the most ingratiating of smiles. "Can I suggest *and* have a choice?"

He shakes his head. "What are you like?"

Ella Jane repeats her blink and continues to allow her smile to play across her face. They've been chatting for months, and now it's real and exceeding the promises she had assumed were exaggerations. One of the phrases he used in his messages rises in her mind, 'The curse of trust.' She's scared but she trusts him, and her trust undermines the fear. The muscles inside her contract at the thought, but there's nothing for them to hold on to.

"Very well, but you only get a choice of two, and I won't promise to include your suggestion."

"So...?"

"So, if you suggest I use a single tail on you tonight, for example, it still won't be a choice."

"Ooookay." Ella Jane agrees after a fashion.

That, however, isn't enough for him, and he hardens his voice and stresses the D of "Deal?"

"I think so. Yes." Her voice is still hesitant, "Can I think?"

"Of course." He kisses her forehead and leads her back to the master bedroom, still lightly perfumed with the scent of their coupling. He lays her down and covers her with the thick, soft duvet then turns away.

"Where are you going?"

"Oh, nowhere special." His voice drips faux innocence and the glance he gives her over his shoulder is filled with mischief.

"That's..."

"What?"

"Nothing."

He reverses course and threatens, "That had better be an innocent nothing."

She stretches her wrists towards the corners of the huge bed and spreads her legs under the covers. "Or you'll?"

Sitting on the bed he pulls back the covers to reveal her nakedness. "I'll do that anyway, young lady," and he trails a finger between her breasts, and bends over her face so his lips are inches from hers. "But I might not make my doing it so amusing for you."

"Oh, in that case." She lifts her head and kisses his cheek. "I'll think while you're going nowhere special."

"Hmm, change of plan."

"You can't take my choice away now."

"I'm not. I'm just going to make it easier for you to concentrate on your nothing while I go to my nowhere."

With previous lovers, she's fought at this point until they either gave up or used the flat of their hand or some other instrument to quell her rebellion.

She expects to rebel, to resist, to force him to unleash on her some portion of his greater strength and his knowledge of the arts of pain they have discussed so long, so often.

Is it that she fears to, God knows he's intimidating, but she's feared previous partners without trusting them so well.

It can't be that cock sureness *arrogance* she insists to herself. He makes her think of all the films where the evil genius is played by an Englishman. That infuriates her.

But he does quite obviously know every nerve and every muscle in her body, oh God, even her bones! Do people even have nerve endings in their bones?

She narrows her eyes, but she doesn't resist. Once having retrieved a set of wrist and ankle cuffs from his bedside drawers, he takes the first of her wrists, wraps it in a soft leather cuff and threads a length of rope through it.

"You have the most interesting things you keep by your bed you know."

"Really? I must say, I've never looked to see what other men keep there."

Ella Jane admires the first cuff and holds her free arm up in the air rather than wait for him to request her other wrist "Can I take it that one of my choices is going to involve me being tied up?"

"We both included bondage in our earliest conversations about what interests us, so..."

"So, I'm right? I detected a theme."

He flips the covers up and snares one of her ankles rather than binding her offered arm next. "You can always make that your suggestion. I'm not going to confirm or deny anything."

It's her turn to attempt a voice of command, "Are you trying to be mysterious?"

But it achieves nothing more than a further lightening of his mood and almost croons, "Are you curious?"

She snaps, "Yes!" and braces for his expected response.

But all he does his touch his lips to her thigh. "Then I'm trying and succeeding." And he looks up smugly.

"If I'd said no?"

He takes and cuffs her other ankle. "If I'd believed you, I'd have said I was trying and failing."

"You're as quick in real life as you are online."

"Possibly quicker." He finally takes her upraised hand, and kisses the back of it. "Though without the benefit of Googling whether I'm right or not and writing out my snappy retorts three times to try them out in my head."

"Do you really do that?"

His smile grows more insufferable still as he ties the final knot. He then openly admits, "I do!" before frowning as asks, "Don't you?"

Ella Jane looks away. "Not saying!" then sneaks a glance back at him and says, "But!" triumphantly and presses her cuffed legs together.

He lets out a disapproving growl, but doesn't tweak a breast or slap a thigh, preferring instead to stand and move away.

Her eyes follow him as he goes to one of the wardrobes, but she can't see what he gets because he hides it behind his back as he returns with his own triumphal look on his face.

She doesn't have to wait long though because he holds it up. "A spreader bar! I love spreader bars!"

"Of course, a chap does listen." She cheerily submits as he clips her ankle cuffs to either end, then tries, and to both their delight fails to bring her thighs together, no matter how she twists her torso.

He sits back on the bed watching her efforts and strokes a hand down the length of her recently bound arm. "Aren't you a little vulnerably situated to be avoiding questions?" Her eyes speak defiance, but there's a different message in the way she touches the tip of her tongue to her slightly parted lips. "When a girl is naked and tied in such an exposed position, a person could do literally anything to her." His fingers skirt around her breasts as the glide across her skin. "Or just tease her for hours on end without ever quite doing anything to her."

Ella Jane remains unrepentantly silent, while her expression reveals an equally unrepentant enjoyment of the situation and of his caresses.

He knows the logical next move, just as he's certain she knows it too, adding little tweaks and slaps, applying pinches and nips with his teeth and neatly trimmed nails to the caresses.

Her eyes study his as he works, only flicking away now and then to watch his hands on her body and to glance down to confirm his arousal.

He drops his voice to a barely audible rumble, "Are you enjoying this?" His question is as superfluous as it is essential.

"Mhm, sort of," she wriggles as much as the ropes allow to complete her own step in the dance.

"And you're not scared?" His right eyebrow rises and his left lowers.

Her tongue wets her lips before she answers, "No more than I should be," in a whisper.

"Do you really trust me that much? Or are you that much of a masochist?"

Ella Jane sinks her teeth into her lower lip hard enough to make it gleam white in the middle of her spreading smile. "Do you remember teasing me about the word 'or'?"

"I do." In answer to her face's Christmas day smile, his grin flows into that of a crocodile homing in on a gazelle that can't climb a slippery riverbank.

She swallows in an effort to summon moisture to her mouth, which is suddenly dryer than it has any right to be. "Then, yes and yes."

"Are you sure you're being entirely wise."

"I'm sure I'm not, but I'm sure I can trust you."

He uses the middle and index fingers of his right hand to trap her hood and make tantalisingly slow circles, while his left takes a threatening hold of the tip of a breast.

All Ella Jane does in response is drop her guard even further, allowing him to see how the pain and pleasure flow through her.

"This is the problem when one meets a bratty masochist."

"A girl could have a lot of fun with a gentleman who responds to every little tease by doing all the wickedly sort of nice things."

"A girl might also want to consider how long a fellow could choose to take to getting to nowhere, leaving her with nothing to do."

She begins, "You wouldn..." but he sounds so confident, that she becomes less so. "You would, wouldn't you."

"Somewhat appropriately, I would in a New York minute." He kisses her pouting lips in delight at his own cleverness, "If you want to play that sort of game with me, you'd best make sure to read my mood, or ask it."

"Hmm."

"Now, there's one more thing to add, and I can go nowhere while you think of nothing." With that he draws a satiny purse from his bedside and opens it revealing a soft padded velvet blindfold.

In her spreadeagle position, Ella Jane can do nothing about him applying the blindfold to her eyes other than appreciate how snug and comfortable it is.

"Is this entirely necessary?"

"No." He tweaks one conveniently erect nipple. "But it does make it easier for me to maintain an air of mystery," and then the other, "And I suspect it will help you focus on whichever nothing you might want to suggest."

Without his hands on her, and their verbal interplay, it takes just a few seconds for the now blindfolded Ella Jane to wonder and to call out. "How'm I supposed to know what else you've brought?"

And just a second for his laughter to answer her.

Not wishing to delay his mission, Ella Jane decides against further protest. The darkness, her bondage, her imagination and the memories of the earthshattering orgasms before she goaded him into binding her, or he steered her into goading him, are enough.

She hears doors open and close, and the sounds of zippers, wicked chuckles of amusement, something, perhaps something leather being pulled between fingers, and chain links moving against one another.

The sonic chorus seems so artful that she muses on whether it is a recording, and he might be sitting on the chair by the bed observing her as she struggles to hear clues to her fate.

Her Choice

Ella Jane feels his weight on the bed and hears him speak, "Well, I've made my preparations." With his lips now on the curve of a breast and then on her own. "Have you got your suggestion ready?"

She twists her hands in the cuffs. "Well, I don't think I need to worry about suggesting bondage or being made to cum, and you're being mean about the single tail, so that eliminates three of my favourites."

"It does." His fingers stroke and in her blindness, she feels them most intensely. "Such a hard life."

"That leaves impact, electricity and temperature. And I've never tried electricity before. Did you bring anything?"

"So, you choose electricity?"

"If you've brought something, yes. If not I'll be very disappointed in you!"

"I'd say I'm going to make you pay for that, but I get the impression that's what you want?" His tone making clear it's a question. Excitement that rises inside her eyes, her cheeks, and then her laughter gives him his answer.

"You're being such a bad girl for such a good girl." He kneels astride her slender form. Her wrists are securely bound, and his weight is on her hips, leaving his hands free to touch at leisure. "I'm trying to decide." His cocky smile speaks of devilment.

For all the sensations his hands give, the darkness in her fears disappointment after the months of anticipation since she first asked him about electroplay. The corners of her mouth fall sadly, "Whether to?"

His laughter cuts her off. "Not whether, when and how. I've waited a long time, and this is your choice." He pauses and smiles, toys with her breasts and takes a gentle hold of their tumescent buds.

She corrects him. "We've waited a long time."

He squeezes harder and pulls firmly. "I want to enjoy this," and harder still, "And I want you to see how much I enjoy it." His voice is level, amicable, conversational, but the cruelty of his hands grows with each word. "I want you to see my eyes, and I want look into yours."

Ella Jane holds her breath and arches her back, lets her voice and face reveal her pain, her arousal and her desire to him. And in the darkness she imagines the daemon in his eyes drinking them in.

"But I know how you love to be blindfold too." His hands become gentle. "If I use electricity on you again, I'll let you try it without being able to see."

He caresses her a while longer. "Do you think it's fair that I should get a choice too?"

Ella Jane grins as she declares "No!" in the certainty that doing so will lead to some form of chastisement, and she squeals with laughter when his fingertips punish her breasts. "Of course!"

"Oh good!"

She swallows. "What have you chosen?"

He settles into his musing and while he does, his hands enjoy the smooth warmth of her defenceless body. "Well, seeing as how my favourites include impact, bondage, and electricity, and you're already tied up." His lips touch her mons. "Wax is out, I'd have to untie you and put some protective sheeting down." The tips of his fingers circle slowly on her skin. "Then there's ice, but I prefer this room to the other and your enthusiasm has already soaked enough sweat into the sheets for the night."

The bound Ella Jane balks at the assertion, well aware that he's equally responsible, but she doesn't speak and spoil the moment.

"That leaves impact or orgasm denial." He brushes lightly along the swollen length of her outer lips. "And it's a bit late for orgasm denial."

Her teeth worry at her lip again. "So, I wanted electricity or impact and your answer is both?"

"What can I say? It must be your lucky, or your unlucky day."

Even now, he isn't sure. There are many women (and many men, though those do not interest him) who watch, and read, and dream. Somewhat fewer are brave enough to step into the shallows of the dark sea and feel its waters lapping at their legs or even just their feet. So, although she has sworn to him that she longs to plunge headlong into their depths, he decides to let her sample those waters first.

With her eyes denied her, she doesn't see the movement, though her ears hear the swish and slap, and her thigh feels the sudden fire. "Is that what you mean?" he asks with demonic smugness, as heat follows fire. He's full of casual arrogance as he delivers the blow, like the way he made her cum, and the passion with which his gaze penetrates her soul. In her blindness, her mind conjures up an image of him looking down at her bound form. That face, the cruel smile, she's certain he wants to kiss her, or to crush her. But she finds herself unsure, even uncaring, as to which.

"Fuck, that hurt." She breathes. "I thought said you didn't like to mark anyone without them asking?" The words were half accusatory.

"I don't. Look, if you don't believe me. Close your eyes." He gives her a moment then removes the black cloth.

She blinks, lifts herself and looks down at the pale skin of her leg, and sees the angry red line fading before her eyes.

"Five, four, three..." he counts down and the mark disappears as he reaches zero; the pain and heat remain.

"Jesus! Where did you learn to do that?"

A hint of ruefulness sneaks into his expression. "I have no idea! Even the friend who taught me how to use a crop doesn't." He laughs, strokes the line on her leg that had briefly carried the vivid mark, and then touches the side of her face. "But I really like it." His kiss is both devil and lover and sweeps her earlier question away.

Next, he shows her a thick, heavy flogger. Its long soft trails fall across her skin.

"Mmm. I like."

He grins. "So you said." And with a flick of his wrist, he sends those falls swirling and brings them down on her in a sensuously warming stroke. "Repeatedly."

She chuckles. "It's true. But a girl can't deny her favourite things."

A long period of him using it to stroke and periodically strike follows. He studies her eyes and how her body responds. He focuses on how hard doing this to her makes him. The blows become more frequent, and he starts varying their intensity. He concentrates on her thighs, and to a lesser extent the smooth muscles of her stomach, but every now and then he catches her breasts or her opening and keeps doing so until her focus begins to drift and her vocalisations merge into a contented crooning.

Having coaxed her into that blissful state, he sits again and shows her two towels. He strokes her with each. Once is cool and damp, refreshing but heavy, the other fluffy and comforting. He twists the damp towel and folds it around. "You said you like thuddy, too?"

Ella Jane's response is that of her innermost self. "All of it," as her voice dreamily confesses, "stingy, thuddy, hot...." her voice fades and, out of words, or at least out of those she can speak aloud, her teeth take hold of her lip to still her tongue. The need in her eyes burns as deeply as before her orgasms and his flogger. "I told you the truth when we were talking, I like the anticipation and the pain." She closes her eyes and lets out a sigh then opens them again and looks straight into his, "The memory of the pain."

He listens intently, as any man would, however, his mind doesn't disengage. "It doesn't actually have to hurt though."

"How do you mean?"

"Beating." His eyes are alight again.

Ella Jane doesn't get it, but her body responds to his devilish look.

"There's a massage technique, pummelling. It centres on impact but not causing pain. There's a beating technique that derives from it." His eyes dance over her body as he speaks, "It's one reason I want to get you stronger if we're going to do this long term..."

He twists the towel loosely and folds it over, swings it, and there's a low whum that makes her insides squirm.

She bats her eyes at him despite the tingling, "But what if I want it to hurt?"

When he stops Ella Jane finds it hard to keep her face straight, and her facial contortions in their turn make his eyes flash darkly. She can't move far with her wrists bound as they are, but she can't stay still so she pulls and twists.

"There's plenty I can and will do in the way of hurting, but I'm doing this first."

Casting her mind back to their many online conversations she narrows her eyes. "Are you going to say you have a talent for it."

He grins evilly then lets his face settle into a level stare.

"Of course you are."

"No, that was online. We're here together now. So I rather think I'll demonstrate." He wraps the dry towel around it. "This is just for your bum and thighs though, and you remember your safe word?"

After the previous ravaging she almost laughs, doubting her body would allow her to speak it, but she understands, and she tells him, "Mhm, red, Sir."

"And you're sure you're ready?"

She has no idea, whether she truly is, but she trusts him. The night has gone so well, and she's filled a burning need. "Yes, Sir."

"I'll have to reposition you."

"How would you like me, Sir?" she asks dreamily, her mind already trying to imagine the sensations to come.

"Face down with a pillow under your hips."

He picks her up and turns her. Doing so puts a twist in the rope securing her wrists to the headboard and pulls her arms still close together, increasing the pressure her bondage applies to her shoulders. He then lifts her hips and slides one of the thick pillows under them.

Everything she has written and said about her submission and her masochism plays back to him in his mind, and he hopes they are all true. He hopes she believes, trusts and wants to experience the hundred things he has suggested.

He climbs above her and leans down close, holding still there until his hardness against her prompts her recently sated body to respond.

She knows what is to come first, but her hips yearn towards him, nonetheless, and she turns to look at him over her shoulder.

It's his turn to bite his lip and give an appraising look. "Tempting though it is, a promise is a promise," He kisses her lips. "And I made the promise to show you I'm not just vanilla first." The next kiss is on just *that* spot on the side of her neck. "But, I'll make you another for afterwards," and he smiles wickedly. "Or perhaps during and afterwards. Now, let's get those cuffs tied down securely, shall we?"

The rush is real, and intense, and consuming. The gift of her masochism is one she hasn't fully given in a long time. She hasn't found someone she trusted enough to give in to for too long. Knowing from their weeks of conversation just how turned on he is by receiving it is as overwhelming as her anticipation.

"Still ready?"

Ella Jane wriggles her raised bum. "Still hope so."

The beating with the towels is like nothing she's ever known. There are elements of pillow fights on childhood sleepovers and some of her experiences with heavy paddles. There's neither girlish giggling nor pain, though. Even the lightest of the blows he inflicts carries a weight and even the heaviest doesn't hurt as such. They all strike right through to the marrow of her bones. Towels in his right hand, he works her with a rhythm, builds up a sweat and although it doesn't hurt, she starts to call out at the fall of each blow.

After a time, the crop makes an appearance. She doesn't see him pick it up, but its bright crisp sting begins to punctuate the methodical thuds. He doesn't strike hard with it, and the blows don't cause more than momentary flashes of pain. Need rises, tears come, and then he's on her again, in her again. She's craning her neck around and their teeth are clashing in a ferocious kiss, and then they are still.

Ella Jane rubs her hips and the back of her head against him as she lies panting and naked but for her cuffs, then grumbles at the loss of contact and warmth when he leaves her. He doesn't go far or for long though, just to get yet another towel. On his return, he begins to tenderly dry her body.

She lies there bound and helpless, sifting through her memory for comparisons and so far as she's able, shifting position to make herself more readily accessible to his ministrations as she processes the exotic cocktail of pleasure and exhaustion spiced with pain still meandering through her nervous system. God! If his vanilla was top shelf! She nestles into him, feels and enjoys his hardness, though she's too far from this plane to take advantage of it or to serve it. So she just lies and processes, revelling in the slow, gentle power of his touch, accepting, and relishing.

Responding to her stirrings, his arm around her eases her more closely into his bulk, and his throat makes a low sound in response to her waking purr. Seeing a patch of her pale shoulder peeking out from beneath the thick carpet of her auburn hair, he lowers his lips to it, kisses tenderly, and delights in her contented mewl of a response.

There's the undeniable feeling of after a beating. Her muscles and bones feel it, the deep sensations and the jangling of her nerves. There's no pain though, just as there hadn't been while he worked her over, not even when she tests her body by slinking and then stretching her back. There's just a marrow deep warmth and a smile that rises from her core.

"Well?"

Ella Jane smiles without fully emerging from her stupor. "Hmm?"

"Did you like it?"

She rouses, and looks up at him disbelievingly only to see a blend of childlike delight and smugness on his face.

"It's important to know."

"Very funny."

"Is that a yes?"

She buries her face between him and the pillows before she asks, "The whipping or the orgasm?"

He gazes down at her with smiling eyes. "Um, both."

She reaches up with one hand and strokes the silver streaked hair above his ear. "Has anyone ever told you, you do too much?"

"Yes."

"And you still do all you do?"

He shrugs. "I do me, and hope others will do the same. Isn't that for the best?"

She lets out a little chuckle. Her eyes seek for traces of insincerity in his face. Finding none, she lifts her head and touches her lips to his then lays her head back down.

He bends and kisses her shoulder again as he continues applying silky sweeps across her now dry skin. "Something funny?"

"Mmm, something nice, vanilla and your salted caramel, and I was worried I'd miss out on dessert."

He lies against her. Being unsure as to how soon she'll be ready, he doesn't press his hardness into her. When the slow, comfortable stretching and slinking of her body against his presses her hips back into his solidity, they feel no such reticence, and the change in the note of her satisfied groan tells him so.

Deciding that no amount of effort can keep the smugness from his voice, he goes the other way. "You still didn't say if it was nice?" His voice is laden with certainty, and he allows his hands to stake their claim to her.

Ella Jane is still processing when she hears the question, and realising that while he's been stroking and drying her, he could have said anything. She hopes it's the first time he's asked and turns her head to see if he's asking seriously or just fishing for the praise he must know damned well his performance has earned.

"Does that mean it was okay?"

It takes her a moment to read his face, and determine the question is genuine, but that the *fuck I'm good* arrogance is too. It takes her a moment longer to formulate the possible answers, "Mmm... Well..." her voice is a little hoarse, "For a first time..." and wonders if he'll read her and respond.

His eyes narrow, and she answers with a laugh and by aligning herself to him. Catching his hardness between her buttocks, she rocks her hips, and, turning her face into the softness of the pillows, she hedges, "Umm, it might have been." And she laughs again, the musical sound prompting a renewal of his rumbling chuckle and provoking him into tickling her.

She tries to escape, but the downside of his strength is that she can do no more than press herself into the bed's warmth and into his. Even straining with her hips and kicking her legs under him has no effect but to encourage his laughter and cause a surge in the stiff heat against her. He only relents, returning to caressing touches, when her laughter begins to sound pained.

He purses his lips in the way he does when he's going to stretch out an em sound for effect. "Might have been?"

"Oooh! You know it was!" Ella Jane cranes around to look at him with accusation in her eyes, but she still presses her lips to his caressing hand when he strokes her face. "Where did you learn that?"

"It was more a case of discovering rather than learning." He sweeps the hair from her neck, bends and kisses her there, then stretches out beside her and resumes his caressing as he speaks. "The funny thing about writing is that you have to learn a little bit about a lot of things."

"Mhm?" With him at her side she rolls over placing her back against his warmth.

"Well, I did a massage course, and while I was doing some research on the Dark series, I did one on enhanced interrogation techniques."

"You make that sound so normal!"

"There are characters in the books who use them. I had to learn enough to be convincing, so I studied interrogation, anatomy and torture." Lying as they are, spooned with her back to him, it's easy for his right hand to take hold of her right nipple and to murmur, "And every now and then, it's proved useful since," into her ear as he tightens his grip.

She arches her neck in acceptance, waits, feels the surge of pain radiate from the captive tip of her breast, and then rides the wash of pleasure that follows as she turns, her lips seeking his.

The kiss is a lingering, and she misses it when his lips break away. "Useful how?"

He chuckles out, "Such a minx." But he still gifts her the pain and pleasure her artful reply seeks to earn. Then he kisses her again, and moves his hand to her left breast.

She suffers and delights under the new assault, and then she nods and presses her bum cheeks into him, waits again, suffers again, and breathes her response into his kiss. When his hand strays downwards, she opens herself to him, uncertain as to what his clever digits will do to her most sensitive places. He doesn't go straight for the target, and she's learning that he rarely does. But, with her rising need, she still holds herself available hoping he'll surrender to his lust even if he won't give in to her own.

She looks back. Her hair and makeup are a mess, and her eyes are still dilated, but there she is sassing him and lifting as if to say, *is that all you've got?* He gives her a look straight out of the seventh circle. It's only meant as a warning, but he sees something in her eyes respond and she twists her hip away from him leaving her buttocks exposed.

He's still looking into her eyes when the flat of his hand lands hard, crazy hard, on her upturned bum, and her body bucks as the sound of the impact bounces back at them from the walls.

Seemingly satisfied with his efforts, he smiles down at her, making her blush and smile. He's hard again. Her libidinous mind's *oh wow* is tinged with a hint of *oh no*. As he looks, he seems to make a decision, and without freeing her wrists or detaching the cuffs from the headboard he turns her back over and manoeuvres yet another towel under her to shield her from the sweat that has soaked into the sheets.

"Wouldn't it have been easier to untie me?" she asks, looking around at him. It earns her another stinging swat from the hard palm of his hand.

"Perhaps, but right now I'm not sure if I ever want to do that."

Those are somehow the perfect words, and she can think of no further response.

He detaches her cuffs from the headboard, but can't bring himself to separate them or to free her legs from the spreader bar, then teases, "Is that enough freedom?"

Spurred on by his taunt, she experiments with the little freedom of movement she has and with some effort, she manages to roll herself onto her front once more. She then stretches out, raises herself onto her elbows just far enough to lift her breasts from the soft cotton. With the spreader, keeping her legs widely splayed, she quickly realises she doesn't have the leverage to turn herself back over. She's trapped, and the sense of being so controlled washes warmly through her again. Finally, she opens her mouth as she looks up at him, smiles and breathes, "Oops!" before lowering her gaze and waiting. This makes her body the perfect offering. Mouth, pussy and bum ready for his cock and every part of her bound nakedness available for whatever delight or torment he cares to inflict.

To think, this is only their first time! She wonders what his instincts will lead him to do. Use her body? Abuse it? Pleasure it? It isn't as though he hasn't already shown his eagerness to do all three. A welter of possibilities floods her mind as he sits down on the mattress beside her and begins to stroke her vulnerable form again.

Ella Jane looks at the toys and then at him and asks the obvious question. "Were you nervous bringing so many through customs?"

"Not in the least."

Of course, he wouldn't be. He'd just give anyone who questioned him that arrogant look and hold it until they blushed to their roots.

"Are you ready for your choice yet or are you still playing stranded turtle?"

She gives him a death stare before admitting she is. "Absolutely not, but absolutely. Just so long as you're ready to explain it to the authorities if I die from an orgasm overdose."

He chuckles and assures her. "I'll do my best."

"Can I have a clue about the things you brought?"

"I brought some of the things you asked me about, and I haven't used all of them on you yet."

She guesses what he's building up to, but teases around it. "Hmm, you've already used a flogger and a crop and you said you won't use a single tail on me tonight."

"There are other things, take your time, I'm sure you'll have a lightbulb moment..."

Ella Jane blinks mock ignorance at him. "You aren't being very helpf-" then her face lights up in a smile. "Oh! You are, aren't you, *electricity!*"

He bends close. "Good girl, go, or should that be come, to the top of the class."

He positions her face up again, this time attaching the spreader to the foot of the bed and tightening the ropes. Once he's satisfied that she can't move, he shows her a black box with sockets and dials then turns it on. "These," he touches two dials, "control intensity from zero to ninety-nine in each channel. The buttons set the pattern. This dial is the speed of the pattern, and you saying 'red' will make me press this." He hits the on-off button and the box's LEDs go dark.

Having shown her, he carefully sets it aside and holds up a little torpedo shaped steel butt plug and a smooth jawed screw and spring clamp, then he strokes her body. "This goes where you think it does, and I'm going to put this over your hood."

Ella Jane swallows and asks querulously, "Not straight on my clit?"

He strokes her hair, touches his lips to hers. "Not this first time, little one." He smiles down at her. "I've been looking forward to this."

She opens her mouth to answer, but her bravery deserts her and nothing comes out.

"Remember traffic lights, and it's okay."

A frown of puzzlement crosses her face. "What is?"

"This!" he winks cockily. "We haven't chosen 'Oh Fuck!' as your safe word."

She narrows her eyes; it's all very well for him to joke! Then again, his delivery of a pain-free beating had been unique and spectacular, and even his twist on vanilla lovemaking had been. So, she waits and trusts as he sets about lubing the plug and fitting it to her. It's only about as thick as the finger he first penetrated her rear opening with, considerably narrower that his cock, and its slick, polished, rounded, and tapered tip slips easily into her slightly reluctant bottom.

"Oh!"

"Okay?"

"It feels good for something so small." She chews her lip at the innuendo, then exchanges a glimmer of a smile with him at their shared understanding.

"So glad." He wiggles it and watches her respond to the sensations, then kisses her again. Next, he holds up the clamp and sets its screw to allow its jaws to close within a few millimetres of each other. "That should be about right." His smile widens. "Red for too tight, blue for it's going to slip off." He then lays a small cloth over her mons and gently pries her outer lips back with the index and middle fingers of his left hand while he prepares to apply the clamp. "Ready?"

He waits while she gives another swallow a nod of her head and a, "No, but yes." Then he applies the clamp trapping her tender morsel of flesh in a definite, but not painful pinch.

"Okay?" He asks, and she nods. He gives a series of little tugs while studying her opening with obvious delight as he does so. Satisfied with his work, he wraps the clamp in a cloth. "Insulation, I wouldn't want the zaps to go where they aren't intended." and lays it on her pubic bone. With her body ready he connects one cable to the plug, another to the clamp and carefully checks both are secure. "Just the two points this time." He says the words with a hint of regret and kisses the tip of each of her breasts in turn. "Sorry, ladies, you'll have to wait for our next session."

Then he settles down to enjoying her bound and vulnerable nakedness, stroking her with his hands and mouth, trailing the soft, heavy falls of the flogger he has so far refused to whip her with and humming happily to himself as he does so. It may only be their first night together, but he knows where and how to touch her so as to set her heart racing and her body pulsating without seeming to try. She's already breathing raggedly by the time he sets the first trickle of electricity flowing through her. It almost instantly puts her on the verge of her first orgasm.

"FUCK!"

He stops the current. "Like?"

"Jesus Christ!" He laughs in response to her exclamation. "Why didn't anyone tell me about this!"

"Ha! No one ever told you about soft towel beatings either."

"Okay smarty." This time he sends a more intense burst of electricity through Ella Jane's most intimate flesh, and she screams at the top of her voice.

"I'd advise you to be a good girl when I'm using these on you."

"Fuck, that hurt! But..."

"The after-effects?"

"Yes, wow!"

"All tingly?"

"Uh-huh."

"Want me to do it again?"

"No. Well, yes." She swallows and breathes out with a whooshing sound. "Give me a second."

"Of course." He strokes her cheek and beams down at her with delight. "Do you want to revise your earlier comment?"

"I admit that you're every bit as much of a master pervert in the flesh and not a smarty pants at all, not even a little bit."

"Thank you, but don't push it." He rewards her with a new pattern and a new, lower level of intensity.

Ella Jane writhes luxuriantly, half testing her bonds and half enjoying their mastery over her. "Mmm, that's so nice."

"I'm glad you're enjoying yourself." He leaves the sensually mild waves of electricity ebbing and flowing between the clamp over her hood and clit and the little plug in her bum, then sets about seducing her captive body with his hands and lips once more. From time to time he stops, kisses or caresses a particular point and lovingly describes the levels of pleasure and pain he aims to inflict on it with electricity and by other means.

The next intense jolt comes while his teeth are gently nibbling the tip of a breast, and the one after while his eyes are inches from her own studying her, and two of his fingers are fully inside her giving her body something to grip onto as shock induced spasm takes control of her body. He kisses her when the pain subsides, then smiles down at her as he sends another, longer burst of electricity through her. He follows this by touching his thumb to the clamp over her centre and making a circling motion. As he does so, he sets his little torture box to an undulating pattern and his fingers inside match the rhythm, pressing against the inside of her pubic bone.

Ella Jane mewls into the kiss that follows, then screams out as when he turns the power up as another orgasm tears through her body.

He lowers the voltage and holds close against her while she calms, caressing her hypersensitised skin and crooning gently either to her, to himself, or out of simple contentment. "Ready for more?"

With him so close, she can feel his hardness up against her. With the tantalising effects of his touch, the softly pulsing tingle of electricity between the plug and clamp and the bondage providing constant reminders of her state of surrender, Ella Jane would only have demurred if, for some reason, she absolutely had to. Instead she tugs against her bonds. "I'm still your prisoner."

"How convenient!" he lifts the box, tinkers again, and this time sets to a regular pulsing, then toys with the frequency until he has it going one second on, two seconds off, before setting it aside again and rolling himself above her.

After the hours of stimulation, her body's more than ready for him. With the bind she's secured in, she would be powerless to do anything but say the safe word even if she were not so eager to have him inside her. She says only, "Won't you get shocked too?"

"Not as much as you."

"So generous!"

"Do you want to share that delicious tingling?" A slight turn of the power dial increases the intensity of the pulses through and spasms in the muscles of her anus and entrance.

"Maybe, if you keep turning it up."

"Meanie!" His fingers chastise an innocent breast as he sinks fully into her. "I do like the way you clench around me."

Ella Jane gasps as he times his thrust with a pulse of electricity causing her to tighten around him. "I have no control over that."

"You do." He grins down. "A little anyway. You can resist it or go along." He strokes a thumb along her jawline. "I gather both can be interesting." He holds still, deep inside her.

Ella Jane tries and, lets her awareness sink into the flow of current through her body. She fights it, goes along with it and rocks her hips as best she's able to in her bondage in lieu of him moving inside her.

He waits, remaining frustratingly still until she's unable to remain silent, before adding his movement and timing his thrusts to hers. There's still no haste about him though. Despite his ferocious hardness and his own vocalisations making plain that his need is both strong and immediate, he builds up slowly. As he adds power, he also turns up the box, eventually reaching a point at which each jolt is on the verge of painful, and each thrust of his hips strikes her with bone-shaking force. Each time his hips meet hers, the impact causes the clamp to tug at her trapped flesh.

83

She tries to focus on him, on seeing how he approaches his point of no return, but fails as she crashes through her own. Her body arches, convulses, strains against her bonds triggering his climax as it does, locking his muscles into place above and inside her. As they cum together, he uses the machine to deliver two last spikes of painfully intense stimulation before he turns it off and wraps his arms around her.

Ella Jane feels his body surrender to their union and sinks into that surrender with him.

As they lie together, she nuzzles against him. "What do you like best?"

He ponders "Various things, the female orgasm is the most fun I can have with my clothes on, but I don't exactly know what it's like to experience one from the female in question's perspective. I've spoken with lesbian and bisexual women who assure me that their feelings *giving* are very similar to my own, but to actually experience the various kinds of female sexual pleasure? That's something that is beyond me."

"I can see you asking people."

"Fortunately, people in the community are quite open. Some vanilla people are quite keen on having someone to talk to as well. I get research students to do it, too."

"There's something rather un-poetic about that."

"Writers are like D types. We pretend we were born knowing everything, but the best we can do is cheat and work at it."

"Was that your way of avoiding telling me what you like best?"

"What do you mean?"

"You seem so happy in whatever you're doing to me. It's hard to be sure what you really want."

"Oh, you mean, teasing, caressing, fucking, torturing or pleasuring you?"

She winces. "If you choose to put it like that."

"I do, and, seeing as how you're still all tied up," his hands trace her limbs and her bonds, "I'm inclined to answer that I'm not sure, but that if you will permit me to do each of those things to you a few more times, I'll try to make up my mind."

"What did you say?"

He pinches the conveniently exposed and conveniently sensitive tip of a breast. "Are you not listening?"

"I am! It's your voice. When you touch me at the same time. I can't help zoning out!"

"Hmm." He repeats himself more slowly.

"That sounds like you just want to keep me here and do whatever you want to me."

His eyes light up, and his voice fills with mischief. "Purely in order to satisfy *your* curiosity." As he speaks, he tightens his grip on her and starts to stretch her nipple away from her body.

She scoffs, "I'll bet!" then yelps, "*Ouch!*" at his latest cruelty when he suddenly grips more tightly and tugs the trapped bud.

"Ha!" He narrows his eyes. "You deserved that." And he allows her tortured breast to return to its natural shape and gentles it.

"I did, Sir." The manner in which she admits it being as unrepentant as he is of his cruelty.

"Do you wish you hadn't told me now?"

"Told you what, Sir?"

"All those fantasies?" he continues caressing. "All of those fears?" His eyes taunt, and her memories rise. Somehow telling her deepest, darkest secrets from the safety of her own bed, with her free hand covering, touching, exploring, pleasuring...

She catches herself looking down and bites her lip. "I don't know, Sir."

Processing the scene "Was that okay for you?"

Ella Jane bites back a laugh and shakes her head, then looks up at him and wipes his sweat slicked neck. "You're not supposed to ask that kind of question." and looks away. "I read that there are three kinds of men who ask that."

"And those are?"

"The jealous ones," she gives him a playful look. "And the ones who don't realise it wasn't."

"That's only two."

"And arrogant bastards like you," His eyes harden, and she teases with hers as bravely as she can while she feels a clenching inside. "Sir."

"Are you trying to get yourself in trouble?"

"No." She looks away, then half smiles and meets his eyes. "Well, only sort of. You want me to admit what you already know."

His wolfish grin confirms the truth of that for her. "I do. And?"

Ella Jane is no wallflower, but she colours as she answers, "Yes." The memory's warmth floods her as she speaks, "More than okay." She rubs herself against him. "You know it was." Then she giggles as a word from her love of PG Wodehouse leaps out at her. "What you might call spiffing."

He tries not to see the funny side. "Serious trouble." But she dissolves in mirth, then complains when her fresh outbreak of laughter hurts the weary muscles of her stomach.

"I'm not sure how that would look as a review."

She tries out, "Spiffing in the sack." And this time he doesn't hold himself back from joining in with her humour.

"Would you like to know a secret in return?"

"Very well."

"When a man asks that in private, it's because he wants you to say yes and mean it. When he asks you that in public, he wants you to say yes and have someone else believe it."

"And why does he do those things?"

"Ah, now that would be telling."

"That's mean!"

"No, I only offered one secret. Telling you would give away a second."

"Hmph." She pouts but it has no effect, so instead she tries to find out more about something else. "What else can my doctor Frankenstein do with electricity."

"So much! I'm afraid I don't have that extensive a kit here."

"What?"

"There's only so much a fellow can reasonably bring with him on holiday."

"You have more?"

"More TENS style boxes, some violet wands, a couple of Van de Graff generators and innumerable attachments for each."

She stretches out against him. "Mmm, I might have to visit."

"That would be nice."

He leans over and her lips part. They kiss with a tenderness and in a silence at odds with much of what has gone before.

When he lifts away, she smiles up at him shyly. "Was there anything else you wanted to show me tonight?"

"There are one or two more things that need taking care of."

She wriggles her hips against him. "Is that so?"

"It is indeed."

"Such as?"

He runs a thumb suggestively across her lips and when she responds by opening her mouth and welcoming its living warmth in, he murmurs, "Guessed one yet?"

"I did say I like that, didn't I?"

"Frequently."

"You make me sound like some kind of hussy!"

"There are whole treatises on how much pleasure a person's mouth can give and receive."

"Are those treatises you've written?" His eyebrow shoots up on cue, and she giggles and takes the tip of his thumb back in her mouth before he can do anything about it.

He growls and, somewhat defensively says, "Not all of them."

She lets his thumb go for just long enough to chirp, "Just most?" then laughs and suckles as his free hand punishes her.

"About fifteen percent, most of them are written by women and gay and bisexual men."

"So, you study treatises written by gay men?"

"Knowledge is knowledge, and some of them have the advantage of experiences from both ends as it were."

She swirls her tongue around the tip of his digit as if it were a real cock, then looks into his eyes. "So dedicated. Is this the only thing, Sir?"

"No indeed, if I have my way, not even your bum will be spared."

"Speared?"

"No, spared, your bum is definitely going to get speared."

"Unless I say red."

"Do you expect to say red?"

"No, you've speared me elsewhere, and I rather enjoyed that."

"Yes?"

"I must say I am rather curious what twist that wicked mind of yours is going to put on it." The imagery in her mind is stark, his height, mass, the power of his hips and shoulders above her tiny frame.

"Is that a challenge?"

"Mmm, might be."

He runs his thumb over her lips again. "Well in that case you should give me some time to think about it, and I have a wonderful idea as to what you can do while I'm thinking."

She briefly takes his thumb into her mouth again. "Won't that distract you?"

"I'm not sure, Why don't you try, and we can find out."

This time she makes sure his thumb feels her teeth before she lets go, and when she looks up afterwards with challenge in her eyes, he takes an iron grip on the tip of her chin. "Behave you."

It isn't as if it's not something she enjoys. It's even better than a thumb or finger, though of course a thumb or finger has the advantage that while she's sucking that, a cock can be elsewhere. And his is intact. A strange novelty to her. It's also one that she's had inside her and not yet had in her mouth. The intimacy of using her tongue to explore something that has known the most private self for the first time is...

Ella Jane kisses her way down his body navigating via the lines of his heavy muscles and the little peaks of his chest. She fails to find any ticklish places to torment him, but does find that every inch of him is sweet with the blend of their scents.

"You don't have any tattoos?" Her question is probably superfluous, given that she is in the process of looking.

"I've never had the inclination." He drawls, more interested in his own exploration of her ivory skin with its dusting of light freckles.

She senses that it's not the time for her to say *my exes had tattoos*, but can't help. "I can't believe I didn't ask."

Unlike some of the men she's known, he isn't fully waxed or shaved, and unlike others, his hair isn't wildly unkempt. When she slips a hand below to cup his balls and stroke behind them she finds he's perfectly smooth there. "Ooh, I like this." The way his already blood-filled flesh hardens further tells her that she's not the only one. "And so do you!"

She kisses his shaft and then the tip of his sheathed cock, lets out a giggle and opens her mouth. She kisses it again, this time more intimately swirling her tongue around its little roll neck. She pulls back and looks up. "It feels nice!"

He's looking down at her with mirth on his face. "I'm so glad."

His sarcasm provokes her into putting her tongue out at him, and having her tongue out, she decides not to waste the effort and runs its tip up the length of his cock. Then she wraps her hand around its shaft and starts to pull downwards. Seeing the skin and opening start to stretch around its head, she stops and asks, "Does this hurt?"

He touches a hand to her hair. "No, it's like your bits, it only hurts if it's done suddenly without warming it up."

She muses, "So much to learn." and resumes her efforts to do so, experimenting with the feeling of having it in her mouth with the sheath forward and withdrawn. "It feels different with your foreskin up."

"Good different?"

She mhms without letting his cock out of her mouth.

"Better?"

That makes her cough, and she lets him slip out. Then she looks up with watering eyes and the beginnings of a smile. "I don't know.

I'll have to keep comparing." She beams her delight as his chuckle shakes his body and makes the engorged flesh in her hand shake. Then she focuses on her efforts.

After that she carries on until her lips, the roof of her mouth and tongue develop the same *I've been fucked* feeling that she has inside. The head of his cock becomes, and stays, swollen and polished in her mouth. Then she looks up hungrily. "Have you decided what twist you're going to put on fucking my ass yet, Sir?"

She's sure his cock's close, but she's not sure whether he's angry or acting when he growls, "Come here, you." He hauls her up on top of him, but when he rolls them both over and drives his full length into her, she doesn't care. Being so close, his cock is hard and hot and having excited herself by sucking him her body is eager and ready.

He fucks her energetically, building up a rhythm until she's breathing hard and matching it. Then he stops with just the tip of his cock inside her despite the continued urging of her hands on his haunches. "I have." He then withdraws, and she lets him. He kisses her fiercely, and she welcomes his energy into her. Moving her to one side and arranging the numerous pillows, he rolls her on top of them. Carefully, he puts the wand within reach. He then settles next to her and adds more of the lube he's used earlier to her rosebud. With slow, tender strength, his massaging fingers seduce rather than force. His lips play a light accompaniment across the skin of her shoulders and the back of her neck. His seduction continues until he has painlessly pressed the full length of his thumb into her rear and is pinching against it in a slow milking action with his forefinger in her opening. Meanwhile his ring and middle fingers sandwich her hood. He now exacts his revenge for her teasing by taking her close and keeping her there until she mewls her frustration.

Once satisfied that she has suffered enough, he stands back to admire his handiwork. While she's looking at him with anticipation on her face, he swings a hand down and lands a resounding spank to each side of her upturned bum before returning to the bed and positioning himself over her.

She's still processing the way the impact turns from shock to pain and then pleasure when he enters her again and gasps as he withdraws and sets himself at her rear.

Ella Jane groans, smiles, pants, and buries her face in the soft pillows.

He holds himself still with the tip of his cock at her rosebud. "Are you sure?"

"I wouldn't have squealed with delight when you started to lube me if I weren't."

Having confirmed her willingness, he enters her more slowly than anyone ever has before. He stops as the crown of his cock reaches her inner, involuntary, ring and waits.

He holds still, and his voice rumbles, "I'm going to take my time," softly in her ear.

That makes her laugh, and they both feels her tight, muscular rings clenching around the intrusion. Between breaths she pants out, "Easy for... you... to say. Oh God! Agh, wait, ow, ah!"

"Ow, not red?"

"Ah! It's okay," Ella Jane assures him she wants to continue. "Just ow, you're thicker than I'm used to."

His responding chuckle makes him swell in and against her, and her panting intensifies.

She has a pretty good idea what the consequences will be, but she says it anyway, "Such a bastard." She feels the pain as his finger punishes the tips of her breasts for her temerity.

He doesn't push further into her, just holds where he is applying more pressure as he takes hold of each of her nipples in turn and slowly, deliberately pinches and stretches them.

He doesn't need to push though. The waves of pleasure and pain, humour and intimacy cause her muscles to ease around him and her hips lifts towards his hips, inviting him deeper.

His slowness continues. It does so frustratingly and delightingly. Time and again he clenches, stretching her and caresses, soothing her until she's ready. Then he advances with millimetric care.

He stops again when he's fully inside her. He kisses, assures, tenses, and begins to rock slowly. He wraps one arm under her breasts and the other down to her hips and grips. He uses them to hold her as he builds his pace and the force with which he thrusts.

In the end, he doesn't need to resort to the wand again. She cries out and her muscles tense around him. By doing so, they force the end to his endurance, and he drives into her one last time, his whole body spasming as he does so.

She doesn't register him withdrawing or towelling her and wrapping her in the covers on a conscious level. She just hums and watches him do so through half-seeing eyes. Half-seeing or not, those eyes notice the look on his face.

Ella Jane has no idea what time it is, only that she's warm and tingly inside and out and as tired as she's ever been in her life. "Have you quite finished with me for the night?"

"Mmm, almost."

She laughs, which hurts her sides and begs, "Please tell me you're kidding."

His answering smile and kiss are tired and gentle. "Nothing major, just a little aftercare."

"Aftercare?"

"Yes, making sure you and your body are okay."

"It's crazy late. You don't have to."

"It's crazy late, and I do have to." He kisses her forehead. "You," and he kisses her cheek, "gave me," and then her other cheek, "a great deal of pleasure." Then he begins brushing his lips against hers, "And anyway," and his eyes are the devil's again, "I like this shit."

She opens her mouth to protest, but he's already turned away and opened his bedside drawer again. This time he draws out a handsome low wooden case which he lays across his lap and opens. "Coconut oil, almond oil, grapeseed oil, vitamins C, E, and K."

Ella Jane blinks at him sleepily.

He taps three small dropper bottles, and the smallest jar in turn. "If you want bruises steer clear of the vitamins C, E, K, and the bromelain."

"You're serious, aren't you?"

"Deadly."

"Can I just lie here while you do what you think is best?"

"You sound like a very sensible girl." Ella Jane blinks as her lips twitch tiredly. "Okay." He kisses her lips, "I'd best say goodnight now, in case you doze off before I finish."

"Night night." Her kiss is to his lips. "It's been fun."

His prediction proves accurate. She sees him pour almond oil into his hands and add drops and a smear from the droppers and jar. She even manages to stay awake while he begins to apply the soothing blend to her skin. But her eyelids begin to droop when he starts to hum contentedly under his breath as he works the balm into her skin, and she's fast asleep before he finishes.

His Breakfast

Ella Jane isn't sure what the first thing she registers is, it's either the cooling space where he had slept, though she may have dreamt that, or him re-entering the bedroom. Enough light leaks around the blinds and follows him through the doorway for her to realise he's naked but for a pair of briefs and glistening with sweat. His body is that of an athlete half his age; His movement that of a dancer or martial artist.

She is sure of the next two things though, the memory of the night before floods her body and his eyes and the rising waters wash over her half way through her next breath.

"Good morning," he rumbles, smiling as he sees her eyes gleam in the dark, and wipes the towel in his hand across his brow. "Should I shower or...?" he lets her mind finish the question as he moves to the bed.

Stretching out in the warmth of the soft bedding wakes a variety of aches and tingles and sets off one of those delicious whole body yawns.

It's early, having been late, and then been the small hours as well. Her brain says it's too early, but the tingles aren't convinced.

She normally wears a baggy t-shirt to sleep in, borrowing one when she's stayed out for a night, but her body insistently reminds her that under the comforter, she's naked. The look in her eyes must have given him hope, or the things they spent the night doing may have given him expectation. Either way he moves close.

Her hand clasps the covers, but she nibbles her lip as she returns his smile, adding something more from her eyes.

He reaches the foot of the bed and takes hold of the soft duvet. tugging playfully against her grip. He's easily stronger than she is, but she clings on while he hauls the coverings toward himself, dragging her with it. In moments, her feet are hanging over the edge of the mattress. It's what he's been waiting for, and in a swift motion, he wraps the duvet under her legs and lifts eliciting a squeal from her lips. Before she knows what's happening, he kneels on the bed, braces, and smacks the flat of his hand into the curve of her freshly exposed rear.

Ella Jane gasps out an *ouch* but doesn't say the magic word as, using her legs as a lever, he tips her onto her side and delivers two more resounding blows. She feels each impact inside just as she feels the strength with which he so easily overpowers her. He holds her thus, and she makes no move to defend or cover herself as he rumbles, "Remember the mantra." His fingers caress her rosy skin.

She can't reach much of him from the position he's put her in, but she can reach a hand. So she pulls it to her lips and kisses the smooth soft skin inside his forearm. His skin tastes different again, and she realises it's his, not their mingled scent she's tasting. "You could have woken me to deal with," her hip rubbing against his morning enthusiasm.

"I would still have needed to do my training some time." His eyes look down to where she's touching. "Besides, I thought you might need your rest."

"Is that so?" Her eyes narrow as her fingers move to the waistband of his gym shorts. "In that case, I need to defend my generation's honour." She starts to lower them. "With your permission that is?"

It takes some time to address his morning condition, satisfy her tingles, and for her to reach a point at which she feels her generation's honour has been adequately defended. By the time she's done so, his skin once again tastes very much of her own as well.

She then lies contentedly at his side idly stroking his shoulder and chest. "You're so big!"

"I'm not that tall."

"No, big as in your muscles!"

"They're not that big that way either. You should see some guys in gyms."

"Professional bodybuilders, strongmen or NFL players?" She looks at him and touches the folds of muscle over his ribs. "How did a writer get to be so *not* big?" Her touches move down to the etched and striated lines at the side of his flat stomach.

"Overcompensation and research. I've always worked in offices or from home. I didn't like what it did to my body. At first, I dug out the old weights kit I had when I was a teenager. Then I went on to join a gym, and finally I started writing about people who trained, which got me properly interested. I got the bug." He shrugs. "The rest is history."

She muses, "I must say, it's a very nice-looking bug." As she strokes further down, her fingertips trail down the line of his V and skirt his scrotum to the soft smooth skin behind. "Is that why you're so smooth here?"

"It's not just vanity." He winces. "I have to shave there or the chafing's awful."

"I always thought older men weren't supposed to be able to..." she touches his returning hardness again.

"I suspect people vary."

The last thing that Ella Jane expects is for room service to turn out to be butler service. The butler's presence when she gets to the dining room explains why, having often talked about keeping her naked, he had been keen to have her wear a robe. Still it is nice being waited on in the privacy of the suite, even if the size of the table is less than intimate.

"This looks fantastic. Would you be able to arrange for the things to be cleared in an hour or so?"

"Will that be all, Sir?" the Butler asks.

"Yes, thanks so much. May I ask you a favour?"

"Certainly Sir."

"Peter, the young man who served us at dinner last night was particularly attentive; I have a small gift for him if you'd be able to make sure he gets it?"

"Yes, Sir, I can do that."

"Thank you again." He already has a copy of the most recent book in the Dark Series signed and ready.

Once the butler has departed, he has Ella Jane stand and carefully eases her out of her robe. She allows him to, revelling in his touch and in that of his clothed body against her nakedness. Then she wraps her arms around him as he kisses her.

"You remembered the waiter's name?"

"Well, I made a note of it. I'm terrible with names."

"That was sweet of you."

He shrugs. "I just try not to forget the people who make me so fortunate." Then helps himself to a slice of toast which he tops with bacon and another egg and tops up her orange juice.

"They didn't seem at all surprised to find a strange woman in your suite."

"You aren't that strange." Her eyes narrow in response to his attempt at humour. "An additional guest or one in a different room is hardly the most outlandish thing they'll have seen."

"Oh, do tell."

"People act as though they aren't there, and get up to all sorts."

"All sorts?"

"So I've been told, best to treat them how you'd want to be treated or find a hotel that caters to that sort of thing. That way you get to like the person in the mirror."

"Are there hotels that cater to that sort of thing?"

"There's someone somewhere who'll do almost anything either for kicks or because the price is right. We live in a corrupt world."

She falls quiet until he asks if she would like another coffee. "Yes, thank you." Then she tries to make up for her silence. "This is bizarrely couple-like."

"It is, so much better than the walk of shameless."

"You mean walk of shame?" She colours again. For him it would be of the shameless.

For his part he shrugs. "You've done nothing to be ashamed of."

They breakfast on the same lavish scale as the suite, and as they had play in the night, or at least he does. Ella Jane is taken aback by the quantity and variety of food arrayed on the table. By the view too. It is quite something.

Each of them senses the other out as they eat, and each also stumbles at the fault line between her wanting to serve and him wanting to be the perfect host. They end up settling here and there, compromising on a touch of their hands when both reach for the same thing.

She pours coffee from the pot. He fresh squeezed orange juice from the pitcher. He eats like a lion and expects her to. She surprises herself with how hungry she is. Then she smiles to herself and blushes to him when, after resisting his efforts to load her plate high, she joins in helping herself to seconds.

He leaves her for a moment when they slow to nibbling, and she has a fancy. The suite has huge windows, and no other buildings nearby are as tall. She rises, slips the soft robe from her shoulders, stands gloriously naked and admires the view of New York. She's plans to go up the Empire State building and to the One World Observatory, but they were places to visit, and there will be people there. This is just the two of them, intimate, as though the spectacular view is just for them. She breathes, "Wow," to herself, not knowing that he's returned.

As he returned, he'd stopped. He'd been admiring a view too, her tiny form and the way her hair tumbles framed against the morning sky but abandons his view to join her. "Not bad is it."

"How the other half live?"

He stands behind her and puts his arms around her. "A few of them, yes."

Ella Jane leans into him. "A few of you?"

"Sort of."

She turns and looks up, giving him a questioning look, but she doesn't press too hard. The glow from the night before and earlier is too warm for her to want to take the risk. Instead, she makes to turn away and muses, "What is it with men and mystery?"

"I suppose it works." He tightens his arms, squeezing her nudity lightly against his own. "We're trying to keep your interest."

"Is that so?"

"That and we want to impress each other."

"You must be easily impressed."

"By some things." He gives her another little squeeze. "But not by others."

"Views?"

He stands tall and looks down, then kisses the top of her head. "Some views."

Their reverie is interrupted by her phone on the breakfast table buzzing into life. She absently reaches over to cancel it, and he lets her slip from his embrace.

"Is it ok if I pop back to my room in a while?"

"Hmm, do you have to?"

She pouts. "Yes. I've got to go to my room. All my things are there."

"What do you actually need though?"

"Nothing much, just my toothbrush and some clothes, so I don't turn up at the conference looking like I crawled there from my lover's bed."

"Ah, good point. You could borrow a toothbrush though. I have spare heads for mine."

"You have a spare?"

"Spare, and spare head for my electric one."

"You must have very clean teeth."

He places a hand on her mons. "If you weren't so deliciously bare down here, I could make an off-colour comment about flossing and spoil the mood."

The line of her lips tightens for a moment before she replies, "That's the reason I shaved," with a perfectly straight face.

He kisses her and decides to risk posing the question, "Then we can decide if you want to check out and stay in here."

"Mmm." She covers herself as best she can, and putting on her best coy expression asks, "What are you suggesting?"

"Let me think." He makes a show of considering before he answers, "Several things we did last night, definitely two we tried this morning, and at least a dozen others that spring to mind." He closes the distance between them as he speaks and sweeps her up into his arms.

Ella Jane squeaks at the suddenness and the ease with which he does so. Then, feeling his obvious enthusiasm against her, she wraps her legs around him. "And then there are all those things we talked about online."

"There are. Though some of them would take a bit of planning, and I'm not going to try to hold you to anything other than safe words or limits, whether you change rooms or not."

"For now, can I just borrow that toothbrush?"

"There are new manuals, if you want. They're in the little toy bag in my bedside, or you can use one of the spare heads for the electric."

"Because you never know when you're going to need to brush your teeth halfway through a scene?"

His lips twitch suggestively. "Because, soft, medium or hard bristles."

"Is there anything you don't look at and wonder how to do something with it?"

"Nothing I didn't think would risk permanent damage, unless it struck me as icky."

Ella Jane purses her lips. "Icky?"

"A turn off."

"Is 'Icky' a domly word?"

"Must be."

"Because?"

He takes a hold of her by the tip of a breast and squeezes and pulls her towards him as slowly as the wicked smile spreads across his face. When he eventually speaks, she's inches from him, and her nervous system is responding to his grip. He looks down, and his voice rumbles, "Because I used it, young lady."

"That's the worst answer I ever heard."

He looms, his face serious, one eyebrow rising fractionally, and she grins. "Sexy, but terrible."

He winks and tightens his grip.

Ella Jane's grin becomes a laugh, and she squeals, "That's cheating."

His free hand roams. "Would you like to discuss that opinion now? Or after you've finished brushing your teeth?"

"Aren't you worried we'll be late?"

"There's still plenty of time to edge you, isn't there?"

"Such a bastard," she accuses but makes no move to break away.

"Is that such a bastard red, or such a bastard, yes?"

"Am I invited back tonight then?"

"Offering to edge you and not inviting you back would break every principle of the kink code."

"Is there a kink code?"

"There are probably several."

"And does it really break them?"

"They aren't worth a damn if it doesn't."

His hands and lips continue through their exchange, and she moves to accommodate them without uttering a safe word.

Her breathing is heavy, and her eyes hooded by the time he breezily declares, "Time to get ready for the day ahead." But her muttered curse only earns her a laugh not the whacking or seeing to she might have preferred.

When Ella Jane finishes brushing her teeth she asks the question that struck her halfway through doing so. "Do I want to know why you have a selection of spare toothbrushes in different styles and firmnesses?"

"It could be because I hoped you'd stay the night." His words are perfectly plausible, but his expression makes it clear that that is NOT the primary reason.

"Is that true?"

He frowns thoughtfully, then grins. "It is."

There's suspicion on her face and in her voice when she demands, "But is it the main reason?"

"It wasn't even the original reason."

"So do I want to know?"

"You'll find out if you come and play a time or two more."

She sets her fists on her hips. "Or?"

"Or I could tell you and spoil the surprise."

"Why do I get the feeling that you're just trying to get me to come back?"

He swats her bum. "Because you're a suspicious soul." Her pout earns her another swat. "I've already given you far too many hints of things you can expect."

"But that was before we met!"

Her protest doesn't win her any sympathy, he merely shrugs. "This morning too. You have a fertile imagination, and a there are a dozen search engines you can access with your phone."

"You'd really stand there and watch me look up toothbrush kinks?"

"I would, but I'd advise you to turn incognito browsing on first."

"You're such a..."

He raises an eyebrow and a hand. "Yes?"

And Ella Jane blinks, bites her lip, shakes her head and smiles. Then she turns away from him. "Bastard!" This time his hand lands on her now offered bum with considerable force. "Yowch! Sir." His hand returns, though this time it gently caresses around the glowing handprint. "I suppose I asked for that."

"Suppose?"

She eases her legs further apart, rests her hands by the sink and looks at him in the mirror. "I asked for that, Sir."

"You did." He runs a finger along the length of her opening. "Are you asking for another?"

"What time is it?"

"Either spanking time or getting dressed time."

"Do I get to cum?"

His eyes sparkle, his teeth gleam, and his fingers idly play with her receptive body. "Now, that's a question..." Ella Jane bites her lip nervously. "Are you starting to wish you'd kept a few more secrets?" He leans over her, and by so doing enables her to confirm his own level of arousal and his hands continue to amuse themselves. "All those messages about prolonged teasing."

Ella Jane rides his hands and presses back into him, and maintains her silence, her insolent expression and their eye contact. It's a game she's loved since she first discovered it. Getting a dominant so hot and hard, and herself so turned on that her pain tolerance spikes, then daring the dominant to do their worst or best, watching every moment of it in his eyes.

Of course, in the past she'd played it with men who hadn't played her body like a fiddle for hours on end beforehand.

The eye contact is as hot or hotter than ever before. Yet it's a two-edged sword, captivating, intense, erotic, a measure of her power and her vulnerability.

But it has a disadvantage to her, as the submissive in their game she has only the power to ask and to tempt.

Ella Jane sees him burn and yearn.

He sees her eyes soften and her will begin to dissolve, and then it's *his* decision.

He stops short of granting the petite American her release and also of taking his own. He wraps his arms around her nakedness and kisses the top of her head.

She leans into his embracing body and breathes, "You're as teased as I am."

"So I am." He chuckles and tweaks the tips of her breasts. "Now get dressed, or we're going to be more than fashionably late."

Her eyes cast around the suite as they make their preparations to leave. "We can always come back, at least, you can." He grins at the way her brow knits. "I'm going to have to. This is my room. I don't have much choice.I It's this or the street." He speaks as though declaring a sacred truth, "I'd like you to come back too, b ut?"

Ella Jane chuckles to herself at the thought that, even after the state he'd got her into, he might not be sure. "Don't you think?"

"I hope." His voice is light, but his face is confident.

She narrows her eyes. "Do you know?"

And he grins. "I'm a very arrogant man."

She colours as his fingertips traces the curves of her shoulders and back of her sides. They tease the sides of her breasts, but don't claim them. She looks down and unconsciously arches her back. Her body makes the offer his hands fail to presume. When she looks up, his eyes are smiling. He touches her chin and lifts her face and kisses her lips.

"I hope, but..." and he kisses her again.

Her heart beats faster, and her breathing stops as he kisses. Her lips part, and they kiss long and deeply. Eventually she eases back blinks up at him and teases, "I might come back."

It makes his eyes narrow, and her teasing turns to a laugh.

His arms tighten around her. "Is that so?"

"Uh huh." She tests the strength of his grip, but does so while enjoying the texture of his skin and the fullness of his muscles without letting her smile slip. "Does this mean you really want me to come back?"

"Yes,"

She presses herself against him and smiles again.

He concedes, "That does too."

"I like that. Can I come back and see it again, not just you?"

He chuckles and shakes his head. "Do you know what happens when a girl teases like this."

"I'm trying to find out."

"More than last night."

"I liked last night."

"And might you like more?"

She takes her lower lip between her teeth, and takes her time, partly for herself, and partly to tease him further. She recalls the pain, the pleasure, the orgasms, his smug arrogance and him cumming in and for her. She remembers taking all he gave her and did with and to her, and then feeling safe in his arms. "I think I might."

This time it's his phone that starts buzzing, but he makes no move to let go of her. "Such a shame we have to go."

"It is."

"We'd best get dressed."

"We had." She makes no move to disengage from him. "Are you going to let go?"

"Yes." He still doesn't let go.

She feels the corners of her mouth curling upwards. "When?"

His face reflects her expression. "Soon." He kisses her once more before letting his arms fall and turning toward the wardrobes.

She picks up her panties from the floor. "Did you mean it?"

He selects a shirt and turns, "What?"

Slipping them on, she answers, "About me moving into your room."

"Yes."

"Hmm." She stops as she thinks, locates her bra and straightens. "Can I come back again tonight and then decide?"

"Of course."

She wraps her bra around her waist with the catches at the front, does them up, then turns it the right way around, slides it up and over her breasts, slips the straps over her shoulders, and smiles at him. It takes a matter of moments.

He nods, "Smoothly done."

"I've practiced." Her smile spreads further. "We girls do."

"Every day?"

Ella Jane smiles. "Most days." She gives him a suggestive wink. "Sometimes more than once."

He picks up and reflects her use of innuendo. "Why more than once?"

"Oh, various reasons."

"Such as?"

She laughs lightly. "While changing or to wash. Us girls are fond of both."

His pout is hopeful, and his, "Any other reasons?" draws a laugh from her.

So she confides, "Sometimes a wicked man is involved."

He raises his eyebrows, "Shocking!"

"Mmm, it is." She lets him kiss her again. "So shocking what some wicked men will do to a woman."

"You'll have to tell me about it."

"If you're lucky I might show you." This time she initiates the kiss. "Or let you show me."

He still hasn't let go, but when his phone buzzes again, he releases her. "Cursed technology."

They finish dressing, and he asks, "Ready?"

"Ready to go back to my room for something suitable."

"Want me to come too?"

"What for?"

He beams in triumph. "So I can see you practicing." She laughs as her response.

"Hey, I'm a writer. How else am I going to learn about the skill of putting a bra on if I don't study?"

"I thought you said we had to go."

"We do."

"Won't we be late?"

"Only fashionably so, so we can make an entrance."

She shakes her head, "Such a bad man."

"I did warn you." He grins a wolfish grin and holds out his hand.

"Mmm, warn and demonstrate." She takes it.

They take the elevator down to her floor. He is content and attempting to continue their light-hearted conversation, while she is stiff in the shoulder and replying only briefly. Her own room is nice. Yesterday she'd taken photos of it because it was so wonderful, but after his suite she's conscious of its modest dimensions, and lack of a view.

His accompanying her is nice, but it presents a problem. "Can I get changed?"

"Okay." He sits down on the room's comfortable armchair.

"Er...."

"Oh, would you rather I waited in the lobby?"

Ella Jane lets out a sigh, "Please."

"No problem, can I tell my driver five minutes?"

She opens her mouth to ask for longer, but decides against it, "Sure."

Five minutes later she emerges from the elevators and quickly finds he is the only man seated in the lobby who's reading a copy of the London Times. When she walks up to him, he's grinning behind the newspaper, "You have a keen eye for detail, Miss Tyler."

He's already rising and folding his paper by the time she formulates a reply, so she just lets him take her arm.

She expects the car to be an Uber or a New York cab. Though, given her limited experience of him those notions are even more ludicrous than what confronts her outside. It's not the seven series that draws her attention, it's the suited driver standing by it. He's not the tallest man she's ever seen, but she guesses he must be six foot six. He is, however, probably the widest. He grins and takes the giant's hand. "Johnson, I'd like you to meet Ella Jane Tyler. She's hitching a lift with us."

"Pleased to meet you ma'am." His voice is even deeper.

She stares up at him open mouthed for a moment before her brain kicks in, "And to meet you too Mr Johnson." She offers her hand, and his envelopes it with a gentleness she wouldn't have credited him as being capable of.

"No change to the destination boss?"

"No, all good. How's the traffic?"

"Very funny boss."

The two men's exchange what she guesses must be a look and a form of words from some past denied her, so she says nothing other than to give her thanks when the giant opens the car door for her without accidentally tearing it from its hinges.

The short drive is slow, but not as bad as the conversation had been led to believe. When they arrive at the conference hotel, the driver is round to the curb side door in time to shut it behind her and wish them both a good day.

As they make their way in, she asks, "Who's that?" in an awed tone.

"That was Johnson."

"He's!"

"Impressive? Yes. Quite the chap, Mr Johnson is. He seems to like you."

Their First Panel

"**Y**our panel starts in an hour, and we haven't eaten yet."

"We just had breakfast!"

"That was just breakfast."

"I'm nervous. I don't know how you can be hungry again."

"You didn't seem nervous about it last night."

"That's because I was too busy being nervous about meeting you!" She gives a half smile at his chuckle, then moans, "I don't know why I said yes to this."

"Because it's good exposure, and you'll rock it. Just be nice and take the time to frame your thoughts when you answer."

"That's all very well for you to say," she complains.

"The press has been great with your first book. This is going to help keep them and your readers on side. It's part of the job."

She narrows her eyes, "A part you're skipping?"

"I've done my time on these things: name, presence, lots of media attention, and the media will love you."

"Will they?"

"Of course, oh, and remember to turn your phone off or put it on mute before you start."

"Do you?" she asks it light heartedly, her eyes daring him to answer yes, no, or by seizing hold of her, but also looking for signs.

He evades, "Not when you try to pin me down," and touches her under her chin, "but definitely when I do the same to you."

"That doesn't seem entirely fair."

"Life," he assures her, "isn't the least bit fair."

Ella Jane makes her way in, nods shyly at her name check as she takes her seat and mutes her phone. It's then she sees a message from Louise, her safe call, checking to see whether she needs to call the police or has any filthy highlights to tell. She fires off a quick message.

Not been murdered, lots of highlights, will call later

She then puts her phone down and hears the panel's chairwoman announce, "And now I'd like to introduce a late addition to our audience panel."

There's applause and Ella Jane looks around. She does a double take when she sees him striding across the stage. He gives the chairwoman a nod, and the audience a shy-looking wave. Then he aims a wink at Ella Jane.

The session begins with a question about getting started. Ella Jane goes to answer it, but her microphone isn't working. He unclips his and passes it over. When she finishes, she offers it back to him, but he waves it away choosing instead to address the room by simply straightening, squaring his shoulders and speaking more loudly to tell the audience some of his tales of rejection letters.

His voice fills the auditorium and the attention of all two hundred people in it without the need of electronic assistance.

Ella Jane takes a question about character voices and writer's block. "It's difficult. Sometimes the writing doesn't flow because you, or the character's stuck, and sometimes it's because you're trying to force the character to do something outside their nature."

The chair picks up the obvious point. "You make it sound like characters are real people, not figments of your imagination."

"When I'm writing, they are real to me in a sense. Their lives matter to the part of me that writes them." she shrugs, "They have to be. I know my character Abigail as well as I do some real people I've known for years."

"Any other answers?"

He speaks up with a smile in his voice, "There isn't much to add. Even an old hack like me does it that way. If the writer can't make themself believe in the story when they're writing it, there isn't much chance that the reader will."

The chair has a follow-up for Him too. "Even with your most controversial characters? The villains, the anti-heroes."

"Even with Dark. When I write him, I could close my eyes, see his face and hear his voice." He smirks wickedly, "He has a fully formed character. It's just not one everybody finds sweet."

Next up is a question about whether male authors can write strong female characters, and an older female panellist fields it first. She begins, "In order to write strong female characters, a man has to understand the struggles women go through."

He glances across to see Ella Jane's eyes flashing and half smiles. When she returns his glance with a look of exasperation he tightens his lips, inclines his head and resumes his smile.

The speaker catches his smile but misses the exchange. "I don't know what you're smiling about."

He raises a hand towards to tiny redhead, "I was agreeing with Miss Tyler that she'd answer before me. Is that alright with you?"

"Hmph."

Ella Jane raises her voice to forestall any further interaction, and turns to the fourth panellist, "May I?" He nods, so she continues, "As my colleagues have either finished or suggested that it might be a question we ladies should have first opportunity to answer. I'd like to put my position."

She looks around the auditorium, "Well, that seems simple, I don't feel oppressed." She looks down at her arms and raises them, "No chains." And here she gives Him a direct look, then touches her face, "No gag and no blindfold." After which she returns her attention from him to the room and shrugs. "I'm sure we all heard our transatlantic speaker before the faulty microphone was replaced, so we know he could shout over me but," here she picks up her pencil and drops it theatrically. The sound is clearly audible. "I don't sound very shouted down."

"With respect, I don't think Ms Tyler's twenty-three years qualify her to speak on behalf of women."

Ella Jane's Hackles rise, "I hadn't finished speaking yet, ma'am. And with respect, I waited for you to have your say, with respect, your life doesn't qualify you to speak for me or to speak for the intentions of others. With respect, I direct you to our transatlantic guest's comment on the way the British use the term, with respect." She continues until the other woman's attempts to interrupt become so loud that she has to shout. Then she shrugs and turns to the host.

"I'm an expert on the patriarchy, and on the oppression of women, and I'm telling you how it is."

Ella Jane fixes the older woman with an icy eye. "Well, thank you, but it seems to me that only one person has tried to prevent me from speaking today, and that person is you. The other woman and our representatives of the patriarchy seem to be quite content to respect social norms."

She then turns to the audience and raises her voice. "If a person seeks to shout me down, they're a bully; it isn't because I'm a woman, or because they're a man or because they're a woman. It's because they're a bully. It doesn't matter whether they claim it's because I'm just a woman, or because I'm someone who just holds an unfashionable opinion. The fact is that they do it because they can't or won't behave in a civilised way."

Ella Jane becomes more animated but less angry as she continues. "We need to try to educate people to respect the rights of others to freedom of thought, and freedom of expression. We need to be stricter in enforcing the conventions and laws that support that, most particularly the constitution of these United States."

The woman demands, "What about people's right to be perceived as they wish?"

"It doesn't exist. I might wish to be perceived as tall, but I'm not. I have a right to be treated with respect, but I don't have a right to demand to work as a firefighter when I can't physically do some of the most important tasks a firefighter might need to perform. My right to be seen as a firefighter isn't more important than your right to not be burned to death because I can't carry you down a ladder."

"So, you don't think men and women are equal?"

"I don't think different people are identical. I wouldn't expect anyone to hire any person of my stature and build as a firefighter."

"I didn't mention firefighters."

"No, you did try to control me by putting words into my mouth though. That's something no man or woman has the right to do to another. I don't pretend to speak for all women, or all redheads, or all people with freckles, and nobody else should either."

When Ella Jane finishes speaking, He clears his throat. "Ahem. Of course, I don't live in the US. Even if I am a semi-regular visitor from a country which has, or at least had a bit of a tradition of freedom of speech, one whose laws and customs informed the great men who set your constitution in place. Naturally, they were mostly great men because the original constitution and most of the amendments were written before women had the right to vote or could sit in on the legislatures."

He does something with his voice as he does so. It stays deep, but holds all of the softness back from it, making every consonant even crisper than usual, making them actually hard. The whole room stills as he makes his little speech.

"Let me ask you where democracy or women's rights would be today if those disenfranchised had not used the freedom of expression our countries allowed them, or gay rights, the rights various heritage and cultural groups?" His voice rises as he speaks and looks around the auditorium as he pauses. "With respect, I suggest to one and all that those groups would be worse off today, and as a result that we all would. Don't for one second think that anyone's feelings should be allowed to trump freedom of expression and associations. They're the bedrock on which all other rights are built. Anyone here want to take those hard-won freedoms away from those people and tell them why? Yes, anyone has the right to try and write a strong or a weak character who isn't identical to themselves. If they plan to try, they should educate themselves and seek appropriate feedback." There's silence when he stops speaking.

The next question is a little less controversial. "How do you write an accent?"

The chair farms the question out, "I think I'll pass this to our English guest first."

"Thanks, though I assure you it's everyone else here who has one, rather than me." He gets less laughter than he'd hoped, but Ella Jane smiles, which is the important thing. "There are three techniques: phonetically, by description, or just saying Joe's such and such accent every now and then. If a character has a particularly strong accent, it can be an idea for others to ask them to repeat things at humorous moments." He looks up towards the questioner to see if that's enough of an answer.

Her brow wrinkles. "Could you give me an example?"

"We could have a bit of fun, if people are up for it?" There's a general murmur of assent. "Everyone got something to write with?" He pauses, then adds, "Everyone who hasn't, really should," to general amusement. "All ready? Good. I'll speak in a couple of tones and accents, and all you have to do is either describe how I'm speaking or write down the words phonetically, with their spellings changed to reflect pronunciation for each of them. He goes on the mimic a brief conversation between a Glaswegian, a Scouser, a Parisian and a Geordie about not being able to understand one another. When he finishes, there's a round of applause. He waits for it then asks, "Everyone got a few ideas?" and he looks back to the host.

The panel chair answers, "Thank you for that, and thank you for demonstrating your remarkable oral dexterity. Does anyone else have anything to add?"

He looks across at Ella Jane whose eyes meet his and fill with mirth. Then her cheeks fill with roses before she finds something fascinating on the table in front of her. Then, sensing eyes still on her, she clears her throat, "The internet can be your friend here. There are local blogs and news channels all over the world that you can listen to and repeat until you're happy. So, you don't have to rely on access to someone with our celebrity guest's remarkable oral dexterity." As she finishes, she locks her jaw tight and fixes him with her eyes, daring him to be the first to crack a smile.

The chair breaks their poker-facing contest by asking for the next question.

It had perhaps been too early in a ninety-minute panel for the grenades Ella Jane had launched, or for his party piece, and the debate and questions after seem tame by comparison.

They both dodge making more than the briefest of contributions to the next couple of questions or add brief comments to what the other panellists say. As they do, he messages her dark promises on the fate of young ladies who dare the wrong lover, each of which she replies to with words and emojis that convey her feelings.

A grey-haired man approaches them as they leave the auditorium, and takes his proffered hand, "Well, you actually came rather than just using it as an excuse to swank around in fancy hotels!"

"I said I would." He then turns to Ella Jane, "Ella Jane, I'd like you to meet Roger. Roger is the leech who pretends to work on my behalf and takes a percentage. Roger, this young firebrand is Ella Jane Tyler."

"Ah Miss Tyler, I gather one of my colleagues snapped you up. Great things are expected of you, I hear." He takes Ella Jane's hand and raises it floridly to within an inch of his lips. "That was brave of you in there, my dear."

Having smiled shyly at the man's initial praise, Ella Jane winces, "What was?" though she's certain she knows what he's referring to.

"Your little tiff with that awful woman. Good put downs by the way."

"I hope I won't get into trouble, but she was making my blood boil." She glances at Him. "I can only imagine how you felt."

He interjects, "I felt it was appropriate to let you have your say then have mine."

"That's unusually diplomatic of you, old boy."

He chuckles, "I'm trying to give a good example."

His agent scoffs, "Ha, there's a first time for everything." He then goes back to answer Ella Jane. "Fortunately for you, if there's much outrage from the dark side they'll focus on this old reprobate because they love hating him, while the good guys will be full of praise for their fresh-faced new heroine."

She frowns. "Isn't that a bit unfair?"

"Life is terribly unfair. Take this hack. I created him and made him too successful for that big mouth of his to get him cancelled, and all he gives me is abuse."

"Abuse, enough money to pay off his mortgages and put his kids through school and university plus," He adds archly, "as much of my Armagnac as he can drink."

Roger sighs theatrically, "There are those small compensations, yes." Then rouses himself, "Speaking of compensations, having found two of my agency's golden egg laying geese, I can use you as an excuse to buy some drinks on expenses."

Ella Jane looks at him.

"Yes, Roger's always like this, except with people he hates even more than he does me. It's best to let him take you to the bar, then leave him when the bottles are empty and order him an Uber for closing time."

Her own agent arrives while the two men are bantering. "Ah Roger, I see you've met my latest prodigy!"

"I have indeed, Cynthia. I met her and heard her speak, too. If her writing is a sharp as her claws, you'll do well out of this one."

Ella Jane complains, "I wasn't that sharp."

"Of course, you weren't. This old goat just likes to tease. He's probably jealous that I snapped you up too." She touches Ella Jane's arm. "All I would say is remember you're here to sell your book and pick up new experiences for you next ones, not just to make points."

There's a separate room for the speakers to eat in peace and quiet. He insists they pop out and circulate when they've finished eating and chatting with the agents, and Cynthia encourages her to go too.

While they're out in the public area Ella Jane pulls him to one side. Ella Jane nuzzles up against him. "What was that thing?"

"What thing?"

She looks up and explains. "You know, the one with your voice!" His brow wrinkles. "Don't tell me you don't know..." His face remains confused, clearly he still either doesn't get it or doesn't admit to himself that he gets it. "The *Cower Brief Mortals* thing." She then goes on to do her impression of it. She's sure she doesn't carry it off properly, but people still turn.

"Oh, that!" It's just how I speak when I'm debating, isn't it?"

She bites her lip to control her smile. "I'd get such a whacking if I tried getting away with telling you something like that."

"It just comes naturally. People tend to shut up and do what I tell them to when I do it, but it only works when I'm telling them to do something sensible."

"Is that so?"

"It might not be if I was a better liar."

"I don't think it always has quite the effect you mean it to."

"No?"

"Some of the girls were closer to jumping out of their seats than hiding under them."

"Really?"

She narrows her eyes, "Really!"

He moves in front her and carries on walking backwards countering her suspicious expression with cockiness in his own. "Was this girl among them?"

Ella Jane's cheeks glow at that, and she looks down. "That would be telling."

When she says that he stops. Partly because he's walked as far backwards as he was sure he had space to, but partly to force her to look up as he repeats his question with that hardness in every syllable.

"Stop it!"

He carries on speaking in the same voice. "Do you really want me to stop it?"

Her breath catches and her pupils dilate for a moment, and her answer comes out in a whisper, "Yes, till we get back, please."

He reverts to a less distracting voice. "I'll hold you to that mind."

And Ella Jane grins. "I'll remind you if you don't. What have you got this afternoon?"

"I've got the afternoon off for bad behaviour, so I'm nipping out to see some friends. I should be passing back this way in time to give you a lift back to the hotel though?"

She bites her lip and says nothing for what he reads as a little too long.

His eyes narrow, and his voice thickens, "If you'd like one that is?"

"Yes, that would be nice; do you have anything planned for this evening?"

"No, I'm footloose and fancy free if you'd like to make a night of it."

She twists a foot on the ground. "I was up late last night, so I was thinking I might get to bed early."

They continue to exchange flirtatious messages through the afternoon, but neither floats the question on both of their minds until he returns to the conference to pick her up.

When he arrives, Cynthia is introducing Ella Jane to people in the author's lounge. He swans in, says hi to someone he knows then a louder and friendlier hi to someone he knows can't stand him. From there, he meanders over to the coffee machine and goes back to his other acquaintance to chat until Ella Jane leads her agent his way. "How was your afternoon?"

"I saw the guys I meant to, Everyone's well. How was your session?"

"Tiring and less fun."

He floats, "So you still want to get to bed early?"

She touches the tip of her tongue to her lips and smile. "Yes."

"I could ask Johnson to come back for you if you want to stay, but I've got a table booked for six, and I'm famished."

Ella Jane enquires, "A table for one?"

"I'm sure they could set another place or two if you ladies are hungry?"

Cynthia makes her apologies, "I have to get back to the office and charm people on behalf of my other clients this evening."

"Oh, that's a shame. I'm sure Roger will manage to line us up a get together while he and I are both over here though."

With that, they make their farewells.

In the car, Ella Jane holds out her hand and he takes it, but they don't talk about the night ahead. When they get back to the hotel, Johnson once again treats her like a duchess.

He makes an assumption based on her earlier question. "Would you like to change before we eat?"

Ella Jane shakes her head. Food sounds good, and the time is close to six. Besides, he's already seen her best dress.

He asks if she'd like wine with dinner, and she shakes her head again and orders something light.

"Aren't you having a starter?"

"No, but don't let me stop you."

It doesn't take a second time of asking. He orders enough starters to share and his main explaining, "I can eat it all, but there'll be plenty if you want to graze."

She replies, "Thank you. I really don't know how you eat so much and stay slim." Though she now has a fair idea.

When his starters arrive, Ella Jane accepts his invitation to pick. The food is as simple, precise and immaculate as the night before. But without the pressure of a first meeting, she enjoys it more and enjoys her main more still after touching his offered hand on the table between courses and whispering. "I said I wanted to go to bed early."

"So you did."

"But I didn't say which bed."

Her Seductive Surprise

"C an I stop at my room on the way up?"

He answers, "No." But he presses the button for her floor. Ella Jane bites her tongue, and seeing her do it, he gives her a sidelong look. "See, you aren't that bratty."

"But you are that much of a tease?"

He shrugs and grins. "Life is so desperately unfair."

"Am I allowed to imagine poking my tongue out at you?"

"Er, only if you imagine me spanking you for it was well."

"Doesn't that put all the onus on me?"

He adopts a conspiratorial tone, "If you want, I can imagine you poking your tongue out at me, and me spanking you as well." He offers her a hand as if to make a deal.

Unable to think of a gracious way to refuse, and not exactly averse to the idea of thinking about him thinking about her, she takes it and gives it a theatrical shake.

When the car arrives at her floor, he makes to follow, but she says, "You don't have to come with me."

"Do you want me to not?" As there's nobody else in the car with them, he holds the doors open button pressed. "I could hold the lift for you."

She stands in the corridor outside the lift and shifts her weight from foot to foot while she thinks. Then she has an idea. She decides his holding the lift will not suit her plan, only there's a problem. "Can I get to your room if you don't?"

"Y-es."

"Then can I follow you up?"

The momentary puzzlement on his face brings a smile to hers, "Of course you *may*." The thought that there's something he doesn't know brings a smile to Ella Jane's face.

Despite his face's confusion, he holds out his room key.

"Won't you need that?"

"It's a spare. That's why there's a way you can follow me up."

"Oh!" And with that Ella Jane smiles adieu and heads off. She showers as quickly as she's able to without getting her hair wet, then takes a minute to get her bits and pieces for overnight. It takes another couple to repack her things, just in case she decides to accept his offer and move into his suite for the remainder of her stay. But it takes her a few more after that to do the other thing. She then straightens herself in front of the mirror, composes her face, tucks her bag under her arm and makes her way back to the elevator with a beating heart.

The car seems to take an age to arrive. She has to share, which makes her doubt the wisdom of her decision, but the couple and two guys barely give her a look. There's an unoccupied corner, so she asks for the top floor number and settles into it, unconsciously holding her bag in front of herself.

Much to her relief, she doesn't have to share the second car for the short ride up to his suite. She takes the opportunity to check her lipstick and hair in the mirrored wall and turns from side to side, studying her reflection to assess the effect. The car stops, the doors slide open, and Ella Jane takes a deep breath and steps out doing her best to walk just so.

It's only on getting to the top floor without him to distract her that she realises no other rooms are up there, just his suite. She has the key, but using it doesn't fit with her plan, so she knocks, waits, and hopes she's judged his mood and his humour correctly. Though with each passing second, she doubts herself more.

Having tired of waiting, she comes to the conclusion that the sound of her first knock might not have carried through the whole of his suite. He opens the door just a moment before she knocks again more loudly, and so he finds her, wearing her raincoat and best heels with one fist raised.

"You..."

She smiles nervously. He's taken his jacket off and rolled up his sleeves. He has his phone in his hand, and there's chamber music playing in the background.

He looks her up and down with increasingly interested eyes, and when he catches on he grins. "You!" and he speaks into the phone, "I'll call you back."

She nods, and her flush changes from one of nervousness to one of anticipation.

"Come in. I've been expecting you." He steps aside to admit her. She steps past him, making sure to move with a hip swaying walk and to pass so close, she brushes against him. He shuts the door behind her. "You can put your bag down." He indicates the small table to the side of the suite's entrance hall.

"Yes, Sir."

He gives a hand gesture for her to follow him into the reception room. She stops in the middle of the group of armchairs and waits.

He leaves her there and goes to the bottled water. There's a hiss when he breaks the seal, and a glugging as he pours himself a glass. Then he makes his way to the chair closest to being directly in front of her, sits and leans back. "You may take your coat off now."

Her smile, and its hesitancy, confirm his guess and his assures her that her idea is welcome, but she doesn't move yet. There's one more thing he doesn't know, and she enjoys his eyes trying to see.

"Well?" He does his best to maintain his poker face, and she to milk the moment. "You aren't turning shy, are you?"

A flash of inspiration strikes her. "The-they told me you like a shy girl."

"Ah, did they, and did they tell you I have some very particular tastes?"

A swallow, a lick of her lips. "Yes, Sir." So as not lose control of the moment, she raises her hands to her coat's top button, and slowly undoes it. "They told me the things you like to do to girls."

"And those things didn't scare you?"

She undoes another button. "Some of them did." And a third while she gives him a defiant look. "A little, anyway." Then she holds the coat closed, so he can't see whether she kept her underwear on

.

Taking to the charade, he raises an eyebrow and tilts his head before rumbling, "Only a little?"

Her hands go to the fourth button. "Mhm," and she undoes it. "I liked some of what they said." She then shifts to make sure the coat's sides stay together while she smiles coyly at him and touches her tongue to her lips. "I even liked that some of them scared me."

"Are you trying to delay what's going to happen to you?"

"No, Sir." She blinks her big grey eyes at him. "But I was told you like to give a girl a night to remember and want her to do the same for you." She finally undoes the fifth and final button and slips the coat from her shoulders to reveal her second-best underwear, the white counterpart to the set she'd worn to dinner the night before.

He stands, and his movement makes it clear how well her act has worked. In an effort to conceal her delight, she sucks her lips between her teeth and bites, but it isn't enough to completely hide her reaction. She holds her place, watching him approach until he stops so close to her, she can feel his body's warmth against her skin. Then he lets out a long slow breath. "Virginal white?" It isn't cold in the room, but the excitement of their play acting has raised a light gooseflesh on her skin.

"White, anyway, Sir."

He brushes the back of a hand over tell-tale dimpling. "Are you sure you aren't scared?"

Ella Jane uses another blink, leans into his touch, and a brief running of her tongue over her lips to buy time. "A little, like I said, Sir."

Then she closes her eyes as his hand touches her, her collar bone; such a brief acquaintance, but such ready familiarity. She draws a shuddering breath and angles her head back offering her slender neck to his touch and her lips to his kiss, should he choose to take advantage.

Once again, it's the opposite of her previous experiences. He touches slowly and confidently. Her senses have been primed by her experience of him and by her enjoyment of her chosen role.

Ella Jane begins to drift into the communion of physical contact. Keeping her eyes closed she listens, concentrates on his touch, and waits as he moves around her, his hands and the sound of his voice telling her where he is. As he gets back to a point directly in front of her and stops, she lets out a long sigh.

"Yes, I think you'll do very nicely, if you can wake up, that is." Her eyes open guiltily to the amused look on his face, and he pours basso honey into murmuring, "The ability to drift so is attractive." Then he takes her chin in a gentle grip and rumbles, "But remember who's here for whose entertainment."

Another lick of her lips, this time with a full eyes-to-toes-and-back-again appraisal of his body, with appropriately inappropriate pauses in both directions. "Yes, Sir."

"Now, you may finish undressing for me."

He steps back, and she doesn't move.

"If you don't mind, that is?"

She swallows, settles herself, reaches out to recapture her mood, and he sits, sips, watches...

There's no urgency about him, even though she can see his physical need as plainly as she can feel her own. But she still doesn't move somehow...

"You aren't as experienced at this as you want me to believe, are you?"

In her mind there's a flick of a thumb and the zing of a coin spinning in the air, "They said you wanted someone fresh, Sir." It takes her a moment to control the look of triumph at her own cleverness before she adds, "Is *that* what you want?"

He raises an eyebrow. "So you aren't as innocent as you're pretending to be?"

"No, Sir, not except for you, tonight."

And he floats, "Just less experienced than you told them?"

"Yes Sir. I needed this, and like I said..." Her hands go up to her bra straps.

"Yes?"

And with a renewed certainty Ella Jane slips them from her pale shoulders. "I liked the idea of the things they said you'd to do to me."

She sets her eyes on his, which lock with hers. The game crashes into reality. The laughter melts away and with it the possibility of picking up her coat. This is more than the game. It's undressing for a man who has taken her in every way. For one whom she has told every secret from the darkest corners of her soul. She's here having chosen to play the part of a courtesan bought and paid for to give him the freedom to do as he wishes to her, and he's looking into her eyes more than at her half-naked body.

Continuing becomes the only choice she can bear.

She swallows, sees his Adam's apple bob, pours herself into the identity of her courtesan, and continues slowly revealing her body's last few *secrets* to a man who knows them and to his character who is about to know them for the first time.

She reaches behind her back and unhooks her bra, lets it fall away from her body, looks around for somewhere to put it and decides to leave it next to the bottled water. She walks over, puts it down and then pours herself a glass and sips. Glancing over her shoulder to look at him and check his responses, she smiles at his smile and turns inexpertly on her heels, then winces as he controls his amusement at seeing her near calamity.

He raises his near empty glass, and she carries the bottle over. Experimenting with crossing her feet as she does, controls a wobble, gives him ample time to see her, the curves of her hips and mons, and of her now bare breasts with their excited tips as she pours water and consciously checks she isn't sending it flooding over the rim of his glass. Then she turns and does a better job of walking away again.

Having put the bottle down she faces him, slips her panties down her legs and steps out of them without taking her shoes off. She bends at the knee to pick them up and arranges them next her discarded bra, before returning.

This time she goes close, stands with her knees between his, against the cushion of his chair, reaches down and touches his hand. Then she kneels.

Once on her knees and in contact with him, her body relaxes. This isn't role play now, not so much anyway, but more a continuation of their night and morning. She looks up at him for permission, the permission men *always* give.

"Are you sure you know what you're doing?"

Her cheeks flare. She remembers demonstrating and if he's forgotten! Then she smiles at the gleam in his eyes, and prolonging her act a little longer, she licks her lips once more and answers, "I've been *told* I do." She makes sure to emphasise the T and D of told and the movement of her lips and tongue as she says the word.

"In that case." He eases his hips forward, lays his hands on the arms of his chair and relaxes into the thick upholstery.

Her position and situation give Ella Jane the chance to press an idea from the story they'd written while flirting online. As she reaches forward, she says, "You're wearing a leather belt, Sir." She undoes it and slides it slowly from around his waist. "It's very thick."

"It is." A corner of his mouth turns up with a hint of a cruel smile. "A belt should have some weight to it." His phrase is from their story too.

She flexes the black leather band and runs her fingers along its length from buckle to tip. "Is it true that you whip girls."

"I do if their behaviour warrants it." He raises a hand and draws a stray strand of hair from her face. "Or if it amuses me to do so."

Ella Jane keeps her eyes on his, her nostril flare and her breath catches. "Even if they do nothing to deserve it?"

"You're here for me to enjoy, aren't you?"

She pauses, touches the tip of her tongue to her lips and swallows again. "Yes, Sir."

He strokes her cheek as he whispers, "So if I were to wish to whip you for my pleasure?"

As close as he is, the quivering that passes through her communicates more than her silence does.

"That's one of the things they told you?"

"Yes, Sir." She looks down.

"And is that one of the things you liked?" Her head hunches lower, and he leans forward, touches a hand to the tip of her chin. He doesn't force her to raise her head, he just waits.

Patience is the key, making him wait to hear the answer, making herself wait to speak it. After an age she looks up, swallows against the welling of desire that threatens to consume her, locks her eyes with his and murmurs, "Yes, Sir."

Her pupils, breath, breasts, and insides respond to the heat the words draw from him and from the man he's pretending to be. Her character joins with her, and her hands lift the belt to him as if it were an offering.

He takes it, bends to her upturned face and their lips meet with a feather light innocence which nonetheless seals their dark compact.

She continues to look up and he down, exchanging silent promises and fire, though neither knows to what extent the other's character is in control, or to what extent the other and their character are one.

An effort sees him move his hand, put the tip of his thumb a millimetre from her lips and, without taking her eyes from his, she opens her mouth and envelops it with the same care she intends to use elsewhere. She swirls her tongue around it and cossets it between her taste buds and the roof of her mouth. She cranes her head forward to take its length into her and holds it there until its presence awakens her body's memory of him inside her there and elsewhere. A knowing smile flickers at an ignited memory of their conversations before either had put a face to the other's words. It's a nod to the girl and the night, to words she contributed *Sucking's different after a man's been inside you, more intimate.* The words remain within the temple of her mind, but a sigh escapes as she places her palms against his lap and lowers her eyes to the waistband of his trousers.

His thumb withdraws, and he lowers his lips to hers in a chaste kiss before sitting back to make it easier for her to do as she intends.

He's hard within his fly, and when she undoes the button and hook at his waist and slides his zipper down, the hooded tip of his cock is peeking over his briefs. She kisses it as daintily as he so recently kissed her lips. It's a gesture which strikes her as either at odds with her role, or intimately in line with it. It's a swirl of thoughts to play, professionalism, passion? Pleasure! It's pleasure, and she repeats the kiss with a smile and an upwards glance.

There isn't room to suck him properly without taking his trousers down, and so far, as she has been able to learn, there's no graceful means known to woman, art or pornographer by which a petite woman can undress a large, seated and trousered man without his active cooperation. It's with a silent upwards plea that her hands go to the sides of his trousers.

Fortunately, he either understands her meaning or is an equal student of women, art and pornography and half lifts himself, so she can slide his trousers and briefs around the curve of his muscular haunches and keeps himself up until she has them past his knees.

More silent communication and her memories of fiddling around with other men on other nights, and she leans forward once again, takes the head of his cock into her mouth. She moulds herself to it, tastes him. And then, with the taste of him in her mouth she bends low, and her hands go to the laces of his shoes, work the double bows free and ease them from his feet. After that, it is a simple matter to finish undressing him from the waist down, though she takes her time, luxuriating in the solidity and power of his legs both while removing his clothing. She returns her attention to what must, at this moment, surely be the core of his being.

Ella Jane's movements emulate his slow certainty, kisses and caresses. She presses her hands as far into the lean flesh of his thickly muscled legs as she is able, gives him a sly glance. Observes, "You must work-out!" She touches her lips to each of his thighs, feels his texture and works upwards at a purposeful pace until she hears his breathing deepen.

She offers a turn of her neck, a look up into his eyes, a hint of a smile and a drawing in of breath. Then she returns her focus to his need, exhales the warmth of her breath onto the twitching limb, wraps her delicate fingers around it, closes her eyes and opens her lips.

The body remembers. That's true of both male and female, and each knows it as their exchanged writings have made clear. She focuses on the night before and senses the echoes of this warm flesh inside each of her openings. Her palate anticipates the strange, new softness of a foreskin against it, and her entrance clenches it's warm embrace reflexively, but finds no reassuring hardness to hold on to.

His sigh half penetrates her reverie, and the muscles of her cheeks respond. A question about the effect of a smiling mouth on a man inside it rises, only to be pushed carefully aside for a more appropriate time.

She continues to hold his shaft and touches her other hand to the loose skin below. Unable to reach lower with him in this position, she applies a gentle pressure to his inner thighs, and he responds by easing them further apart. Still, she doesn't reach lower without looking up for permission.

It comes in the form of a hand's touch to her hair. The touch doesn't seek to guide, or control her movement, a reassurance rather than a grip to enable him to fuck her mouth.

Ella Jane turns her head, rubs against the flat muscle wall of his stomach without releasing him from her lips, and slides her own touch lower. She cups his orbs, presses her fingertips into the tumescence behind and works his flesh with her hands in unison with her mouth.

The tip of her tongue explores the tiny ridges on the sides of his shaft that the smooth softness of his cock's delicate skin hides, but the folds of her canal remember flowing over them.

His hand grips her hair, and relaxes, withdraws, releases her to continue, and he breathes the word, *Fuck* as he yields himself to her enjoyment of and gift to him.

She answers by lifting her mouth from him, smiling up to him and taking him in again. Her hands still keep their strokes short, leaving his cock's hood forward as her tongue plays with its opening. Its tip dances with it as though it were a lover's kissing tongue, though its silkiness is so different and so new to her.

Tempting though it is to continue, she takes him deeper, squeezes the muscles at the back of her mouth around his tip, presses her tongue against the springiness of the underside of his shaft and uses her hands to perform matching caresses to beneath and behind his sack.

A hardening and swelling of the head of his cock signals his enjoyment and a juddering breath confirms it. Having spent the night before being subjected to the delights of his tormenting teases, she lifts away, resumes her attention to his foreskin, pulls it back, tastes the first hint of his clear sweet saltiness, and allows her mouth to spend time comparing and contrasting the smoothnesses of his glans and foreskin. She slides his sheath back, then forward again alternating between exploring his glans and the tiny lips of its opening and its silky natural covering.

She works with her tongue and palate until a sigh escapes his lips. Then she takes him deeper again and repeats her earlier touch. Ella Jane remembers an hour spent with him, alternating between the head of her clit and other sensitive parts of her vulva and inside her and she shifts and presses her legs together.

Positioned thus, she tenses the muscles of her inner thighs around her opening in time with each squeeze her tongue and hands apply to him. Then she mewls her own pleasure around him.

He raises his hips, lets out a brief laugh, and whispered oath. Then she feels him set the cool leather of his belt unrolling down the length of her back. It reaches to, and a little beyond, her buttocks letting her know the wickedly sensitive skin at the top of the backs of her thighs and around her openings is within his reach.

"Are you trying to take your pleasure without permission, little one?"

She locks her jaw open and presses with her tongue and the grip of both hands. Then she consciously, clearly and visibly clenches every muscle in her hips and thighs and waits for the seemingly inevitable.

There's no immediate response. None in the time it takes her to relax herself with an audible sigh.

When she tenses again, he slowly lifts the belt, and she locks her jaw against the impending blow.

Surely!

His cock feels ready to explode and the little involuntary muscles inside her twitch in anticipation of the belt's bite on her vulnerable opening.

The whum of the thick, heavy strip of leather passing through the air warns her, and she grips white knuckle tight.

She redoubles the lock set of her jaw.

Tightens the muscles around her opening still further.

And arches her back just that little bit more.

His aim is true, and her convulsions are close to the explosion of full orgasm.

Deep in the back of her mouth the head of his cock swells, and she braces herself for him to erupt but his body, too, pauses on the brink.

Ella Jane lets out her breath in long, slow waves and hears him do the same. She feels his hand on her shoulder and his hips rock. The motion partly raises her head and her mouth, and she kisses the tip of his cock with a passion. She pulls his foreskin back again, runs the point of her tongue along its tiny lips and tastes the further traces of sweetness there. It's close, so close... but...

She looks up with animal need, sees the heat in his eyes, and the beast behind them howls. She rises to her knees and wraps her arms around his neck as he lifts her.

He doesn't carry her far, just clear of the furniture. before he lays her down. He doesn't hesitate as he enters her, not that the way her legs cling around his hips would allow him to. She pushes his shirt up his back, pulls hard against him and he thrusts into her. Their teeth clash in a fierce kiss, and their bodies join in a primal coupling.

At last, they become still.

And eventually the cooling effect of the slick sheen of sweat evaporating from her naked body rouses her enough to speak, "Wow!"

He's still in and above her. His weight is supported by his knees and elbows and by her hips. Her legs are still pressing against his sides and her hands are clasping his.

"Wow indeed." He brushes his lips against hers. "What gave you that idea?"

"I wanted to do something, but I wasn't sure what. It just came to me in my room." He frowns, "I really only stopped off to get my toothbrush and to think." The intimacy of his laughter while still inside her draws first a crooning from her lips, and then a shared mirth. "So you liked it then?"

"Hmm. That depends."

"What on?"

"On whether you're going to charge extra, should I want you to stay the night?"

She bats him with a fist. "Such a bastard!" He presses his stubbly chin into the soft skin of her neck.

They laugh until he softens and continue as he withdraws from her. Then he stands and leads her through the suite and on until she's wrapped in a robe and streams of hot water are cascading into the bathroom's huge tub. Only then does he finish undressing. Though unlike her, he doesn't bother with a robe.

Having him standing there in the warmth, with steam rising around them and his cock hardening again and still laden with the scent and taste of their union is too good an opportunity to miss, and she kneels again.

With him standing, his peachy bum is available to her curious hands. Ella Jane cups it before first placing the most chaste of kisses on the opening of his hood and then taking him into her mouth once more. She carries on holding his bum with one hand and uses the other to draw his protective sheath back, and bathes his still hypersensitised inner tip with her tongue until she has drunk in every trace of their mingling.

She then pulls back and holds her hands out for him to help her up.

He does so with a courtly grace, though there's a smirk on his lips when he enquires, "Tiles too hard?"

"No Sir, I just wanted to kiss you while my mouth still tastes of us."

Unfamiliar with gigantic tubs and mutual bathing, Ella Jane earns herself a punishing swat for daring to begin by starting to soap her own body rather than his. However, once chastised she quickly realises the benefits of mutuality. Still new to one another's bodies, each bathes the other slowly and with long questioning looks, seeking to learn the details of their taste and preference.

He finds and kisses each one of her fine dusting of freckles. With much giggling, and even some coughing when she comes up for breath, she tries to use the tip of her tongue to do a join the dots on his. They then stretch out as his hands knead a thick lather of shampoo into her hair.

She purrs as he continues far longer than strictly, or even approximately necessary, then on until his chuckle rouses her.

"Mhm?"

"I was just wondering?"

"Yes?"

"What else they might have told your ever so innocent, but ever so talented, young courtesan?"

"Mmm, let me try and remember..."

Her fingers idly caress his heavily muscled forearms as he continues to massage her scalp, and her back feels him hardening against her once again, "Ah, that was it!"

"Hmm? What?"

"They said you liked to tie girls up."

"They did, did they?"

"Uh-huh."

"And what did they say I liked to do with girls after I've tied them up?"

She turns and gives him a mischievous look. "I'll have to try to remember exactly. I must confess I was quite distracted once they mentioned that."

"Oh, were you?"

Ella Jane nods. "Uh-huh." She smiles a kiss-inviting smile which works most satisfactorily.

"Was there anything about edging?"

"Ah, that's right. I remember now." Her eyes sparkle and the corners of her mouth turn upwards as she embellishes. "They had to explain what edging was!"

"Did they?" She nods again her eyes full of mock sincerity. "And did you like the idea?"

She laughs, "No! I hated it, but it turned me on so much that I still took the job even after they said you like to do wicked things to a girl's bum." She wriggles her bum against his now once again fully erect cock.

"Did they tell you about safe words?"

"Yes, but they said I wouldn't get paid if I used one."

"Hmm."

"B-but the-the lady took me aside afterwards. She said I should say red if something hurts too much, or yellow if I get too scared, or I want you to slow down." She reaches into her memory and smiles. "A-and she said something funny too."

"Yes?"

"She said I could say, *Oh-fuck, cramp!* if I had to, as well."

He chuckles and kisses her lips before whispering, "Lunatic," in her ear. Then he straightens. "A cramp," and he strokes her cheeks and down the side of her neck, "is a passion killer. If you get it, tell me, and I'll untie you, and sort it out."

"But..."

"I can always tie you in another position afterwards."

She smiles. "I've had fantasies and read stories, but I didn't think people really did those things until they said you'd do them to me."

"Yes, little one, there are quite a lot of people who do those things, and those who enjoy being tied, too."

She smiles, then looks away in order to hide her amusement at the outrageous pretence that, after their last night, she is in any way innocent. Though of course, a girl looking away while discussing such things creates a rather different impression.

"So." He touches her arm solicitously as he exhales a slow count of three to control his own mirth. "Would you like me to tie you up?"

Ella Jane nods but still doesn't speak or look up.

"Not just because it's your job?"

She looks up at that. Her lower lip is white where her teeth grip it. She blinks, then swallows. "I-I would, Sir."

His hand strokes her wet locks away from her face, "That's a very good thing, because you're going to spend much of the night in bondage." He then touches his lips to hers, and she twists around to face him, opening in the most passionate of kisses.

The change in position puts her slick, eager nakedness against him, and his hardness against her mons. She presses, rubs, wraps her arms around his neck, and uses her buoyancy to move him to her entrance.

He supports her, his hands cupping her buttocks. He holds them as his index fingers slip between, cross over her now supposedly virgin rosebud.

"Oh, Sir!"

"Does that feel nice?" he asks the question, his voice thick with need.

"Do you really mean to take me there as well?"

"I do, by the time you leave; I aim to know every part of you in every way."

At those words Ella Jane closes her eyes and lowers herself, taking the head of his cock inside her and placing more of her weight onto his supporting hands, and onto the tips of his fingers. The pressure there tightens her around him and she rocks her hips to enjoy the sensation. "Does this feel nice, Sir?"

"It does." He leans his head down and nips the tip of a breast, then straightens, "I just hope you're doing it all for my pleasure, not your own."

"Ah, fuck! Er, yes, Sir!" She tells the lie right to his face, then closes her eyes, moistens her lips and allows him to lean her back so that his teeth can punish her other breast for her dishonesty. Tender kisses follow the little bites, and she presses her cheek against his head as he bestows them.

After a while, her mewling and his need persuade him to abandon his ministrations and he allows her to slide herself lower, taking him fully inside her. They find they have to keep their lovemaking gentle while in the tub though, as every time they accelerate their rhythm the waves begin to splash over the brim.

"I'm sorry Sir. This was a bad idea."

He answers, "No," quite firmly. "It was a good *idea*, but we should get out while the water's still hot and mostly in the bath."

"I'm sorry, Sir."

"Don't be. There are ways of dealing with this problem."

"Sir?"

He reaches out of the tub and picks up a curved black rod, "I'd put this in here in case my room guest from last night showed up and wanted to do something in the bath."

"What is it Sir?" she asks the question with her eyes wide, but full of a complete lack of innocence.

"Why it's a waterproof wand vibrator."

"And you want to use it on me?"

"I do indeed."

He brings her to two sweet, intimate orgasms while he's inside her, only stopping when the water begins to cool, and his own need for release becomes so intense that he requires something a little beyond the sweetly intimate to distract him from it.

Being on his lap, Ella Jane is the first to rise. "We spilt quite a lot of water Sir."

"So, we did. Can't be helped now."

Ella Jane injects a note of disappointment into her voice. "Are you going to punish me for making a mess, Sir?"

"Of course I am, but that doesn't mean it was a bad idea. You remember the trick with the towel from last night?"

"I do."

"It's even more intense if the outer towel is wet too." He touches his index finger to the tip of her nose.

She takes his finger and kisses it. Then, having registered its texture on her lips, she looks at it and then at her own. "Our fingers have gone all wrinkly, Sir."

"They have. I shall have to remedy that after you've dealt with the mess you made."

He sets the bath draining and supervises her while she mops the bathroom's floor cropping her bum whenever she slows or the desire to do so takes him. When she has one towel soaked to dripping, he swaps it for another and wrings it out. In this way she manages to get the floor mostly dry. And by the time she has, he has two heavy, wet towels which he twists together and folds over. He then commands her to bend over the side of the bathtub.

Ella Jane looks at him, then at the twisted mass of wet cotton in his hand. "Sir?"

"How many strokes do you think would be appropriate?"

That's a poser for her. the night before it had taken more than she'd been able to retain the awareness to count, but he'd bound her with a vibrator in place. "Please Sir, I don't know how much it will hurt or how many I can stand."

"You can touch it if you wish."

Both towels being wet has changed the texture, removing some of the softness. It adds weight too. She looks at him twice, the first time with excitement, and then with artfully nervous eyes. "A-and you're going to hit me on the ass with this?"

His voice is firm and his face serious by the time he replies, "Your bum and the backs of your thighs, yes."

"But..."

Then his eyebrows join in on the act. "You did agree that you deserve to be punished?"

"Yes, Sir."

"So how many strokes do you suggest?"

Ella Jane squeezes her face up in an effort to seem scared and repentant. "One?"

He sighs. "Let me explain. If you guess too small a number, I'm going to give you double the number I'm thinking of." She swallows. "Would you like to make another suggestion?"

"Yes please, Sir!""And that suggestion would be?"

"Ten, no, twelve Sir."

"Very well. Now get in position."

"But Sir?"

"Yes?"

"I'm not sure I can hold still."

"Allow me to offer you an incentive. If you hold still and thank me after each blow, I'll use this," he shows her the vibrator he'd used on her in the bath, "on your pussy for thirty seconds before the next stroke."

She looks at the towel, and at the vibrator and swallows theatrically, then up at his face. That proves to be a mistake, at least from the perspective of maintaining her role. Laughter lines spread from the corners of his eyes and set her off. In the end, he calms them both by touching a hand to the underside of her chin and his lips to hers. "Now get into position, you little minx."

She turns, positions herself, kneels, and spreads her arms along the side of the bath. The side is too high to bend over it with her knees on the floor though, and she has to lift herself and put her hands down onto the bottom of the tub.

"Spread your legs."

Ella Jane knows why, but she asks anyway, "But Sir? Why?"

"Because I say so, and now you can count thirteen instead of twelve."

"Please Sir, no, that's not fair. Thirteen's an unlucky number." There's a pause before he answers, though she never finds out whether his silence is due to thought or an attempt to control either his amusement, or his other responses to seeing her so perched.

He dismisses her objection. "Then count to fourteen."

To which she protests, "Sir!"

Which prompts him to caution, "Should I make that fifteen, young lady?" in a dark tone.

"No Sir!"

Her acceptance earns her a gentle touch to a shoulder, and a kindly, "Good girl."

So, she positions herself with her legs splayed, her *innocent* derriere raised and her openings on view and waits for his *justice*.

The first blow lands with a jarring force across both of her buttocks. It is the heaviest she has ever known, but, just as the night before, there's little, if any pain. It's just a shockwave that rolls through every fibre of her being and echoes in her centre. She breathes, processes the sensations, and imagines more of the same.

His voice, quite calm, comes to her. "You didn't count or thank me, so that's still zero." Then, without further warning, she senses his movement and a moment later a second blow lands in the same place. Its effects are at least as great, though this time, while she's dealing with her body's response, he touches a hand to her back. His voice asks, "Is there something you've forgotten?" She remains silent. "Or do you just want me to carry on?" and he lands a third.

Once again, her body allows the blow's full force into her already jangling depths. "Whu-uh-one."

"And?"

"Thank you, Sir."

"That's better." He kneels beside her, strokes her hair with one hand and she hears a low buzzing start. He doesn't go straight for her clit. Instead, he runs its bulbous head along and around her swollen outer lips, pausing a little above her hood and over her perineum at each end of his cycle. After three long, slow delicious circuits, he removes and silences the device and stands again.

"Ready?"

Ella Jane is, but her character? "I-I don't know."

That is good enough for him, and the towels fall again. Once again, she misses her count, and once again he repeats the strike, "Two, Sir, thank you."

True to his word, he sets his bludgeon aside and resumes his ministrations. They aren't enough to get her there, not by a long way, not even enough to get her close. They are just enough to leave her more aroused and more ready for him to continue than the first time.

Her mind drifts, both into and away from the scene. She misses the sixth *official* stroke, and he warns her, "If you miss another, I'll start again from zero."

It isn't fair, but with the bones of her hips thrumming to the beat she answers, "Yes, Sir," and it continues. By the time he reaches twelve, she knows that fifteen is not going to be quite enough. "Please!"

"Please what, little one?"

"Just please, Sir."

He chuckles and strikes again.

This time he stretches the thirty seconds to allow him a fourth circuit, and he makes one of the pauses directly over her hood, but it's still not enough.

After fourteen, she's even more of a mess and after fifteen, she begs to be allowed to cum. But her pleas fall on deaf ears, and he lifts her into his embrace. "Will you be good now?"

"Please let me cum!"

"Will you be good?"

"Yes, Sir."

"Excellent. Then I think it's time I took you to my bed and got my money's worth out of you, don't you?"

Ella Jane smiles up at him, well aware that it isn't just an orgasm his strange painless beating has left her body in need of, but his live warmth filling her. "I'm here to serve, Sir. Just lead the way."

He swats her behind with the flat of his hand. "I have a better idea. You aren't here for me to display my body for your amusement." He guides her from the bathroom in front of him.

On entering the suite's master bedroom, Ella Jane casts a backward glance. "My what a huge... bed you have Sir!"

To which he answers, "All the better to tie you to," with a wolfish grin. She giggles and turns to face him, raising her hands with her wrists pressed together as she does. "Anyone would think you were eager to be in bondage."

His words, or the prospect of being in bondage, bring a quite natural flush to Ella Jane's cheeks. She chews her lip and looks down, but keeps her arms raised while he goes to the bedside cabinet and retrieves the cuffs he'd used on her the night before. She looks up when he returns though, and her eyes study every detail of his actions as he secures each of her wrists in turn.

"Lie back now."

She does as bidden.

"And offer me your ankles."

Once again, she obeys placidly and in silence, moving further back onto the bed with a wriggle. She then bends her knees, leaving her feet at the edge of the bed for him. She holds her cuffed wrists to her nose and draws in their heady leather scent.

He stops to watch, and his stillness draws her attention. "Enjoying yourself?"

"Mhm, I love the scent of leather."

"I'm so glad." He finishes fitting the ankle cuffs and muses, "It's a shame I don't have a longer spreader bar here."

A brief squeak escapes from Ella Jane's lips as she prepares to ask, "What's a spreader bar, Sir?" She then bats her eyelids at him curiously, as if daring him to vocalise the laugh she herself is stifling.

"It's a strong pole that attaches to your ankle cuffs, here and here." He illustrates by taking hold of the steelwork of her ankle cuffs. "It holds your pretty legs nice and wide open so all of the sensitive places between are available, and the captive isn't able to do anything at all to prevent them being enjoyed."

She lets him spread her legs wide and leaves them apart when his hands begin to glide upwards.

"How would you go about enjoying them, Sir?"

"Would or will?" He continues to caress, his eyes and hands making it clear that 'will' is the more appropriate word. "Do you want me to spoil the surprise?"

"No, but will it hurt?"

"Some of them will, but certainly not all." He kisses the inside of each of her thighs. "I've been told some of the things I plan to do to you can be quite pleasurable."

"And the others?" she asks the question querulously.

"While I'm doing them? That depends on how much you enjoy pain afterwards. The intention is to intensify both your pleasure and my own."

At that, Ella Jane surrenders herself, but not without letting out a plaintiff, "I hope I can bear it, Sir," in the voice of her role.

With her body relaxed, and her will seemingly absent, it's a simple matter for him to finish binding her. First, he secures her wrists to the midpoint of the top of the bed, and then he arranges the pillows, three on either side of her. Finally he spreads her legs widely over the pillows before finally threading a rope through the D-ring of one ankle cuff, under the bed and to the other. He ties the rope off carefully allowing her legs only an inch or so of movement. Thus bound, her hips are tilted forward, making her openings easily available and her breasts are drawn up.

The tie also has other effects too. It applies a tension to her body, and particularly to her hips, shoulders and the muscles and soft tissue of her torso. Doing so multiplies their sensitivity and her awareness of how vulnerable she is. As a result, when he stands to admire her body and his own handiwork, she's already close to drifting, and it takes little effort to make her *Oh Sir!* sound entirely natural.

She opens her eyes and observes him observing her. Her body is more than ready and a glance shows that he needs to fill her emptiness as much as she needs him to.

However, he isn't ready to submit to either her desires or to his own, and leans over her. He trails confident fingers down the length of her arms and the side of her neck. They skirt and circle the yearning flesh of her breasts despite her desperate pleas, moving on with inexorable slowness. He denies her folds their caress too, preferring for now at least, to explore the less widely appreciated sensitivity and softness of her inner thighs.

His lips come next, placing feathery kisses everywhere his hands have been before them, and her knowledge of his intended path makes every nerve in her skin hypersensitive as it awaits their touch. She aches in anticipation, dissolves in their arrival and her burning need cries out at the seeming inevitability of denial.

He straightens when he reaches the arches of her feet, looks down at her and asks, "Nice?" in an offhanded tone, as though unaware of the effects of his actions.

Ella Jane lets out a cry of exasperation as she struggles against her bonds. "You know it is." Then she gives him a mischievous grin. "Why Sir, you beat me without hurting me, and now you're torturing me with tenderness." He turns away in response, raises a hand to his lips and bites down on the fleshy pad at the side of his thumb, but still lets out a laugh before turning back to her with a serious expression. There's mirth in her eyes, but there's also sincerity in her voice when she murmurs, "Sorry."

"Don't."

"Okay." She bites her lips closed.

"Ready again?"

She closes her eyes, nods and in her assumed voice whispers, "The waiting makes it more intense, doesn't it, Sir?"

Back in control, he sits on the side of the bed and strokes her. "It takes years of study, practice, and experimentation, but the right woman," he touches his lips to the tip of first one breast, "in the right mood," and then the other, "makes it all worthwhile, and more besides."

Her eyes are open and fixed on him when he lifts his head. "Thank you."

He gives her a wink and touches a fingertip to her lips. Then he lets her take it into her mouth for the briefest of moments and then resumes his sensuous exploration of her defenceless form. This time she watches as his hands glide over her skin and sink into her muscles. Their touch lingers longer and finds its way closer to her most sensitive places. By the time he reaches her feet she's mewling, and when he goes to begin anew with his lips, she cranes up in the hope of a kiss.

Ella Jane closes her eyes and lets out a long sigh as he kisses his way down her body, then smiles to herself. "Oh, Sir! Shouldn't I be the one pleasuring you?"

He stops his lip-trailing kisses just as he reaches the faint line between her side and front muscles of her abdomen, looks up, narrows his eyes, and lifts himself. He takes a hold of her by the tips of each breast. "And who, might I ask, is whose plaything for as long as the meter's running?" He then applies a wicked pinch sending spears of pain through her tender buds and lightning bolts of intensity down into her centre.

"FUCK! I'm your–" She gasps while the intensity peaks, "plaything."

His answer is a chuckle and a softening of his grip to a rhythmic massage. "So what should you do?"

Ella Jane takes another steadying breath before answering, "Anything you want me to, Sir?"

This time he kisses each tender bud while still chuckling. The rumbling of his deep, wicked voice sends vibrations through her breasts and into her chest. "Good girl." He then resumes his cruel tenderness, trailing his tongue along the length of each of her outer labia and blowing cooling air over the slickness he leaves behind and her own on her inner lips.

She sighs, and he rumbles his amusement, "Good girl. Relax into it. It's going to be a long, slow trip, but I think my little plaything will enjoy both the journey and the destination." His voice is deep and his mouth close to her opening. Close enough that her stretched body conducts every perfectly enunciated syllable into her core.

He teases her so artfully and for so long that at times, she struggles. When she does so, he chastises her both verbally and physically. The words shame her, but although the physical admonishments force her to do her best to hold still, they also send rivulets of delicious heat flowing through her body.

She mewls and begs, but he does nothing more about this than chuckle, cast slyly arrogant looks her way and continue his tantalisingly slow enjoyment of her nakedness.

By the time he starts kissing the sweet taste of her opening to her mouth, she's so far lost in her sensuous daze that she doesn't even think to pass comment on the decadence of enjoying her own nectar from his mouth.

The second time he does this, he does so from atop her with the needful tip of his hardness between the lips of her desperate opening. The bind however prevents her driving herself more than a few millimetres further onto him as every fibre of her being desires her to. In her powerlessness, she lets out a low sob and a first tear of frustration trickles from the corner of her right eye.

He kisses it from her skin and kisses it back to her lips and then does the same when her second leaks from her left. He murmurs, "Hush, little one. You've been very good so far," before he starts kissing and caressing his way down her body again.

With every few cycles of kisses and caress he adds a little more, entering her, swirling his fingers or tongue around her hood, sucking her clit between his lips, running his grooved tongue upwards lifting her hood away and dragging the little nodules of his taste buds over her aching pearl. With each new delicious torment he adds, she becomes more aware of her bonds, of her body's capacity for pleasure, and of the absolute power that he holds over her bound form.

Only when her tears of frustration cease and her mewling pleas to be fucked and to be allowed to cum fall silent does he begin to focus on her building orgasm rather than his enjoyment of her body. He brings her close with his tongue and then with his hands. He kisses her taste into her mouth as he slides into her, tweaks the tips of her breast and then repeats. He reaches inside her and presses against the front wall of her canal while he sucks and sets the tip his tongue dancing around the centre of her pleasure.

Ella Jane does her best to hold still, but her will has long since faded in the face of his tormenting and her own rising heat. He does his best to hold off while still moving forward, but it takes even more effort to hold her convulsing hips still enough for his hands and mouth to continue. She rises and tumbles and flies instead of falling and he sucks hard and holds on for dear life while her slender body bucks with the strength of a mustang.

He clings to her, and she to her bonds until her cries, her struggles and the shockwaves flowing from her centre leave her limp with exhaustion. He then enters her and holds her until the last echoes of her eruption fade. He holds her until the skin of her outstretched limbs begins to cool before he undoes the knots, wraps her in his arms and the covers, and takes her with a tenderness neither Ella Jane, nor her character had ever realised a dominant man could.

He Grants Her Wish

They spoon afterwards, and he nuzzles the back of her neck. "We never talked about role play while we were chatting online, did we?"

"Mmm." She hugs his enfolding arms. "No, we didn't." She begins kissing each of his increasingly familiar fingers in turn.

"Would you like to try it?"

Ella Jane playfully bites the digit in her mouth and wriggles her bum against him. Then she answers in her faux innocent voice, "If you'd like to Sir, after all, I'm your plaything till morning."

After a while of dozing and of togetherness, he asks, "Does the real you remember asking if I brought a single tail?"

"Mhm, I do." Her lips emphasise her answer with a kiss to his knuckles, and her hips do so by pressing backwards so that his hardness nestles between her buttocks.

"Would it surprise you to learn that I did?"

"Uh-huh, no. Nothing would surprise me from you."

He nuzzles her. "And do you remember telling me how you like the feel of one?"

"Yes."

"And how you wanted me to use the one I showed you?"

"Yes, Sir. I do."

His arms tighten around her, and his voice murmurs, "I think it's time."

Ella Jane swallows, "Yes, Sir. I'd like that if you say so."

"And in your role?"

"Hmm?"

He breathes, "It'll be her first time under the whip," into the side of her neck.

She smiles at the stirring of a sensuous memory, "So it will."

"How does she feel?"

Ella Jane stays where she is hugging his arms, nestling into the warm, strong safety of his body, facing away from him so she can focus on her memory and her truth, not on him, or on their game. "Hmm, let me think. I was excited my first time, but it was nothing like this." She punctuates her words with kisses to his hands and with silences for thought, and he remains still against her. "We hadn't just done all the things we have tonight." she kisses his fingertips. "I never have, not like that, not until last night, and he wasn't so sure of himself as you are." Her next silence is punctured by the sound of her laughter. "I wasn't sure at all."

His hardness surges against her, but his voice remains still.

"I was turned on, but not so much, and I trusted him. At least a little." Her next laugh is wry. "Although I probably shouldn't have." After a long pause she continues, "This is so intimate. I know you know how to hurt me, probably a lot better than he did, and do other things, too." She kisses his knuckles again. "Is it the whip you showed me?"

He breaks his silence, but only to confirm, "It is," in the softest of tones.

"Then I've got an idea, and how wicked it is, but I want you to do it." She kisses his hand again and whispers, "And I want you to have done it."

"And your girl?"

"She wants it. She wants her first time under the whip, and she wants it to be at her client's hands, yours. She's ready for it, and for him to take her afterwards while the pain and submission to it are still fresh in her body."

She turns then, and blinks up at him, raises her lips to his and abandons herself. He kisses her, enters her, holds her, surges as she quakes around him. He only disengages from her when she stills.

"I'm going to whip you now."

Her innocent courtesan voice answers, "Okay." Then she nervously adds, "I haven't been bad though, have I?"

"No, little one, this is just because I want to, and because I want to be the first to whip you."

"Will it hurt?"

"Yes, little one. It won't be anything like the towels were."

"I-I won't be able to hold still, Sir."

"You won't have to. I'm going to tie you with your hands over your head.

"So I can't get away?"

"That's right, and so you can't defend your body from the strokes of the whip you haven't earned."

She clasps his wrist. "I'm scared."

And he raises it, cups her cheeks in his palm. "It's supposed to be scary." Then he touches his lips to hers. "And it's supposed to hurt. I want you to always remember your first whipping and who inflicted it on you." He kisses her again. "And that I did it for no

163

other reason than my desire to whip you and to be the first to impose such a torture on you, defenceless, innocent. I want to see, hear and feel your pain and your acceptance of my right to do as I please with your body."

There isn't a suitable attachment point in the ceiling, so he ties her in a spread-eagle between the tall posts at the foot of the bed. Her compliance and the cuffs still secured about each of her limbs make it a simple task for him to do so.

Rather than fetch the whip straight away, he lingers in his appreciation of his handiwork, of her body and of its readiness. Ella Jane is breathing raggedly by the time he leaves her. He does so for just long enough that her eyes are eagerly focused on the doorway by the time he returns with the wicked coil of plaited leather in his hand.

Despite her familiarity with whipping, and her clear memory of seeing his photograph of this exact whip, she still blanches at the sight. This is reality, not fantasy. The whip is a wicked looking thing, and he's a strong man. She understands full well that he could use it to inflict grievous wounds on her body should he wish to

.

Fear isn't the only emotion though; her body and mind are still flooded with the passion of their couplings and the art of his caresses. Her anticipation is something in its own right, almost a third person in the room.

He shows her the whip up close and has her kiss it and then him. Then he stretches it out and flexes it. Having done so, he strokes his fingers across her shoulders and back, her buttocks, stomach and thighs and finally over her breasts, mons and vulva. Even her delicate rosebud doesn't escape their caresses. "These are the places I'm going to whip."

"No, Sir! Please!"

"Hush." He strokes her cheek and speaks as though comforting a skittish animal, then shows her a padded leather bar bit. "I want you to bite down on this when you want to scream, and if it gets too much, I want you to let it fall from your mouth."

There's writing embossed in the pristine leather of the bit, *Whipping girl*.

"This will be a gift for you when I finish as something to keep as a reminder of your first time. Now open."

Ella Jane licks her lips and then opens wide and takes it between her teeth.

He touches a hand to her cheek. "Try not to disturb my neighbours too much."

There are places that are more sensitive, and there are parts of the whip and of the stroke that cause more pain. Not all of the sensitive places are well known. The inner thigh and where the thigh and buttock meet for example. Everyone knows about the breasts and pussy, but less know about those. Likewise, any fool can swing a whip and hit a back or a leg, particularly if they have no mind to control where the whip's weight falls and where its tip bites, or whether its impact is oblique or directly with its full force.

The first blows he applies are with the whip folded and to her buttocks and upper back, each giving a reassuringly solid impact. Compared to Ella Jane's previous experiences of similar tools, there is a lack of sharpness, something she finds herself beginning to long for even though they land with a force and infuse her body with familiar delicious heat.

It isn't as if rhythm isn't thrilling or there's a complete absence of pain. The sight of his hard expression and muscular frame and of the black leather snaking out and striking her defenceless body is innately frightening even though she trusts him.

Before long, he releases the tip and aims another lash. Only the higher pitched sound of the full length of whip moving through the air warns her of its approach and when it lands it wraps around her and bites into the inside of her right thigh. She's still processing the certainty of pain while he moves to the other side of her captive form and unleashes a mirroring blow that wraps and sears her left. Her body reacts to the double assault as though to a single blow.

The wooden bedposts flex as her body spasms, and the bit fails to fully muffle her cry, but she doesn't spit it out.

He pauses, moves close, traces gentle fingertips along either side of each burning line on her flesh. The touch is comforting. However his whispered, "That was just a taste," is anything but, and the way his hands move to even more sensitive places carries an implied threat.

She tilts her head back and swallows, and he touches her lips. "Are you trying to avoid the embarrassment of drooling on yourself?"

With that he steps back and resumes his work. He demonstrates a dozen ways in which the one whip can strike: with the handle, coil, folded, unfurled using half wrap and full. He changes the force he uses, points and angles of impact with each. By doing so, he applies everything from bone-shaking force to the most superficial of glancing blows and from thud to searing bite.

Her twisting tests the strength of her bonds and of the frame, but there's no escaping. Bound as she is, there's no protecting any part of herself from the wicked leather tongue that snakes out from his hand.

At least he leaves the blindfold off so she can see him move. By seeing his arm and the whip, and by hearing it move through the air, she is able to prepare her mind at least a little. This does however mean that she sees the blows to her breasts and vulva coming, and she whimpers helplessly even before they find their targets.

Despite her earlier enthusiasm, Ella Jane yelps and struggles as he warms, caresses and stripes her body. She glows when he pauses, and his touch finds her opening swollen from more than the whip's blows. Her jaws still cling onto the padded leather bit. So still he whips her, playing her body like an instrument, picking out sensitive points and those where the whip's impact sends messages clear into her core.

The tips of her breasts are already in pain. He pulls back again. This time she sees his muscles tense and his body unleash it's full strength, aiming a blow that's surely heavy enough to slice through her tortured flesh like a knife.

Time slows. She stares at the whip as it lashes out.

The room fills with the sound of its gunshot crack.

But there's no accompanying explosion of pain to her gag-stifled howl.

The whip's crack is an inch from her breast and a moment later his arms are around her.

He runs his fingertips through her burning folds while she gasps and mewls in her efforts to process the aftermath of her fear then lifts his hand for her to see.

She looks fearfully, half expecting to see her blood on his hand. But there's nothing but the slickness of her own passion.

He strokes her tousles away from her face, eases the bit from her mouth and holds her so she can't do anything but look back into his eyes. "Was it as bad as you feared?"

Ella Jane swallows to clear her mouth of saliva, licks her dry lips and looks down in acknowledgement of his physical reaction. She uses the little freedom her bondage allows her to lean into that proof so he can no more hide his body's delight than she can her own swelling and slickness. "Better and worse." She gives him a crooked smile, then blinks slowly, looks up coyly through her lashes, draws her lower lip between her teeth and breathes, "Oh, Sir! I'm scared you've whipped me so bad I won't be able to work for a week."

Catching her cue, he hardens his voice. "Work? Or work for anyone else?"

"Sir?"

He brushes his right hand lightly over the side of her left breast, pausing to run a thumb along the hot, tender raised lines there. "If I've hurt you or marked you so much no other client will want you, then I might as well use you myself."

She buries her face against him to give herself time to think her own and her character's thoughts through. She lets her mind review the pain and pleasure, being pampered, and tortured, being the absolute focus of this powerful man's attention and the means by which he has slaked his hunger.

When he frees her arms she wraps them tightly around him and, without looking up, she asks, "Would you keep doing the same things to me?"

"Some the same, others different."

"Torture me?"

"Yes, of course." He caresses her tenderly. "That gives me almost as much pleasure as the other..."

Another lick of her lips. "As having me?"

"And pleasuring you, yes."

"I don't know if I can bear a whole week, Sir."

"That's the beautiful thing about bondage." He idly toys with the cuff about one of her wrists. "You can revel in your powerlessness." He threads a finger through the cuff's D ring and uses it to pin her arm. "While knowing you have no control over what happens to you."

Ella Jane opens to his kiss, and to his hardness. She clenches around him and her body moulds itself to his in readiness for him to begin moving inside her once more, but he just sinks into her and holds still. "Having whipped you for the first time, I'd like to do something else for the first time too."

She blinks up at him again. He touches another fingertip to her rosebud and raises an eyebrow that asks if she understands.

She understands immediately, but her character takes a little longer. In her smallest voice, she says, "Very well, Sir. I am here to be your plaything."

He tastes her and has her do so herself. "Your body responds well to the whip."

Ella Jane breathes as she suckles and avoids his eyes, thinking instead of what is to come.

He unties the ropes securing Ella Jane's legs to the frame, but leaves the cuffs on her, lies her down, kisses or caresses each of the places his whip had bitten her flesh, then lovingly applies coconut oil to each. As he progressively works the soothing oil into her derriere, his hands stray into her valley. They tease around her supposedly virginal rear. They linger and move close enough to make her body anticipate them doing more, a great deal more. They also awaken the sense memories of the night before when he and his hands did all of those delicious *more* things to her there.

In reality, it's far from the first time a man has taken her this way. It isn't even the first time he has, but he still prepares her as though it were. She lets out a cry if delight when he eventually eases the well-oiled finger into her narrow passage. But he continues to work with a slow, tender patience, taking more time and showing more consideration than her partner had on her real first time. He takes longer even than he had the night before.

This time he arranges her on her back with her legs raised, though he still slides a pillow under her hips in preparation.

He draws out the kisses and the long slow application of the power of his hands. He gets her close again and again as he stretches and lubricates her with slow movements of his finger in her narrow passage. She moves against him and practices clenching around his intruding digit. He looks her in the eyes and holds still. "Are you sure?"

Ella Jane grins, and her courtesan gushes, "Oh Sir, I wouldn't have squealed with delight when you started to lube me if I weren't."

His eyes laugh as he manoeuvres the tip of his cock against at her rosebud. He eases forward until her body resists, and then stops, staying barely in her, rocking gently without pushing deeper. His tip slips past her first muscular ring and presses firmly against the tighter, involuntary inner one. His hands work their wonders as he does, and he smiles down with his wicked eyes and places the palm of his right hand over her mons. "Touch your breasts."

She bites her lip, and her hips move against him, meeting his motion with a will of their own.

"But don't cum yet."

She lets him guide her hands, smiling up as he does and she murmurs, "If you hadn't taught me to do what I'm told, I wouldn't have dared to touch myself like this while I was with you."

"Is that so?"

"It is." She gives a little shiver as she begins to tease her sensitive mounds, and her lips twitch with her continued amusement as the pleasure begins to flow. "As it is, I don't dare not, Sir."

The pressure on her pubic bone and against her tight opening, and the way he moves his hand creates a liquid fire inside her that flows to her chest as she teases the swell of her breasts, and her hips undulate with its waves. She doesn't know whether it's her recent orgasms or the multiple sources of stimulation, but she finds her body racing toward another climax. As it does her inner ring pulses, relaxing and contracting, allowing his lubricated cock to ease itself deeper. It still hurts, but the pain is now a secondary sensation. It's adding spice and a feeling of submission to the transporting mix.

He half enters her eager rear, chuckles and goes back to his teasing.

Her lips part, and her back arches. He stops and commands her, "Stop!"

She's so close that he has to repeat his command and to take hold of her slender wrists and move her hands away. She whimpers and mewls as her needed is denied.

Only her role and her fear of an embarrassing encounter with a keen eared neighbour hold her back from crying out for him to *Just fuck my ass!* She knows her impatience is a sign that he knows what he's doing, so she bites her tongue, and her fingers dig into the swells of her chest.

Her fingers grip her stiff buds, punishing her achingly aroused flesh in an effort to control her arousal as his hardness begins to press forward again.

Even with their four hands at play, her readiness and his eyes burning into hers, he takes his time sinking fully into her rear and holds still to give her body time to adjust. That still isn't enough for him though. He takes up the wand, plays with its controls until it's humming low and slowly and applies it to her perineum first.

Ella Jane's eyes widen as the vibrations travel along his cock up and inside her. "Oh, Sir!"

He chuckles, "I thought your virginal bum might enjoy that," and starts moving inside her.

The welter of sensations gets Ella Jane to the edge quickly, but the confusion of stimulations prevents her from cumming right away. She goes beyond it without finding her release as he builds up a rhythm.

She arches, bucks, clutches her breasts, pinches down on their tips to try to create the necessary focus, and he moves the vibrator to the centre of her pleasure.

His body begins to develop a sheen of sweat. Their voices mingle, and he commands her, "Hold the vibe." Then he uses his arms to support his upper body as she releases one breast in order to do so. He moves one hand to claim it. She holds the device to her clit and thumbs the little plus button, as he begins to drive into her with a fury.

Her scream begins before he locks deep inside her, and his cock begins to pulsate against her spasming muscular rings. Still she doesn't let go of the vibe or of her breast until he stills and quiets.

When she does, she wraps her arms around his slick shoulders and heaving chest. He makes to withdraw from her, but she tightens her hold. He flexes and rumbles, content to stay within her warmth.

When her own breathing calms she kisses the sweet saltiness of his sweat and chuckles to herself.

"What's so amusing?"

"Nothing, I was just wondering. Can we re-do all of my first times?"

"Ha! Now there's an idea." He touches his lips to her offered mouth and answers, "I don't see why not," in a tone that suggests to Ella Jane that they have just made a deal.

The night before, he'd disappeared to the bathroom alone after sodomising her. This time he commands, "Come with me." He leads her into the shower and has her stand to one corner with him before adding, "It's your job to bathe me afterwards," and turning on the stream of water. He holds her there until the water is steaming hot.

His words and tone are harsh, but his expression and the touch of his hands give the lie to them.

Ella Jane apologises, "I'm sorry Sir. I didn't know I was supposed to."

He allows his hands to brush lightly over her skin. "I think I shall make allowances for your inexperience as that was your first time." He kisses her cheeks as one would kiss a lover. "You're to wash me in the shower and make most especially sure that you've cleaned me. When you finish, you're going to take me into your mouth again."

She'd have lingered in her task even without his threatening tone. Her hands further familiarise her with the cock she now knows so intimately and his body that's both a visual and a tactile delight. "Make sure to use the body glove." She looks up puzzled and he soaps an exfoliating mitt and passes it to her.

It isn't as much fun as using her bare hand, but his contented growling as she rubs its rough surface over and between the folds of muscle on his back is still enjoyable.

She kneels and uses it to scrub his thighs, then stays in that position to give him the proof he requested, that she has cleaned him well. She then rises dreamily when he guides her to her feet and abandons herself to the strength and skill of his hands.

After their shower, he has her dry him before drying herself. Then he slowly unwraps the towels from around her body and has her look in the mirrors as his fingers trace the places where he made the single tail's tip bite. There isn't a mark left on her body for all the pain he put her through.

"I can't believe you didn't mark me. I was sure I'd be bleeding by the time you finished."

"I rarely leave a mark unless I plan to."

"Will you mark me another time?"

"You, Ella Jane, or you my little courtesan?"

"Either; both."

"If we see each other for long enough, and you consent, then I will mark you occasionally. If your courtesan is sent for just a night again, I think I can guarantee that I'll mark her enough that I may as well keep her for a few days."

"Mmm..." Ella Jane squeezes herself up close to him and presses her warmth against his."

He hugs back and lets out a low rumble.

She enquires, "Hmm?" without moving.

"The way you played up being *made* to touch your breasts had me. You almost hammered your way into another whipping."

"Mmm, sorry." She rubs her head against his chest and presses her lips against him. "I was enjoying myself while you were doing all the work."

"That's okay. In case you didn't notice, I was having a good time too."

"I did get that impression." Ella Jane's fingers tentatively stroke his cock. "I can still feel him being in me everywhere."

"That's good, though I think now it's time for him to be in you again."

She bites her lip and tightens her hold on his erection as she looks up at him with her tired eyes. "In here?"

"Not this time. I think something more vanilla flavoured, and in bed, would be more appropriate."

He takes her hand and leads her back into the bedroom rather than making her walk in front of him.

Ella Jane's too tired to do much, but he's too close for her to need to. He's no longer focused on her need and with every nerve in his cock so well-worked by her body's embraces, her welcoming is all it takes.

She drifts after he cums but still makes a grumbling sound when he makes to withdraw, so he stays in her a brief while longer.

Hours later, he rouses her with a kiss and disengages himself with a regretful sigh, "You really should read the rules."

She follows him and his body's warmth as she sleepily asks, "Any rule in particular?"

"The one about it being the guy who falls asleep afterwards."

She giggles and then frowns and finally grins in triumph. "That only applies when he cums, and she doesn't."

He raises an eyebrow, "Is that so?"

"Yes," she announces smugly, and supports her position by telling him firmly, "I've watched all the videos on YouTube about it."

"And?"

"And if a girl has lots of orgasms, she's allowed to be the first one to fall asleep."

"Hmm." His voice is dubious, and his hands seek out sensitive places. "How many is lots?"

The unrepentant Ella Jane resorts to reason, "I don't know. Lots isn't a precise value."

"Oh, isn't it indeed!" He asks, "And how many did you have?" somewhat archly.

"I don't know that either." Ella Jane gives him a big-eyed look. "But definitely lots."

His fingers skirt around places that would be easy to use to inflict flashes of chastising pain or rewarding pleasure. "There is a theory that I should punish you for not counting."

For her part, the petite American lets her body yearn towards them heedless of which he might choose to impose. "I could tell you that me not being able to remember is a sign of your virility, or I could fib."

"There's a definite thing about punishment for fibbing."

"Even for white lies?"

"Depends." He grins and playfully pinches, then caresses her. "Maybe something more funishmenty for them."

She grins and lets him kiss her, before realising how hungry their night's fun has left her. She climbs out of bed. "Can you funish me after breakfast?"

"I can, but I get the distinct impression that this system might tempt you into telling all sorts of white lies."

Tea-potting her arms in response gets her nowhere, nor does pouting, so she tries tilting her head and blinking her eyes through her curls. When that doesn't work, she lifts her foot.

"If you stamp that foot young lady."

It's as much his tone and the set of his eyes as the words, but she lowers her foot. "Can we order?"

"We can and have it delivered after your morning exercises."

"Owh! That's so not fair. You had me tied up most of the night while you did things to me."

He blinks and remains silent, well aware that he has both time, and breakfast on his side.

Her Quandary

He seeks to encourage her with kisses and caresses, but the sweet nothing he whispers in her ear when she starts to show an interest is, "It's time for our morning exercises."

Ella Jane tried to get out of it be complaining, "I don't have any fitness clothes."

"You don't have any dangly bits to need keep tucked away either."

"You're just going to make me do it in my underwear like a schoolgirl who forgot her gym kit?"

"No, I'm going to make you do it naked like a submissive doing what her Dominant tells her." He pulls the covers from the bed. "Doing it like that'll keep you on your toes, and aware of who's in charge." He emphasises his point by raising the long thin dressage whip already in his hand.

She touches his cock in an effort to entice him. "Aren't you at least going to let me attend to your morning needs first?"

"Maybe after, when I attend to yours."

"How do you know I have them?" She asks the question knowing she's in the mood, but also knowing that his body's mood is quite literally staring her in the face. After a short silence she pushes her lower lip out. "I'm going to get nowhere, aren't I?"

His cheeks tighten with suppressed mirth, and he touches a fingertip to the end of her nose. "That depends if you're obedient and work hard."

"This doesn't seem fair. You and that call girl kept me awake until the small hours."

"Did we?"

"You did. She was quite shameless!"

"Then the next time I see that young lady I shall have to have a very severe word with her, but if you don't move that cute little bum of yours soon, it'll be you I'm having a severe word with now."

When she hesitates further, Ella Jane learns that he's as much the dab hand with this whip as he is with each of the others he's used on her. "Yowch!"

"You were warned."

She rubs her stinging thigh as she gets out of bed then watches that vivid red stripe fade and gives him an accusing look. "I think I've decided to still be that young lady."

The next flick of his wrist produces a matching flare of pain on her other leg.

"Ow! Do you practice using your whips every day?"

He smirks.

"OMG You do!"

"I don't practice with every kind every day."

"That's a comfort."

"There wouldn't be time."

"I pity your regular practice target."

"I don't currently have one. If your courtesan would like, I can have a word with her agency and arrange for her to be offered the job. Now..." the whip's cracker snaps around to sting her bum, "move or the next one won't be a warning shot."

He starts by guiding Ella Jane through some basic exercises, nothing extreme, but he still pushes her to a level of effort she hasn't reached outside of scenes since she was in high school. The resulting aching intensity isn't entirely unlike that she's experienced while in strict bondage or when she's been subjected to thuddy beatings.

He flicks his wrist, and the crop slashes across her thigh. "Stand up straight." He touches the crop's tip to her chin until she holds it high enough to satisfy him, taps her shoulders until she holds them far enough down and back, and then taps the undersides of her breasts. "Push these out as if you're trying to impress me."

She grins but obeys. Then, when her posture satisfies him enough to stop tapping away at her sensitive flesh, she asks, "How do you keep a straight face?"

The question draws a sharp slap of the crop against the curve of a breast. He cracks a smile momentary as her sensitive flesh bounces under the impact. "I take this very seriously."

"Thank you, Sir." And she tenses her cheeks in an effort to match his face's seriousness even as she processes a mixture of pleasure and pain.

With her naked, he trains in just a pair of shorts, working until his body is rimed with sweat. He pushes her hard despite her continuing attempts to divert him and despite his body's desire for him to be distracted being clearly visible to her. It's hard enough that if she didn't want to prove something to him, she would have given up.

Her efforts earn her smiles and swats hard enough to make her skin tingle both from the palm of his hand and with the crop. Ella

Jane can't help sneaking peeks at her body to see the pink and red marks rise and fade. By the time he calls an end, the last mark has faded.

She admires herself, and him, and surrenders to his attentions when he holds up a towel. He starts to clean the worst of the sweat from her tingling body but doesn't get far. Her vocal responses and the urgency of his need see to that, and he finds her not merely willing but complicit when he forces her down onto the carpet.

He wrings an orgasm from her before the beginnings of carpet burn to his knees convinces him to adjourn to the bedroom. Then he pulls another orgasm from her before he decides to plug her, and finally erupts inside her as the combined effects of their exertions and the pressure of the plug inside her drive her to the third and most intense climax.

Only afterwards does he finish towelling her slick skin. She starts laughing before he finishes, and he enquires, "I didn't think you were ticklish?"

"That wasn't ticklishness. I was wondering how you knew how much I needed that."

His chuckle and his kiss come before his answer. "I had no idea. All I knew was that I did, and you were ready."

"Huh."

"I knew you had your safe word."

"So, you get to do anything to me, so long as I don't use my safe word?"

"I'll stop if I don't think it's safe, if I don't think it's appropriate to continue, or if you safe word." He gives another kiss, which she sullenly returns. "Other than that?" He chuckles again, "Anything you've agreed to in principle, yes, just as you can stop me at any time."

Over breakfast, he enquires, "Did you have any plans for the next few days?"

She sucks her lips into her mouth before brightly reminding him, "The conference."

"After that!"

"I was going to recover from going to the conference."

"And now?"

She grins and makes sure she's far enough from him to avoid any instant reprisal. "Now I'm planning on recovering from my time with you!"

"Owh, don't be like that." He rises and moves around the table to her, but all he does is kiss her cheek. "I thought you were having fun."

"I was, I am, but you, Mister are hard work."

"That's a shame. I'd rather hoped you'd be able to stay on over the weekend."

"Oh, you had, had you?"

"Yes."

"You do realise not everyone can afford to just stay a few extra days in a swanky hotel whenever the fancy takes them?"

"I do, but I was hoping you'd check out of your room."

She feigns misunderstanding. "And sleep on the streets?"

"You could, but I suspect my suite might be more comfortable than a doorway."

"Why Sir? Are you propositioning me?"

"Not at all." He places a hand over his heart. "I have a spare room, so there's every chance that my intentions are strictly honourable."

"I bet you say that to all the young women you wake up with."

"Of course. I have a spare room, but I don't want to risk them sleeping in it by telling them about it before we go to bed."

"Beast!"

"I know," he confesses. "I'm terrible."

He's been making decisions for them, and for her, since she stepped into the restaurant on her first day in New York. Nothing she hasn't enjoy but still, Ella Jane decides to make a point and reaches for a third egg, leaving the plate empty with him not having had a fourth. She keeps her eyes on him as she does.

He raises an eyebrow, and she waits, then continues with putting it on her plate.

Looking at the now empty platter he asks, "Would you like me to order more?"

"No thank you."

"You're sure? I could cook you some."

"Pardon?"

"There's a kitchen. It has a fridge, a hob and a frying pan. There are supposed to eggs. I'm going to do another for myself, so it's no trouble."

"And you can cook in real life?"

"I gave you no word of a lie when I told you I could."

"I thought it was one of those things guys just say."

He frowns. "Did you really?"

"Yes! like I *give head* and I *know how to give you an orgasm.*"

"I said those things too."

"Yes, but you weren't just saying..."

"See?" His smile spreads as he raises his teacup.

"Why aren't you married Mr Smartypants?"

He offers, "I must have been too busy learning to cook and give orgasms I suppose." Somewhere between disinterestedly and in self-satisfaction at having turned the conversation so swiftly in a circle.

She snipes, "Very funny." In response, his face begins to shape with different emotions again. The stern lowering of his brows above the slight crow feet of amusement at the corners of his eyes and his jaw pushed forwards even as his he tightens its muscles to suppress a chuckle. "Okay, quite funny. How do you do that?"

His eyes widen.

"Be stern and laugh at the same time."

"I think it's an English thing. We're supposed to be miserable and funny." He gets up and takes his plate to the little kitchen. "Fancy keeping me company?"

Realising that he really is going to cook more eggs, she adds a rasher of bacon to her plate and follows him.

She manages to clear her plate while she watches him rifle through the cupboards and fridge, before cooking two eggs easy over. He's as casually competent in the kitchen as he is in the bedroom, and as presumptuous of huge appetites, offering once again to cook her some more.

"Thank you, I'm stuffed though. I probably shouldn't have had all I did."

"Ha, terrible."

She toys with her lip while pretending to think. "Too terrible for me to want to stay with you?"

Having cooked he makes his way back to the dining room. "I rather hope not."

When they sit, she comes to a resolution. "Okay. If I decide to move, how do I do this?"

He shrugs, "I have no idea. I suppose you check out and ask them to move your bags in here."

She hedges, "I'm not sure I want the staff getting my things."

"Then we can get them ourselves."

"Is fetching bags around a hotel beneath you?"

"We can find out. If I have a seizure on the way up, then yes."

"Lunatic. My bag weighs less than your dumbbells."

"Phew."

"Let me see if I can get a refund on my flight." She takes up her phone and taps away. After a few clicks she announces, "I can, and it's cheaper to fly back during the week!"

"So, is it a deal then?" he offers his hand.

Which she takes and shakes. "A deal and a bargain." Then she sends a message to her mother to tell let her know she won't be back until Monday.

"So pleased, though if that little courtesan turns up again, one of you might have to sleep in the spare room."

"Her!" She sets her jaw. "I want you all to myself."

With that agreed, Ella Jane helps herself to more to eat. A second long night of debauchery, followed by starting her morning by literally whipped through her first gym session in a little too long have given her a bigger appetite than she's used to. It's still not enough that the plentiful breakfast the butler serves doesn't fully satisfy, but it is enough that his eyes fill with mirth. "Hungry?"

She finishes her mouthful, "Yes." Then another. "Somebody's been making me work."

"The cad."

His Diversion

The debate on the second morning that they're both on stage for is on the subject of tense and perspective in fiction. He makes a face going in, and as this is a topic that had been dear to the heart of one of her dullest professors, she can't help but share his feelings.

After ten minutes he has to cover his mouth to stifle a yawn, and after fifteen he sees Ella Jane's head nod and messages,

Nap buddies time?

Ella Jane gives him a mortified look, which he responds to by covering his mouth and making a coughing sound to disguise his smile.

What's a nap buddy?

We watch each other for signs of dozing off.

Ha, yes, we have another deal.

A little while later, Ella Jane notices Him looking down and tapping away in his tablet while others give their answers to questions and messages:

What are you doing?

Shopping.

Where?

Home Depot [evil grin].

Without thinking she sends a humorous reply.

Make sure you spend enough to get free delivery.

A few clicks later, he replies with a link to their website. Continuing with her whimsical thread she sends:

You could save even more by spending enough to use that discount code at the top.

In reply to which he sends another evil grin, as he starts replying to someone in the audience. Thus her next message goes unanswered for some time.

You aren't!

When he finishes speaking, he sends her:

I am. [smug] Is there anything you'd like me to add? [angel].

He then raises his head and suggests that her thoughts on the question would be interesting, and she splutters a little but manages to make some sort of coherent reply. Then she casts him a dagger drawn look and an hastily tapped:

You are a completely filthy man.

True, and you are going to pay for that later.

He looks across and winks at her in person rather than sending an emoji. Then while giving his opinion on character development, he sends her a copy of his shopping basket.

It's all Ella Jane can do to control herself. He's selected lengths of a half dozen different types of rope and three kinds of chain, a heat gun, an assortment of dowels, numerous electrical cabling and polyurethane piping, sand and a half dozen padlocks. Then there are several power tools, bolts and lengths of sawn timber.

She almost misses her cue to give her views and casts him a look before beginning her response. When she finishes, she fires off:

Am I really in that much trouble?

[raised eyebrow] You're in as much trouble as you want to be young lady, and just maybe a tiny bit more. [wink, evil grin]

She messages back:

Please don't tell me you're having this delivered.

He doesn't message back right away, and when she glances across at him, he gives her a swaggering look. Seeds of doubt sown, he ponders whether to leave her thinking he'd had the makings of a thousand bondage games delivered to his suite. She looks nervous, embarrassed, and he loves that look on her, and slowly lets his wolf smile spread as she fidgets,

I got them to gift wrap it.

How on earth did you do that?

[Money, Shrug] And seeing as how you insisted I save money on this stuff, I got you something to wear with it.

From Home Depot?!

No.

Something nice?

Something sort of nice.

You're not going to tell me what it is, are you?

Of course not [smug, laugh]

Ella Jane sucks her lips into her mouth as she remembers his suggested emoji for hands on hips then sends him:

[Teapot]

She looks across at him with blinking innocence.

He doesn't bite right away, but just like her, he can't resist looking down, seeing and understanding. On doing, so he raises a hand to cover his mouth to hide his reaction. Though as close as she is, she sees his shoulders and cheeks betray a suppressed chuckle.

They lunch together with the other speakers and panellists. It's a buffet service, and Roger and Cynthia are elsewhere so they fill their plates, one for her and two for him, and find somewhere to sit side by side. The attention paid to him, and the somewhat different attention paid to her, is a little overwhelming for Ella Jane.

"I'm commercially successful, but I write the wrong kinds of books. Most people don't care, but there are a few who don't approve of action, fantasy, or filth."

"How dull."

He looks over at a small group across the room whose members are less animated than most and nods to her. "If you want, I can introduce you to a couple of them so you can find out how dull."

Ella Jane catches herself laughing while looking at them. She bats his arm. "Don't. They'll see."

A woman she recognises and wouldn't have dared talked to is passing with a drink and on hearing pauses and looks around. "They won't. And even if they did, they're already offended." She then looks at Him with recognition and extends her hand. "You don't often grace these things."

He takes it with a smile, and sighs resignedly, "Releases and long-deferred promises to my agent and publisher."

The woman then turns back to Ella Jane. "He's such a martyr."

"Ah, allow me to introduce Miss Ella Jane Tyler, a rising star."

"I'm not!"

The woman raises an admonishing finger to her. "Don't listen to that voice. There are enough other people queuing up to tell us all we're not that special without telling ourselves it."

Ella Jane flushes. "I just can't believe I'm here and meeting you."

The other woman smiles and leans forward. "It's alright. We're quite a solitary breed, so you won't have to meet us very often."

They talk on for a while before the woman's friends drift over. She introduces them to Ella Jane, and they too exchange pleasantries before the group heads away.

He watches her eyes follow the group and offers, "Are you sure you want to hang around with me rather than meet everyone?"

Her hand touches his leg under the table. "Don't leave me!"

"Is there anyone you'd like me to introduce you to?"

"Can I just take this slowly?"

"Of course. It gives me an excuse to be antisocial too."

"There you go, making a joke of everything."

"Not entirely. There's a reason why people are surprised to see me."

They sip and exchange a few nods and hellos. One of the organisers comes over to them and does his hostly thing, and then they're free until their next panels.

He gives her a *Good luck*. And they each go their separate ways, him to a discussion on dark futures and Ella Jane to try to avoid answering questions about coming of age. She doesn't entirely succeed but does find speaking in public in such company easier than she'd feared. And when the session breaks up, having overrun, the chair praises her answers, which sends her off with a warm glow.

Left to her own devices, she checks her phone and notes a series of messages from him. They're a mix of dry observations and encouragement. She composes what she hopes is a witty reply, asking if he spent the whole session thinking of clever things to say.

His reply arrives a couple of minutes later

Have you escaped then?

When she confirms that she has, he follows it with funny face emoji and:

I'm trying to escape from a conversation about the perils of fan fiction.

I'll let you know what I think if/when I get my first piece.

You'll get a lot in time. You can stop by if you'd like.

Not having anything better to do, she makes her way, listens, and tries to put herself in the mind of a writer whose characters or world have been adopted by others.

When the conversation breaks up, he asks her thoughts. Having checked that they're safely far away from prying ears, he leans close and hints that somebody might need to put her over his knee if that's what it takes to make her speak her mind.

Ella Jane frowns up at him. "I'm more used to that happening because I've given my thoughts."

His brow furrows. "That's not how it's supposed to work. Provided a sub isn't rude or disrespectful, it's their D's responsibility to help them grow."

"What about slaves?"

"That sort of play is a long way down the path, and not for everyone." He then lightens the topic. "Anyway, you've heard all about my session. Tell me about yours."

She starts, then looks around. "I've barely been outdoors since my flight. Is it okay if we go around the block?"

"Of course, nothing stops a conversation being overheard quite like New York traffic."

There's a side entrance that leads to an alleyway, and with his charm and her looks they're through it in no time with a smile, a *But you can't be serious* and a *Thanks awfully*. He unclips his delegate pass as they step onto the sidewalk. "And this, is how we play hooky from school."

"Aren't you supposed to be a good influence on me?"

"If Roger asks, I know nothing."

"That's not very gallant."

"Fortunately, he won't push, and is terribly good at coming up with white lies."

"Is that so?"

"It's part of the selection process for agents, and terribly important for writers, publishers and the press, because we all have more aspiration than ability. Agents keep us from one another's throats and in some cases from the bottle as well."

"You're a goldmine of information."

"Why thank you."

"Is this a way of avoiding talking about play partners, submissives and slaves?"

"More a circular approach. We've been talking for a long time, but we only have these two days and nights under our belts."

She steels herself and asks, "As we're in New York City, can I make it a linear question then?"

Then she relaxes when he accompanies his, "When in Rome?" with a smile.

"Yes."

"A Master has the same responsibilities and more than a Dominant. A slave needs to be more sure of what they're offering than a sub. But relationships should be entered into only with deep knowledge, and after trying things out for size. The submissive or slave should be protected as far as both are able in the event of a parting of the ways."

"Protected how?"

"Somewhere to sleep, things to wear, funds or an income to see them back to life outside of a dynamic."

"So having a room to stay in?"

"Yes, that's one thing."

She checks her phone. "I suppose we should go back in, shouldn't we."

When they return, a harassed looking member of the organising committee nervously approaches Him.

"We've had a speaker drop out. Is there any chance you'd be able to join one of this afternoon's panels?"

He grins, and wobbles his head drunkenly then slurs, "Has somebody got a 'sick-over'?"

"Uh, probably. But I don't suppose you could...." The committee member's eyes plead.

"What's it about?" His voice is suspicious.

"Trigger warnings, cultural appropriation and sensitivity reading."

Ella Jane interjects, "Ooh, I'm on that one!"

"You do know who I am and what sorts of books I mostly write, don't you?"

"Yes, I spoke to your agent, and he said you might be willing to help out by sitting in on this one."

She joins in the effort to persuade him. "Please. It might be fun seeing you get into trouble instead of me."

He looks from Ella Jane to the organiser, both of whom are wearing their best ingratiating expressions. Then he ponders the possibility of Roger's stirring, whether this is payment in kind or an effort to help him out by nudging him and Ella Jane closer. "Oh, very well. But don't say I didn't warn you." It isn't as if he isn't curious to see if Ella Jane plans on a spot more hunting.

In the session, Ella Jane keeps her answers and comments considerate. He does his best to stay out of it, but listens and reconsiders his views as he forms some new ideas. When somebody finally annoys him enough. he joins the conversation.

"Those of you who know my work will probably be aware that I'm something of a *Free Speech Absolutist*. As a Brit, and a guest in your fine country, I'd say our shared tradition of allowing people to say what they want is part of what makes ours the best and most creative of nations, top universities, patents, books, stories and music. We produce more than any other cultures. That said, trigger warnings are an interesting one. You'll find some readers treat them as a shopping list. Meanwhile if you put them on a book that might upset some people, you might stop them picking up a book of yours they won't like and which might put them off other books they might." He shrugs. "Overall, I think it might be better if we, the industry and public, were to consider them as content descriptions and to make them standard." He pauses expecting some response, but the room remains silent, so he adds a throw away. "After all, when we go to a restaurant the menu usually includes some description of the food." That gets the ripple of laughter and applause, so he finishes there.

"I like that. What I'd say is *Write what you know and what you imagine*, get friends to read and give you feedback. Wherever possible, find someone appropriate to get feedback from, whether a friend or a professional. Then don't be shy about making sure the reader knows what to expect." She's about to yield the floor, when she remembers what her agent had drummed into her. "When I write a passage about interactions between male characters, I badger guys I know to read it and tell me if I portray them believably, and if not what I've got wrong. I don't know if anyone here's read my book, but I'm sure those who have will be able to identify the scenes I made sure to research and run by others."

There's more applause when the session comes to a close, and some of the attendees approach the stage. He descends the steps and spends a while signing autographs and allowing selfies. Ella Jane steps down too and finds a couple of those who approach to speak to others pointedly avoid her. But more approach her shyly to ask questions about starting her career in writing and to praise her for standing up for her views.

Eventually the panel's chair rescues them after a few minutes by announcing that the room will be needed. He takes Ella Jane by her elbow with an apology that they've arranged to meet someone. Guiding her in front of him, he squares his shoulders and assumes a thunderous expression. Nobody obstructs their passage and by the time they're in the corridor and he withdraws his guiding hand, they're well clear and he's relaxed to the point on humming cheerfully.

Ella Jane turns to him over coffees in the author's lounge. "Well, you made it."

"Hmm, so did you."

"What was that about?"

"There's a chance some fool's going to want to get a selfie of themself confronting one after one says something unfashionable. Best avoided."

There's a *Meet the Authors and Agents* session in the afternoon, and they're kept busy answering questions about the industry, working with editors and experiences of being published. He also gets to say hello to a few acquaintances, and Ella Jane is able to meet one of her inspirations.

Shortly before it comes to an end, Roger and Cynthia round the pair up and Roger wheedles them into agreeing to go to a cocktail bar where each works on their client to agree to more promotional work. Promises given and first cocktails drunk they make their apologies and swear solemnly that, should either be asked, they will swear they were being plied with drinks for the whole night.

With that, they make their farewells and Johnson sweeps them back to the St Regis.

Their Gifts

Ella Jane is excited on their way back to the hotel. She has a surprise to give him, or for him to discover.

However, when he lets them into his suite something else steals at least a little of her thunder.

There's a collection of neatly wrapped packages, large ones. Well, most of them are large. On the top of one pile is a single slim parcel with different wrapping.

Ella Jane's mouth drops open. "You really ordered it all?" He nods and grins. "And you're going to keep it in the hotel?" Thoughts of what the staff will think flood her mind.

He shrugs. "I was planning to use it in the hotel so..."

"Have you gone insane?"

"Gone?" He grins. "You wanted me to be more adventurous with your body."

Her words that morning had been meant in jest. "Holy crap, we can't just turn your suite into a dungeon!"

He shrugs. "We can. If we don't damage anything, or anyone." Then he smoulders towards her and takes her in his arms. "We can do anything we both freely consent to, so long as we don't impose on anyone else."

"Safe, insane and consensual?" she asks with a winsome look. "You're crazy for getting all this, and I must have been crazy for egging you on."

"I wish I'd thought of that." He smiles before putting her down. "Now, did you want to help open the packages?"

Ella Jane wants to stamp her foot. *He's cheating* rages one internal voice, and she tries to build anger as she colours. In response, he smiles a we've-got-new-toys smile. She curses the months of openness with her fantasies and his understanding. *Of course she wants to see what's in the packages!* But that's not the point.

"How long are you here for?"

"Another few days after the conference for work and pleasure. Then I've got a few work things and some more downtime planned around the states. Why?"

He tears open the plastic envelope taped to the outside of the largest parcel. "You're the one who suggested I buy enough to get free delivery and a discount code that had a minimum spend."

She stares at him with her eyebrows raised and her eyes wide as she takes it. "You're insane, aren't you?" He frowns, so she tries to explain.

"How much does this suite cost?"

"I don't know. I didn't book it."

Ella Jane knows how much her own luxurious, but comparatively modest, room cost and does a mental guestimate at the price of a penthouse suite ten times the size. "And you saved a few bucks on DIY kink toys we might never use?"

"I didn't get that much!" He gives her a lopsided smile and hands her the slim parcel. "And I got something for you."

"You must have bought enough things to do a different session every day for a year!"

She continues to stare, and to try to work out whether he's taking the piss. But he's either serious or acting well or just engrossed in running a finger down the two sheets of the note. "I suppose it'll be best if we take these things through to the reception room then check this."

"You expect me to help carry them?"

"Not till you've opened yours. Fair's fair." With that he picks up two of the stacked boxes and carries them through.

Ella Jane follows him and watches him cheerfully transport and arrange the rest of the boxes. He disappears into the bedroom and returns with a wicked looking little lock-knife and a marker pen. One's in each hand. He holds both up. "Want to open or check off?" She shakes her head disbelievingly, and he notices something. "Didn't you want to open your present?"

Still shaking her head, she looks at the package. The paper is pretty and the tape hard to peel. "Can I borrow your knife?"

He opens it and passes it to her handle first. Then waits while she carefully slices the tape without touching the paper. As soon as she's done so he holds his hand out for her to return it, which she does, before peeling the paper back. Doing so reveals an elegant black box labelled with the logo of an exclusive lingerie brand.

"You bought this with the money you saved?"

"I might have rounded up a bit."

She lifts the lid, then sets the box down and lifts the contents out. There isn't a lot of contents, so it doesn't take much effort. Only having to use the one hand leaves her other free to feel the fine lace, which is just as well. The material's fine texture goes some way to make it better.

"They call it an open bodysuit."

Holding it in both hands in front of the suit she's wearing demonstrates the irony of that description. It looks as though, while it might frame everything quite beautifully, covering anything isn't a possibility. "Calling it a body whisp might save them from being sued."

He shrugs. "I did say it was sort of fun. I can send it back if you want." He reaches out to take it.

She steps back. "Don't you dare! If you get to tease me with it, the least you can do is let me try it on." With that she scoots past him into their bedroom.

Rather than just wait, he sets about unboxing and checking the contents of *his present* on his own.

In the bedroom Ella Jane looks at her case and wonders ruefully at what now looks like a failed attempt to surprise and impress him. She then peels her clothes off a little sadly and examines the network of lace in an effort to work out how she's supposed to put it on. Having done so, she decides to shower first in case she does choose to ask him to send it back, or her emergence wearing it prompts him to do something that would make an effort to return it somewhat inappropriate.

She isn't quite sure how the makers have the nerve to describe the tiny cut-out bra and frame thong linked by a few lacy straps as a bodysuit, but whatever tiny amount there is of it fits the curves of her body like a glove. It feels and looks incredible. Posing in front of the mirror, she decides it could only be improved if, rather than the thin bra straps, the top came to a halter to give the hint of a collar.

A short while later, a showered, made up, and not exactly dressed Ella Jane makes her way to the living room. She steps in and stands, holding her case in front of herself, though not high enough to hide any more than the nothing the bodysuit covers.

He hears her and looks up from the neatly arranged hardware store full of tools and materials. A look of delight and lust spreads across his face.

As he stands, his eyes travel downwards, taking in the case, and then light up as his brain processes its meaning. "Wow" He covers the distance between them in long strides. "So, you did decide to let the hotel move your bag."

Her eyes drink in his happiness, but she can't help herself. "No, I'm just on my way to the other hotel I'm moving to."

He puts one hand by hers on the case's handle. "If you'll permit, ma'am, I'll escort you and carry your bag."

"Don't you dare! I wasn't being serious."

She pokes her tongue out at him.

He ignores her brattishness, preferring to admire the way the lace frames her breasts and hips, or else sets down the memory of her teasing to use against her once he's finished. "Do you like it?"

Ella Jane rocks first her shoulders and then her hips back and forth, showing herself off, and delights in the ways his eyes stare while she does so. "Maybe not quite as much as you seem to."

"Phew, it's so hard to know what's appropriate."

His relief makes her smile. "It's the most inappropriate piece of not quite clothing I've ever seen, but I love it." Then to wind him up, she opens her mouth to say something mean but thinks better of it. "It's probably not the sort of thing to buy for someone you haven't already had kinky sex with."

"Thanks. I'll bear that in mind, but first there's something I need to do."

He casts his eyes back to his partially finished unboxing and cataloguing project, and she starts to wish she'd gone ahead with her mean comment.

Then he looks back towards her. "If you really don't want me to send it back that is."

Her eyes slit at the prospect.

He exclaims, "Good!" With a laugh, he lifts her from the floor and carries her past her case and into the bedroom.

By now, Ella Jane is used to him wanting to suck her and used to the fact that, short of using her safe word, there's no way she can stop him. She's not a girl to use her safe word to get out of either being edged or of having an orgasm. That doesn't mean she doesn't wriggle or put up just enough resistance between the kisses and caresses to force him to be forceful.

While going through these motions, she learns one advantage of the parody of a garment. He doesn't have to strip her for the swats she quite consciously provokes to be able to find her bare buttocks, mons, and vulva.

She's already pleasantly tingly by the time he pins her down and lowers his lips to her opening to begin.

The orgasm is nice. It isn't one of the monster ones he's given her over the last few days, but it is one that a week ago she's have noted well enough to describe the next time she gathered with her girlfriends. It's just not him taking his time with and for her; rather it's him getting her ready for him to take her. And, that he does, testing her readiness and entering her before the quaking subsides.

He spends some time inside her, moving slowly, applying his hands and lips to her. They talk, touch, commune through their connections eye to eye, skin to skin sex to sex.

The do all this without building to a frenzy.

She makes to complain when he suggests they finish unpacking, but he tells her to sort her bag out, spend five minutes making some notes on how her heroine would cope with her first experience of New York City, and then join him so they can enjoy their night.

With that he pulls a pair of jeans on, opens a wardrobe and leaves her. Moments later, he puts her case through the doorway and calls, "Come on sleepyhead."

It takes her a while to get out of bed, though hardly any time at all to unpack her things, and it only takes her a moment to put them away. She considers the additional items she brought and smiles to herself. Then she thinks a second time, gulps and leaves all but her curved nJoy dildo where they are before tucking her case away.

Out of curiosity she opens another wardrobe and finds it filled with dark suits and crisp white shirts. She runs a hand along them, shakes her head slowly and muses on how the other half lives. After that she opens her laptop and tries, but for most of the time, instead of writing about Abigail, she writes of herself and him. She sets the gleaming steel toy down on the bed, then goes out to join him, and hopes he doesn't make her show him what she's written.

Her Surprise

He's set a mix of classic and modern hard rock playing and has already set up the workbench and begun measuring and cutting when she joins him and starts taking in the full scale of his lunatic purchase.

His array of new possessions is quite something, including as it does lengths of PVC plumber's piping of various thicknesses, dowels, a half dozen different weights of electrical cables, and as many varieties of chain. There are even numerous kinds of rope, coconut, jute, hemp, nylon, cotton, and even silk. Each of these, he assures her, with its own texture. He chattily explains that several of the ropes can be used to make a traditional cat-o-nine-tails and how to weight sections of piping using water, sand, and lead shot.

"Is this what I get for not being able to tell you my favourite kind of rope?"

"Of course." He beams his delight.

"And these?" She lifts one of the thicker dowels.

"All the better to beat you with."

"You really have bought an instant dungeon, haven't you?"

"Not really. I looked at pulleys and ceiling mounts, but I couldn't think of a way of fitting them without damaging the walls."

"You had no fear of damaging me though?"

He sweeps her into the air. "You said you trusted me."

She giggles. "That was before all of this arrived."

For Ella Jane, exploring the hardware starts off as a pure turn on, touching, stroking, exploring the different materials, feeling the weight and flexibility of each, and wondering how he plans to use each. By the end though, he's convinced her that he's every bit the sadistic master he promised online. Only online it was just exciting. In the flesh, it's wow, scary. Very scary, but he's *Ohhh!*

She looks at the pile. "Tool cases? Dust sheets. A workbench! Two spools of paracord? What can we possibly do with two whole spools in a couple of days? There are probably hardware stores that don't get through that much in a month!"

"Cut, shape, and make things. The two colours let you include patterns."

She moves on to next things that catch her eyes. "How about the tools?" There are a number of hand, plug in, and rechargeable.

"Have you ever tried doing DIY without them?"

"Power tools?"

"They're better for some jobs, and I could hardly get a non-powered heat gun."

"Won't the hotel mind?"

"Mind what?"

"You setting up a workshop in their Presidential Suite."

"Why should they?"

She salutes. "President McGyver." Then she laughs with him. She carries on giggling uncontrollably when he tumbles her over his knee, and she squeals, "I pity the fool who let you stay in their Presidential Suite!" between spanks.

Having once again done his best to not quite beat the brat out of her, he goes about starting his first construction project while she takes over going through the delivery list and checking it against what has arrived. At the same time, she further familiarises herself with the weights and textures of each item. She watches him too, enjoying his cheery mood and the sureness with which he uses the tools.

A little experimentation; a little thought; and the G-clamps, cleaning cloths, and the sections of wood he cuts turn the double doorway to the capacious reception room into a surprisingly effective bondage frame without denting the plaster or marking the paint.

"I get the impression that you've done this sort of thing before."

"Some of it."

"Not all?"

"No, just some."

"And why's that?"

He shrugs. "I think up or learn new things all the time." Then he gives her a disgusting look. "Besides?"

"Besides what?"

"I'm not always inspired, and –"

She cuts in, "I inspire you?"

"You've been inspiring me since before we met in real life, since we first started exchanging filthy fantasies every day."

"So, what's the *and*?"

He humphs. "I'm not sure I should tell you." He raises an eyebrow when she scowls at him. "Okay, if you're going to be like that about it." He pauses for effect and to make sure he's out of kicking range.

"There's the way you squeal with delight at every new thing I want to do with you."

"I do not! Well not everything."

"Want to try out the new whipping frame?"

Ella Jane bounces to her feet. "Yes, but I'm not going to squeal until you start whipping me."

"Best take that off then. I don't want to damage the lace."

"But you don't mind damaging me?"

"I might just pretend you're that call girl they sent last night and damage you just enough so I can't send you back."

He cuffs her, cuts sections of rope, and secures her wrists and ankles. "Try to move for me."

She does.

"More secure than last night?"

It is, but she's not prepared to let him be the only one who can refer to their previous adventure. "I wouldn't know. You were with that hooker."

The spank is sudden and loud and satisfying and so are the warm glow and stroking that follow.

"Much more secure, Sir."

"Excellent."

For the next while he cuts sections of rope, dowel, timber, and tubing. He tests them on various parts of her body, various songs come on, some appropriate to her situation, others filled with driving force and a couple hauntingly beautiful. At times he unconsciously moves or works in time with the music and at others he matches the nature of what he does to her to it.

He uses the heat gun to seal one end of a section of tubing and fills it with sand before sealing the other end. This new toy is heavy and thuddy when he lays it across her buttocks, and it sends a satisfying surge through into the strong bones of her pelvis and the delicate places within and beyond. The more satisfied he is with the sound, feel and effects of each tool the more times he strikes her. He whacks her six times with this. Each time using greater force, and each time forcing sounds from her lips.

"You like?"

"Fuck, yes, sort of."

He kisses her in response, then aims a final blow at her mons. It's enough to set her shuddering and he places a hand over the point he struck curling his fingers into her opening. "I think I'm getting to know your body better."

For Ella Jane, the assault on her senses is enough to tip her into her warm, glowing place. She clenches around his intruding fingers and welcomes his renewed kissing. When he goes back to his work, she watches him as though through a veil.

He crafts implements to use on different parts of her body than just the tempting curves of her buttocks. For example, he fashions a bundle of foot long sections of soft cotton rope and strokes her with them. They're too light to have any effect on her buttocks or thighs, but he applies them to her her breasts. The sensations the soft, light ropes cause as they curl around her body and impact her tender orbs and their tips are another new and alien delight. It's as pain free as the towels had been the first night, but the heat being whipped with them stirs in her breasts, though equally sexual, is a different thing entirely. He whips her long with them, until she's close to a form of delirium and until something other than exertion makes his breathing become urgent.

When he sets this whip aside, it isn't to fashion another, but to let her down and then take her up in his arms. He carries her straight to their bed and lays her down there with the greatest of tenderness. Then he belabours her hungry sex with the fury of a madman while she clings to him and urges him on.

It takes him an age to cum and another beyond that to drive her to her own climax. When he has, he holds her to his sweat-soaked body as if clinging to life itself and gasping in great lungsful of air.

"Did you need that?"

"Mhm, maybe."

"I did too." She stretches, luxuriating in the sensations still flowing through her body. "How much of what you bought have we used?"

"Not a lot."

A thought strikes her that he may have missed an important detail in the evening's excitement. "You noticed my luggage?"

"Yes, I did. Sorry, I should have said how glad I was."

"Did you get distracted?"

"Yes, but only twice."

"Can I take it you really did want me to move in?"

"Ha, something like that. I suppose I should welcome you properly."

"Haven't you just done that?"

"I could do it again if you'd like?"

"Now?"

"Now would be nice."

"Don't you ever get tired?"

"Of course, that's why I sometimes have to tie you up to stop you struggling, and sometimes I use toys on you."

"Hmm, does this mean you're going to tie me up again?" He grins and she puts her hand to her face.

"You walked into that one."

"I did."

He bounces from the bed. "Don't go anywhere."

"I'm too exhausted to go anywhere!"

It doesn't take him long to return, and when he does, he comes bearing a magic wand vibrator, a coil of his new rope, and an ostrich feather.

Ella Jane holds each of her limbs up in turn and he hums contentedly as he secures them. She waits until he's finished tying her before she says, "Do you know a man your age has no right to have a bum as peachy as yours is?"

He responds brandishing the feather, "You'd be in a lot more trouble than you are right now if this was a bit more intimidating." And with that he strokes the softness down the side of her face.

The feather's touch is sweet and delicate. It neither tickles nor sends her rushing towards one of the climaxes she's getting used to him giving her. But he doesn't have any urgent reason to be up early, and the simple pleasure of caressing her skin with it keeps him entertained past the point at which she begins to plead for more.

Eventually he holds the wand up. "Did you want this instead?"

"I want you!"

He looks into her eyes. "Oh good."

His hands, lips and the wand are all capable of doing more than teasing her bound form, but that's what he does with them for almost an hour, until she needs to cum with a wild desperation. Her threats and pleading vie with the raging need in her eyes. He bends over her and kisses her breasts. His lips trail downwards along familiar ways. and her body responds once more. They reach her mons and trace her lower lips. His tongue circles her; then his lips seal around her clitoris and hood. His thumbs press back, and he sucks as his tongue circles in the partial vacuum maintaining contact despite the bucking of her hips. As she begins to cry out, he breaks the contact and, eyes closed, she wails in frustration and finds his mouth on hers transferring her taste. She's half out of her mind, and the animal part of her considers biting that talented tongue hard to pay him back or simply wailing its way over the border into madness. But she does neither.

"You'll like this," he whispers and the heavy mains powered wand hums into again life. He presses it firmly into the top of her pubic bone so his vibrations shoot through her entire pelvis. Then the tips of his clever fingers once again, unerringly find the centre of her pleasure, circling slowly, pushing her back to the edge, but not letting her escape over it no matter how her hips try to force him. His fingers slide lower, enter her yet again, and she feels the item in his hand. This too bursts into humming as his hand traps it against the bottom of her pubic bone when his thump nudges under her hood. The vibrations transmit along his fingers and thumb into her g spot and clitoris and through the bone itself where then meet and form a symphonic wave with those from above. She flies over the edge, her body bucking in the restraints again and again. She senses his left hand caressing her breasts, drawing further lightning strikes of pleasure to course through her and she half hears the words *You are so beautiful.*

As they lie together afterwards, he strokes her body gently, doing so intimately even though he avoids the places men usually touch when searching for intimacy. "May I ask a question?"

"Of course."

"When did you decide you were sure?"

"To sleep with you or let you torture me?"

"Both."

"I started thinking about both when I read your story about electroplay. So wicked but so erotic." She kisses his chest. "But I wasn't quite sure about either until you were nice to that waiter who recognised you."

"Really? Not something I said."

Ella Jane casts her eyes around and lowers her voice. "Are you hinting at all the naughty things we talked about before?"

He tilts his head and allows his lips to twitch. "Maybe."

"I was always interested, but that moment made me sure I trusted you to be someone to do them with. You could have ignored him, but you took the time. It's one thing for a person to say they believe in something. It's another to see them live it."

"So, nothing to do with the laughter and orgasms then?"

"God, we had so much fun even just chatting, didn't we? I hadn't thought about it like that till the other night though." She puts a hand on his chest and cranes up to place a kiss on his lips. "Yes, from now on I might not agree to play with anyone who hasn't done a bit to prove himself first."

"And about the safe call?"

Ella Jane frowns. "Hmm, it's a good idea, but I'm not sure I like the idea of you trying to keep me safe when I see other people, when I've only just moved into your room!"

"I asked you to move in because I wanted you to. I still want you here with me, but I also like you. I don't have any claim over you in years to come. Don't tell anyone, but you matter a bit more than my short-term wishes."

"That's the nicest thing anyone's ever said to me."

"Yeah, sorry. I won't put that in a book."

"Unless you write a book of bad lines. It's a good thing I've already let you fuck me, or you might be in the spare room."

"It's my spare room, and I'm the dominant."

"True, but it was that bad a line."

His eyebrows rise in the middle. "Really?"

The moment of uncertainly draws a smile to her face. "Possibly worse."

"Oh well. Are you hungry?"

She hadn't been, at least, she hadn't realised being, but the word speaks straight to her stomach. "Starving!"

"Then I suggest getting up."

He allows her up, but rather than leave her arms free, he has her put them behind her back with each hand gripping her opposite elbow. Then he uses a length of his new rope to bind her in a box tie.

Her *Is this strictly necessary?* is not the most cautious thing she's ever said, and his reaction is perhaps predictable.

The bind doesn't just keep her arms out of the way and prevent her from defending herself by holding her shoulders back and forcing her to arch her back. It also thrusts her breasts out temptingly in front of her. The tension it places on her after the lingering excitement of their play session also make the buds at their tips stand out at their most proud.

Pride may come before a fall, but in this case, it also provides two convenient handles. Handles which he uses to pull her to the full-length mirror in their bathroom.

Having positioned her facing it, he moves behind her. "Tell me what you see."

"Me, us, mostly my tits."

"Correct." He caresses them and she purrs. The same tension and post coital feelings that have made her nipples so still have also made them even more than usually sensitive. "And how to they look?"

She knows the answer he wants, just as she knows he knows she's shy of talking about her own looks. But there really is not denying the truth, so when his patience wanes and his fingers and thumbs start rhythmically squeezing and stretching to her nipples and applying slowly rising pressure and tension, she doesn't wait for either sensation to become painful. "Good."

He bends and kisses her shoulder. "And can you feel me behind you?"

It would be hard not to. Compared to her he's big, broad, and warm, but those qualities aren't what he's referring to or what her attention is on. His cock, so recently inside her that her body's memory is filled with the experience of satisfying it, is hard again. "Y-es."

"And how do you feel," he movies his right hand lower and holds it with cupped fingers a fraction of an inch from her sex, "Down here?"

Her lips curl upward and her cheeks flush.

"So is it entirely necessary?" His voice is warm against her, his fingers are so close.

"Well, not entirely, but..."

"But it's nice?" He continues to massage the tip of her breast.

"Yes, Sir."

"So I should keep you tied like this?"

She sees him lowering his head in the mirror and turns, opens to his kiss, and when their lips part she murmurs, "Yes, Sir."

He stands up straight and swats her bum. "Good! Now that's decided, it's time for some nibbles. If I'm not very much mistaken, they should be ready.

There's noone in the reception room when they return, but there is evidence that there has been. A tray with a decanter, glasses and a selection of cheeses with bread, biscuits and nibbles sits on the table. She wonders how long ago the butler left, and if he heard them and guessed what they'd been doing while delivering the refreshments.

The scents of the cheeses assail her senses as he leads her towards them and she makes an involuntary effort to reach, which of course, does her no good at all. She turns to him, "Can you let me go?"

"No."

"Please, I'm starving."

"That's why I'm going to feed you."

Her mouth opens on hearing the words.

"That's right."

She shuts it again.

"You have a choice. Here or at the dining table, but I'm not untying you."

Having given his message, he sets Mozart's Eine Kleine Nachtmusik playing, goes to the table, selects a grape, and pops it into his mouth. He then takes the stopper from the decanter and pours himself a glass of the thick dark port, which he sets down before cutting a sliver of soft ripe brie. "There's plenty."

Ella Jane is still standing naked, hungry, bound, and staring at him with a battle of wills playing out across her face. It isn't a battle he chooses to involve himself in. He knows that she'll either choose to stop the game or continue playing. He's done all he can by delighting her senses, showing his capacity and desire to take her beyond her experiences and to guide her safely back again.

The first step she takes towards him is small and slow, but it's the most important. It's the one that ignites his smiles and unties her heartstrings.

He sets a cushion on the floor and guides her to her knees on it. Then, one morsel at a time, he satisfies her need for food as he continues to nurture her other hungers.

Every instinct tells her it should be a cacophony of the senses. The cheeses, each overpowering in its own right. There is brie, richer than a farmyard after the rain; a cheddar, whose acrid cleansing washes through her mouth like a burning river; and stilton, whose myriad metallic and floral tones boil despite its clotted cream texture. But served with celery, redcurrant jelly, grapes, and the powerful vintage port, it is a symphony played in her senses by his feeding hands. It's one that drains and fills her, and as she allows herself to be consumed in the act of consuming and ends enfolded in him.

When she can eat no more, he holds her as he finishes his own meal and takes the leftovers to the kitchen.

Ella Jane is kneeling and waiting when he returns. She welcomes it when he pours a final glass of the dark red wine and tips it to her lips.

She tastes and waits as he drinks then tastes again. He drains the glass, stoppers the decanter and carries her to bed before untying her.

He lays her on the soft sheets, strokes the fading rope marks on her arms, sinks his strong hands into her aching shoulders and sinks himself into her aching need.

He strokes her cheek with a crooked index finger. "Glad you moved in?"

Ella Jane lies back against him. "How long are you staying on after the conference?"

"In New York, or the states?"

"Umm." She idly doodles her fingertips across his chest. "Both."

"A few days here. Then the rest of the month dotting around, half-holiday time, half working trip. Why?"

She looks at him, until she realises that he really doesn't understand, "I'm staying in your hotel room."

"Ah, so you are. That's a good point." He leans forward. "I'm in New York till next weekend, and you're welcome to stay the whole time or just take things a day at a time."

Having got the writing bug just before college, and studied her arse off as well, it's been a while since Ella Jane has taken much of a break. "I'm bad at taking holidays."

"So am I. If you'd like we could be bad at taking them together."

"The whole week in New York?"

"Why not?"

"Let me think about it. I didn't bring enough clothes."

His Invitation

"That's not kind." The tousled Ella Jane is lying on her left side. On being roused, she looks up at him blearily and complains.

"That's the sort of thing you told me you should be punished for saying, young lady."

"Sorry, Sir," she apologises still half asleep.

"Hmm," He ponders, sitting on the bed, and looking closely into her eyes. She's too sleepy for anything much, and she looks so sweet lying there, so he decides to wake her more gently.

He lies down, sliding the covers from her shoulder and easing them low enough to reveal the curves of her firm young breasts. Their buds are stiff before he touches her, ready for him well before his teasing caress reaches them. So capturing her exposed right nipple is easy.

Ella Jane knows what's due but doesn't shrink away. Instead, she steels her will and breathes in, arching her back slightly to press her tender flesh into his hand while offering it to his scant mercy.

Even tired as he is, the gesture of willingness captivates him. They're both too tired for much cruelty to be fun for either of them. Instead, he treats it to a blend of pinching, kneading and pulling that sends mixed jolts of pleasure and mild pain through her. "You seriously need to practice morning-ing." He bends down and kisses her lips, "I won't always be so kindly."

The lovemaking that ensues is gentle. He doesn't take his full pleasure or grant her release, but it is tender, fulfilling, surprisingly satisfying. Though when she feels the wave rising inside her and he withdraws she is disappointed. "After you've at least done something, young lady."

And with that, he guides the naked Ella Jane into the room he's had configured as a mini-gym. Being forced to exercise in the nude is still a novel experience for her. It's exotic but embarrassing, even if the sight of him shirtless and sweating and the way he freely enjoys her nudity do provide some compensation.

Other than being left exhausted, she's unharmed by the exercise session, so long as one doesn't count a dozen or more spanks and strikes from his whip, or the effects of his encouragement and praise. Together, she must classify it all as little, if any, distance short of deliberate edging.

Her protests about this lead to a further spanking as they shower, which delays them.

In the end, he only has time to give her a single orgasm before breakfast is served.

Having allowed him to beast her through twenty minutes of exercises to the sound of Judas Priest, and a gentler while of intimacy with Palestrina playing faintly in the background, Ella

Jane is even hungrier the next morning. Eating in his room is certainly nice. "If I didn't know what I already do about you, I'd wonder how you aren't overweight."

He humphs. "According to BMI lovers, I am." Ella Jane wrinkles her brow. "It doesn't matter. Pet peeve." He gives her an apologetic look. "I like my food, and I like living energetically."

Her face responds flirtatiously. "You certainly seem to." Then she pushes her food around, selects a morsel, eats, looks away and comes out with what's on her mind. "Are you sure you want me to stay?"

"Yes, why wouldn't I?"

"It's just..."

"Ella Jane Tyler, I would be honoured if you'd continue living in my hotel room for the remainder of your stay, or even my stay."

She tries to keep her face serious. "Now you're teasing."

"Yes, but I'm also repeating. I would very much like you to move in. I have some good reasons to."

"Is this so you can keep making me do my morning exercises?"

He frowns, smiles lasciviously and starts counting on his fingers. "That's about number seven on the list."

She licks her lower lip and sways her hips. "What's above it?"

"Six other things." His brow knits. "Having you with me, saving your pennies, your company, um..."

"Yes?"

"Having someone to use all those toys I brought with me. Er, making sure you eat properly."

"I can eat properly by myself."

"Ah, but can you eat properly enough to cope with doing your morning exercises and having lots of naughty fun with me?"

"I might not need to eat so much if I wasn't with you getting worn out!"

He smiles innocently. "Don't you like naughty fun and good food?"

"Hmm, very smooth."

Her concession brings a relieved smile to his face. "So those are your six reasons."

"I'm not sure confirming I eat enough to cope with your cruel exercise regime can come in above the exercise regime."

"Then making sure you eat enough to be able to handle the naughty fun comes in below the naughty fun and that comes in at eight." She hmms again. "Worst case, if you decide to move out of my bed part way, you can stay in one of the other rooms."

"That is a little excessive."

"It was intended to help persuade you to stay the whole week," he winces, "And to sound better than it did."

"I was talking about having a spare room in your hotel room."

"It's just where my management booked me."

"There wasn't anywhere else?"

"I didn't ask them. It's just the suite I stayed in last time I was in this hotel."

"It's so big!"

"Not compared to a lot of houses over here."

"Compared to the hotels I've been in, and the apartment I shared at college, it's big, and they weren't in New York. My things rattle around in the wardrobe."

"We can get you some bits if you'd like."

"No, that's okay. I'm not here for long."

"You don't want to try some proper clothes shopping in New York?"

"I'll be at the conference today."

"I know. I'll be there too. After the conference, if we're hanging around New York for a while, we can do some touristing too. You can show me around."

"I've never been to New York before, but…" she stops, intimidated by the opulent surroundings, not wanting to admit that even with her advance, she can't exactly afford to lash out a fortune on new clothes. She's also desperate for him not to spoil their brief time together by treating her as a hooker in real life rather than just in their game. "I'll just order a few bits online or pick them up nearby if I need anything."

"Then if you fancy being shown around."

"That feels wrong."

"Why? I lived in London for years but didn't know some of the museums and theatres as well as people who only visited. We live our lives mostly in our own little parts of the world.

"What *touristing*," she emphasises the new word, "did you have planned?"

"Nothing much. There are a couple of things you might like, and there's all the usual: restaurants, skyscrapers, galleries, museums, shops. If it's your first time we could take a helicopter tour."

"Are you making this up?"

"Just trying to remember everything they put in my calendar and the things people do here. There are a few bits I want to see in museums, and a couple of restaurants I've promised to visit. Roger would love to take us to dinner, so Cynthia can get you to agree to the details of your publicity work."

Her Final Statement

Having escaped the second day without any particular drama, the third and final morning takes a turn for the worse.

It all begins innocently enough, the theme of his session is 'Violence in Literature' which, given the brutal nature of some of his book series, is appropriate. Ella Jane is at a loose end, so she wrangles herself as an extra guest on the stage. It doesn't take much to convince the chair to do this as her presence conveniently balances representation.

Things start off well. People ask about methods, and he and others explain their avenues of research. There's a hotly debated point on whether morality has a place, and whether it should cover classic literature and movies.

And then...

"I have a question for our English speaker."

The host looks across at him and He nods. "Go ahead."

"It's about portraying sexual violence against women in your books."

"I think you'll have to narrow it down a little more than that, consensual or non-consensual violence?"

"All sexual violence towards women."

"You are aware that I've touched on both consensual and non-consensual violence by, and to, both sexes. Have you any examples from my work where you feel I've glorified any non-consensual act?"

"That doesn't concern me."

"So, all sexual violence towards women makes you feel uncomfortable, whether it's something the character consents to and can stop at any time, or not?"

"Yes."

"That's your right. Tell me, is sexual violence something that happens in the real world?"

"Of course it is."

"And is it the responsibility of writers to write about the real?" The woman nods but doesn't speak. "Do you accept that a character carrying out a sexual assault sadly has basis in human experience and that it is appropriate for fiction to highlight the harm done and the possibility of judicial or extrajudicial retribution?"

"Well..."

Ella Jane weighs in, "Do you feel it's okay for a male character to be raped, but not okay for a female one to like being spanked, by someone she trusts, when she has safe word that can make it stop any time she needs?"

"No, of course not."

"He's written about both consensual and non-consensual violence against men too. Why do you focus on women?"

"Because women are more often the victims."

"I'm not sure that's entirely true. I read that incarcerated men rank high among the many victim groups of sexual assaults. But even if it is, isn't one victim of assault or rape too many, whatever the anatomy of the victim?"

He raises his hands palms up. "Then I think we're all agreed, aren't we?"

The questioner splutters, and the chair rapidly seek another.

The rest is relatively routine. Ella Jane learns He and other panellists are interested in a sport called HEMA, in which participants *fight* with medieval weapons. Another panelist has a heartrendingly in-depth knowledge and understanding of in-family abuse.

Once he judges they're at a sufficient distance from the auditorium he puts his arm around her shoulders and squeezes. "Thanks for standing up for me."

Her Satisfaction

With the conference over, they escape from the final reception as rapidly as decently possible. Johnson drives them back to the St. Regis. When they get back inside their suite, Ella Jane leans against the door and sighs. "Free at last."

He sets his laptop bag down and toys with a curl of her hair. "Apart from the signings, publicity, and interviews your agent just conned you into."

"Don't. I just want to enjoy a day off." She remains leaning firmly against the door as if holding it closed against a world of people eager to break into their private sanctuary.

His lips come teasingly close as he enquires, "After three days working."

And Ella Jane plays up to his teasing by turning her head away. "Three days *and* three nights."

He swats her bum. "Did the nights feel like work?"

"No." she giggles. "They were harder!"

That gets him, and he sets his hands against the door on either side of her head. "I was rather hoping you didn't want to take tonight off."

"Don't be silly. Of course I don't. We've barely scratched the surface of what I know we can do with all those things you bought, let alone what your filthy imagination can come up with."

"Ah, so you expect my imagination to work overtime while you skive off, do you?"

"You've done nothing but exercise your imagination, when you haven't been eating, showing off, or exercising your domly rights."

He sets his teeth in the gentlest of bites on the side of her neck and rumbles, "So now they're domly rights, are they?"

Doing her best to remain serious, Ella Jane manages to get out all four words of *Did I say that?* before she corpses. His face is serious when she stops laughing and looks though. "Very well, just for tonight you can think of them as your domly rights."

"Oh good. I'm going to take full advantage of those rights now that I don't have to leave you in a fit state to get up at an ungodly hour in the morning, young lady."

"You already keep me up most of the last three nights!"

"Is that a complaint?"

"I don't know. Do I want it to be a complaint?"

"Don't you mean do I want it to be?"

"Not necessarily. I'll keep you updated." He then registers that there's something different about the place.

"Ah, I see housekeeping has acknowledged your arrival." Ella Jane gives him a puzzled look and he nods toward the table. There's a large floral arrangement in place of the masculine austerity. There are vases with fresh arrangements in every room, and even in the hallways.

"For me?"

"I prefer to not have that sort of thing in rooms when it's just for me. I cancelled the cancellation, so sort of for you."

Ella Jane goes to the elaborate arrangement on the coffee table. "I'll have to have someone book the most expensive suite in a hotel and say they don't want the complementary flowers in my next story."

"Feel free."

"They have roses."

"They do indeed." He goes to a vase, selects one, and lifts it from the arrangement. "But their roses have no thorns." He pushes out his lower lip and pauses a long moment as he eases close enough to her to stroke the pristine white bloom down the length of her throat and décolletage. "So, I'm afraid they have reduced fun potential." He then falls silent and allows his devilish grin out of its cage again.

Ella Jane looks at him and at the flowers and judges his intentions. "You never stop thinking, do you?"

"Overactive imagination, I'm afraid. Bit of a professional curse. I've always thought it was one of my more interesting qualities."

"I remember. You came up with so many wicked things you wanted to do to me."

"You had a few of those ideas yourself."

"But most of mine were only fantasies." He humphs, and she looks down. "Well, some of them were."

"One or two of mine were theoretical, and a few would need a certain amount of monitoring equipment to make them safe."

Ella Jane mentally ticks through some of his wilder, but still exciting ideas and smiles. "Shocked!"

"In my defence, there was very little risk of me causing you hypothermia while you diddled yourself under your comforter four thousand miles away from me. And any risk of burns would have been of the friction kind."

"Filthy man. Dehydration was more of a risk." She blinks slowly as she appraises him, and her level of trust. "I started taking a bigger glass of water to bed with me after a few nights. Are you going to try some of your new toys on me?"

"May-be."

"You are, aren't you?"

"I thought you'd never ask. Want to see my creation?"

The *creation* is a strange frame fashioned from plumber's tubing, wood, rope, and sections of chain. To Ella Jane's eyes it doesn't look strong enough to hold her. "What does it do?"

"I put it on the floor or a bed. You kneel over it, and I tie you to it. Then I have access to all of you."

She asks the obvious but foolish question. "What do I get out of it?"

"Me having –"

"Access to all of me."

"Correct."

"Are you sure it's strong enough?"

He takes a hold of the two raises sections and tenses. Even with his strength, the frame barely flexes. "I'm sure we'll find out."

She chooses to trust him once again and lets him secure her wrists and elbows and her knees and ankles. He ties her at the waist and shoulders too.

Ella Jane tests the strength of the cuffs, ropes, and frame. It's not to get free so much as to prove to herself that she can't, that she's powerless and that he can do anything he wishes.

For his part he watches. It takes him a moment to work out this was important to her the first time, and half of his mind spends that moment enjoying her struggles as he does so. Now that he gets it, he enjoys them even more as he sits on the bed next to her. He still speaks as though he doesn't though and purrs, "They'll hold you fast no matter what you do." While trailing his fingertips lightly over the fair skin of her slender body, he adds, "You're going nowhere until I've had my fun."

Ella Jane can do nothing but kneel there mounted on the frame. She tells herself that, and the bonds which hold her naked body in place, ready for his amusement, tell her the same thing. She doesn't think safe words or aftercare. She doesn't see the skilled lover who does fantastic things to her with each of his hands and that wicked mouth of his. Nor does she see the man whose tomfoolery makes her laugh. She just makes a fresh, futile attempt to escape the strength of the leather, ropes and chain holding her and tries to imagine what torments he has in mind.

The delicate buds of her breasts are already erect, but he teases them further. His touch is light, but that doesn't stop them becoming so stiff they hurt even without his direct cruelty. Cruelty she's certain their defencelessness will suffer.

His words, his bonds, his touch and their confident slowness creates a sense of ritual. They all serve to get her to this place, in her mind, floating on vulnerability. His caresses consume her as she waits in delicious despair for whatever his imagination has contrived. She sinks, or is that rises quickly, her heart pounding and yes...

At this moment his hand touches and yes, she's ready, eager, in need. If her limbs were free, she would seek to pull his teasing digits into herself. If her body were free, it would hungrily impale herself on them, but she can't.

A burst of pain radiates from the tip of her left breast, and she cries out. He must have said something that demanded a response, and she was too wrapped up in her other senses to register it.

"That's something else we shall have to address young lady." His voice is menacing though he's now gentling the flesh he so recently abused. The fingers of his other hand are still going about their skilful exploration of her pudendum. He knows every millimetre of her, but he still takes to time. After all, with her as his bound captive, there is no need to rush, and with the heights she reaches every reason not to.

His touch is just enough to set her on her way. She guesses he's unlikely to grant her release so quickly, but there's always a chance, with the skill he's already demonstrated, he could. That gives her a seed of hope, and in that hope, her body anticipates despite her mind knowing how faint it is. They don't have to be up early; he has all the time in the world and the many new toys and potential toys from his online shopping to try out.

The thought is delicious. The hours ahead and the weekend ahead are exquisite prospects, and although she put her phone on silent, she hadn't turned the vibration off. It buzzes. He looks at her with a question on his face, and she mouths *Ignore it*.

He smiles and resumes his tactile exploration. After a moment her phone stops buzzing.

It doesn't stop for long though, just long enough for her to start recapturing the mood. This time she lets out a groan of frustration.

Fearing that either there may be a real emergency, or that whoever it is just won't take a hint, he picks her phone up. "Who's Louise?"

"Shit! She's my safe call. I said I'd ring her back."

"Want to answer it or turn the phone off."

"I'd best answer in case she calls the cops." His face questions the possibility. "You're the one who made me make the call!"

"Fair enough." He accepts the call and holds the phone to her. "Hi Louise."

He starts silently laughing, and she mouths a curse.

"Yes, I'm fine. Better than fine." She rolls her eyes, and he starts shaking with mirth. "Yes, the conference was amazing." She mouths *Fuck off* at the phone which does nothing to help him solve his attack of the giggles. "No, I haven't been murdered. Actually, I'm staying in New York for another couple of days."

This time she uses the time her friend spends replying to mouth *Sorry.*

Starting to get a grip of himself, he shrugs, mouths *Okay* and signals *Roll it up* with his free hand.

"Listen, I'm a bit tied up right now."

His renewed wave of amusement takes the phone further from her ear, and she lets out a laugh too. "I promise I'll call you in the morning and tell you all about it." She rolls her eyes for another half a minute and finally announces, "I've really got to go now, bye!" and he hangs up.

"Sorry."

"That's alright. Can I take it you've lost the mood a bit?"

"Something like that. Sorry."

His hands knot at her right wrist.

"You don't have to start again."

"I think we do."

He orders food and they shower together while they wait. Then they eat at leisure while he tells her a dozen things he plans to do to her while she's secured to his Heath Robinson frame. This includes punishing her for leaving her phone on, but doing so less severely that he would if the experience had not been what he refers to as comedy gold. After they eat, he has her get the still generous remains of the night before's cheese board out of the fridges and then come to him in the bedroom.

When he ties her again though, he doesn't start with a punishment. Instead he pairs the rose he'd selected earlier with a Wartenberg wheel.

For her part Ella Jane delights and suffers, and delights in her suffering. He takes her close to the edge by playing a wand on the tip of her clitoris and then over it. Then for the first time forces her over the edge again by using his fingertips in the same place. She bucks and screams at the overstimulation, but the frame holds her still.

He fucks her and has her suck him while she lies there and accepts each, doing all she can to make her mouth and her pussy active agents of his pleasure rather than mere passive vessels for it.

When she feels the beginnings of cramp in her hips she curses, and he guesses and frees her. The he gently berates her for not calling yellow.

During an interlude, Ella Jane lets her fingers play with his body in the ways that have quickly become her habit, exploring the novel delight of the striations, folds and curves of muscle, and the silky softness of his foreskin.

He smiles indulgently and observes, "That's why men don't have breasts too."

"What?"

"Women don't have cocks and men don't have breasts because we'd never get anything done if we did."

And Ella Jane blinks at him in puzzlement, though she doesn't stop idly stroking his cock.

He expands, "We'd spend all of our time playing with them." His look is that of a child explaining to a slow parent.

That draws a sudden laugh from her lips. "Lunatic."

"Moi?" True to his fears, he reaches out and brushes the backs of his fingers across her breasts.

Ella Jane laughs and then forces herself to make a disapproving face. "Promise me one thing?"

"What?"

"You'll never try to get a job as a biology teacher."

With his ego piqued by her demand, his clever hands start to demonstrate, and he growls, "You were saying I had a knack for biolog... oh, quite."

"Uh-huh. Stick to your salons and your submissives, and you will go far, Sir."

"Now who's the lunatic?"

She scoots around to allow his hands easier access and enable herself to use her mouth. It ensures that her answer is unintelligible because her mouth is now full and that she avoids the just punishment she feels she would undoubtedly receive if he were to understand.

He sends her for port and cheese, and they eat and drink in bed. In that convivial time, she asks, "Am I going to see you again after the weekend?"

"I'll be in New York all next week, and I haven't any plans to kick you out."

"Hmm, that's generous."

His fingertips circle the tip of a conveniently vulnerable breast. "It is, and I'm being even more generous by not pinching this little bud till you squeak."

"Are you going back to England?"

"Not right away. I'll be dotting around for the next couple of weeks. I've got some work and a bit more tourism planned. You said you were taking some time before working on your next book, didn't you?"

"I did, but then *somebody* made me start working on it."

"You've got your laptop though."

"I do."

"Then there's no reason why we can't meet up, or you could join me for some of it. I could stop by your home town on the way back to England. If you're feeling brave you could even hop over the pond yourself. Besides," he holds up one of his improvised canes, "We've only barely started working our way through all the things we can do with the Home Depot stuff."

In her present state, it's hard to deny that she is interested, and given her experiences with his lunatic purchases and his wicked imagination, it's tempting. "You were crazy to buy all that."

He shrugs and repeats his defence. "I just spent enough to get the discount."

"There's a male logic to that. If you take it with you, it'll cost a fortune to transport."

"Hmph, it would be female logic if it had been clothes."

"Sexist."

His brows rise in disbelief. "Et toi?"

"Guilty." Ella Jane's expression and tone are at odds with her confession.

"But definitely not guilty?" His artful fingers inflict a little stab of pain, which they follow by with a delicious caress. "All the best people are playfully sexist." He further rewards her for her honesty, but not by untying her. Then he settles down next to her and holds her close.

Ella Jane tries to give him a hint, using the fact that he has only secured her arms, by lying on her side and laying a thigh over his erection. Then she stares at him while licking her lips.

"Where would you like to visit if you stay on past the weekend?"

"Me?"

"If you're going to be my guest, I've got a table lined up at some good restaurants, and there are a few other things I've been roped into. It's only fair that you get a couple of choices."

"You'll laugh at me. They're silly."

He shrugs, "If we can't be silly on holiday..."

"The Empire State Building and the Statue of Liberty."

He agrees, "Done." And holds out a hand considering himself to have got off lightly.

Ella Jane makes a show of trying to respond, and he releases her from her bondage.

She then takes his hand and shakes it. "You don't mind?"

"No!"

Her eyes narrow suspiciously. "You've been to them both before, haven't you?"

"I have, but only with someone even more jaded than myself who thought he was doing his duty. With you it'll be like doing it properly."

"It feels wrong getting shown around New York by an Englishman."

He shrugs. "Hardly shown around. We're just going to a few places. I rarely come to New York, so if you need showing around properly, we'll need a guide."

"You know what I mean. Rarely is more often than never."

"You've years ahead," he assures her with a firm nod of his head. "And if your career carries on its current trajectory, you'll get to travel the world to your heart's content."

She humphs, "You're much more confident about my abilities than I am."

His response to her self-deprecation starts as a low growl.

"Sorry, but you are."

He reaches to the bedside and retrieves her wrist cuffs.

"Are you really going to..."

His eyebrow rises and he lowers his head. She decides it's not worth resisting, so she lets him cuff her and set her lying across his lap.

"Your first novel is doing very well, both in sales and reviews. That's a good indicator." His words are measured and positive and punctuated with firm smacks to her upturned bum cheeks.

Ella Jane protests, "Not as well as your twentieth."

But that gets her nothing but further explanation with accompanying spanks. "I've had a long time to build up a reader base. My first sold slower than yours is, and there are reviewers who cordially hate every book I put out."

She asks, "Really?" Then she braces herself, but his hand strokes comforting circles instead.

"Uh-huh, and my second and third only charted after a couple of years."

"What if my next one doesn't sell?" This earns her a hard spank.

"Then the next one after will, and the people who like it will read your back catalogue." His arms squeeze, and he kisses the top of her head. "Anyway, that's tomorrow's troubles. Are you sure you only want to spend a day doing the tourist stuff?" He helps her off his lap and seats her at his side but conveniently forgets to free her hands.

"Could we eat at the Plaza too?"

"Probably."

"I'd love that, and it would give my mom a kick."

"I'm sure we can do something. Is it because you like architecture, or Hitchcock?"

She puzzles at him. "Hitchcock?"

"It was in a classic film, North by Northwest."

"I was thinking Home Alone." Then she laughs. "Your face." His dark look only makes her laugh harder. "My mom used to put The Tenth Kingdom on when my sister and I were kids too." He frowns. "The Plaza's in the opening credits. It turns into a fairy tale castle.

"Ah, so you like grand architecture?"

"That's one reason I went to Duke."

"We could go to St Patrick's, too. Then you'll have to visit England." He chuckles. "Just don't go while I'm still over here."

"I promise not to go while I'm still naked too."

"But while you're still tied up is okay?"

Ella Jane bravely but unwisely begins, "I might..." and he slowly pinches one of her nipples and draws it towards it himself, "Ah... Ow."

"So impractical to try to do anything complicated when you're tied up."

"Except distracting wicked men?"

"Well, there is that. I suppose I could take you while you're still tied up?"

"Would they let you take me onto a plane like that?"

"Oh, I'm sure there are ways." "What excitements did you have planned for tomorrow if I hadn't said I'd stay?"

"I was going to lunch, then the range, and I have a box at the Met in the evening. Fancy doing some shooting?"

"Are you one of those European tourists who *has* to get their hands on a gun when they come over here?"

"Johnson shoots and likes to demonstrate how much better he is at it than me."

"Oh, okay. Why didn't you ask about the opera?"

"It was a bit of a tossup on which marmite idea to try to rope you into first. Besides, it's a box and there's a seat for you, so that's easy to sort out."

"I've never been to the Opera."

"It's Turandot. It's a grand opera. The Met's stage and production style should suit it."

"You say that as though you expect me to know."

"I say that as though I expect you to Google it or let me play you some of the music. If you like it, I'd love to go with you."

"What if I don't?"

"Then we can do different things and meet up, or I can tell my friends there are a couple of spare tickets."

"Why do you have a spare ticket?"

He grimaces, "Because it's a box. My friends are forever trying to match-make for me, and I prefer my taste in women to theirs."

"And you don't want to be tied down?" He raises an eyebrow to that, and Ella Jane corrects herself. "Sorry, pun not intended."

"I generally don't like people trying to do things for me without being asked to. For anything else? I'm prepared to see what life throws at me."

"As long as you can shoot it?"

"Ha, quite, at least metaphorically. That or take it to the opera, for dinner, to bed, et-cetera. If I'm feeling especially mean, I might threaten to read one of my books to it."

"I love being read to."

"Really?"

Her eyes drift away and she muses, "Uh-huh, makes me feel all cosy." Then she pulls herself together and asks, "So if you take me, your friend won't try to set you up if you say you're bringing someone?"

"I'd hope not."

"I'll come and protect you then." She makes a pistol with her fingers and pretends to be defending him from an imaginary adversary. "I don't want to do something different, then come back to your room and find out you've been match-made. So long as you don't mind me being underdressed that is. I only brought jeans, a couple of dresses and my suit with me. I didn't plan on staying beyond the end of the conference, so I only packed enough for a few days."

"No problem. I can get you another dress."

"If I'm staying longer, I'll need other things too, and you can't just buy things for me."

"If you're more comfortable, I can hire you a dress."

"Hire?"

"Yes, lots of people do it. They don't wear the things that often."

"And you know this because?"

"Research. I've never hired myself a dress in my life. Closest I've got was buying a miniskirt to wear to a tarts and vicars party about twenty years ago."

"Not because you hire dresses for all your mistresses?"

"I've known people who've hired them. A lot of people dress up for the Met, people including my friend. I wouldn't want you to feel out of place."

"Are you going to get yourself a tuxedo?"

"I have evening dress with me."

"Of course, you do!" She shakes her head. "I wouldn't want to pay your luggage excess."

"I get a special deal."

She raises an eyebrow and guesses, "Like on hotels?"

"You'd be amazed."

"Oh, I'm already amazed."

His Teasing

With the conference over he puts her through a more intense workout, and as soon as she finishing it, he cheerfully informs her that he has a surprise.

"A good one?"

Her frown only makes him laugh harder. "Don't you want your surprise?"

"Depends. What it is?"

He raises his left hand holding the wand.

"I'll be too tired to do *anything* today."

Next, he raises his right, in which he holds her nJoy. His eyes don't waver, but his cheeks do twitch.

"You're going to do this anyway though?"

"Of course. The conference is over, and there aren't any other pressing demands on your time, are there?"

Ella Jane sighs and offers up her wrists with a martyred expression. "No, Master."

He plays along, all seriousness, setting the two toys aside with a solemn expression on his face. Then he binds her wrists and secures them to the head of the bed.

She lifts a leg and waves her foot from side to side while looking the other way, so she doesn't see his eyebrow rise.

"What happened to your reluctance?" This time he fails to keep the amusement from his voice.

Ella Jane turns her face as far away as she can in an effort to keep her cat-that-got-the-cream smile from him. It's an effort her vocal cords don't quite match. "I'm submitting to my master's will."

"You aren't taking the piss at all, using the word *master*?"

"No, I'm trying the idea on." She turns her head to face him and teases her lip between her teeth.

He *Hmms* darkly but collects another pair of cuffs and secures one around the offered ankle. He then makes a show of deciding which spreader bar to use, even though he's already decided on the longer and to adjust it to a length that will put a strain on the muscles of her inner thighs. There's already a length of rope threaded through it. Once he's cuffed her other ankle, completing her bondage is a simple matter. "Are you trying to work up me up to doing the splits?"

"Yes." He tightens the rope until the muscles along the insides of her thighs are drawn taut. But he doesn't explain why as he ties the rope off, preventing her from closing them even a millimetre. "Are you lying comfortably?"

"No, Master."

He reaches to his pre-prepared set of toys and fetches his bottle of almond oil. Then he spreads some onto the palms of his hands, applies a firm pressure to the top of her left thing and sweeps slowly down to just above her knee. "Good?"

"Yes, you know it is."

He repeats the motion, then copies it on her right moving from one leg to the other, working still more slowly and with ever greater force until satisfied he has done all he can to ease her suffering without releasing her or reducing the severity of her bondage. "Are you ready for me to continue?"

Ella Jane nods as her body becomes more accustomed to the stretch under his sure hands. "Mhm."

He lifts his hands away and starts vigorously working the oil from them. "No *Master*?"

"I was only trying it out."

"Hmm, does that mean I shouldn't punish you for your teasing?"

She blinks away a smile. "Of course, not."

His eyebrows rise, and he lowers his voice as he continues to towel his palms. "Are you sure?"

"No."

He tests his grip on the nJoy's polished steel, and satisfied, he holds it up. "Shall we revisit that question after? Only I'm looking forward to trying this on you."

Ella Jane closes her eyes and nods. "I'd like that." Then opens them and watches him bring the gleaming steel toy towards her moving with all the seriousness of a surgeon with his scalpel.

She's familiar with the way the heavy, curved sex toy feels on her skin, her outer and inner lips, around and over her clit and its protective hood. She knows how it feels inside her. But not how it feels for the heavy curved steel toy to be in someone else's expert hand.

He runs its thicker end over the lines of tendon and muscle standing out on the inner surfaces of each of her tortuously spread thighs.

His doing so causes her to focus her mind on the steel's hardness, on his strength and on how vulnerable she is in this bind.

It also transfers the almond oil's slickness to the polished steel, so when he draws it in a horseshoe starting from one side of her perineum around her outer lips and mons it glides almost frictionlessly. When he completes the motion, he touches it to the sensitive bulb of flesh that separates her openings and then into the mouth of her vagina. He presses down rotating his hand as he does to ally pressure to the delicate folds there and the swollen eager tissue beneath.

He keeps this up until Ella Jane starts using the minute freedom her bonds allow her to rock against it. Then he moves up around her pink opening without allowing it to move further into her, even though he knows the places she wants him to apply its unyielding hardness, the points inside her pubic bone where she holds it while using her fingers or her vibrator outside.

She can't do that though, can't do anything but wait, that or safe word and spoil the moment. It would risk breaking the laser focus evident on his features, interrupting the painfully slow build up in a self-defeating fit of pique. Her lips let out a long sigh as she surrenders herself to his will and his art.

The round steel head completes its circuit, and he sets it on another, this time between her inner and outer lips.

His eyes remain fixed, but his lips twitch as he presses the curved toy over the thickest, most blood swollen point where her opening reaches the front edge of her pubic bone. Then again as he stills his hand with it above her hood just where she herself touches when her clit's head becomes too sensitive after cumming. From there, he lets out a long slow breath until he's at her fourchette once more and begins to push into her unresisting canal.

He doesn't go quickly, or deep. Instead he guides the unfamiliar toy to a familiar destination. Once there, he slides it back and forth until her voice starts to respond to each movement. Then he bends to her, breathes out heat and places delicate kisses across her skin. He circles outside her hood with the tip of his tongue all the while stroking inside her with the rounded hardness.

Shifting his position, he places the tip of his tongue against the top of her opening and strokes it slowly upwards. She knows what comes next. It's the way he grooves it and drags it slowly so as to lift her hood away and envelop her aching bud while licking both sides at once. Then his tongue swirls, sucks her into his mouth and continues. She knows how fully and how fast her body responds, too.

This time he changes up. Rather than his tongue swirling, his teeth take a light hold on her most delicate flesh, and he begins to hum softly and deeply. It's another new sensation, a vibration that is at first almost too faint to feel, but which once her senses become attuned to it, grows in her awareness.

She does all she can to abandon herself to the sensations, and her bonds help her to do so, holding her legs wide despite the uncontrollable tensing and flexing of the muscles of her legs and core.

He hooks his left arm around her right leg and presses the toy more firmly inside her. He lets go with his teeth while he draws in air and resumes his delicate bite and humming.

Ella Jane mewls her need as her body battles the bonds and his strength, but they hold her still enough for him to satisfy it.

He doesn't choose to satisfy that need so swiftly though. Instead he pulls away, eases the dildo's gleaming hardness from her.

She breathes, sighs, groans and draws in lungsful of air as she seeks to regain her composure and rhythmically tenses the muscles around her wide-spread opening in an effort to retain the heat he has stoked there.

He looks into her eyes, then down at her flexing muscles as he sets the nJoy down with a solid thunk. "I almost forgot this." He holds up the vibrator. "It would be remiss of me not to use both toys on you."

He slides the nJoy back into her and holds it still against the inside of her pubic bone as he runs the wand's humming head up the taut tendons and muscles of her inner thighs. Unlike his hands, it doesn't have the power to melt into them, but it's vibrations do set them thrumming and that thrumming carries into where they connect to the bones on either side of her opening.

"Fuck! Is this just another thing you picked up?"

"Sort of, that or came up with." He presses it against her perineum and above her hood, everywhere but against the nJoy's shaft or over the shyly peeking head of her clit. As he does so he sighs sadly, "If it weren't your first time like this..." and with that expression of regret he grips the vibrator's rounded tip and the dildo shaft where it passes into her. His hand carries the vibrations to the steel and the steel carries them inside her, but this isn't enough for him. He also reaches upwards with his fore and middle fingers and uses them to sandwich her hood and carry the vibrations there as well.

Ella Jane bucks and curses, prays and whimpers and the bonds hold her, and he carries on until the cries fade to sobs.

He frees her while she's still lost and holds her until she's found, and stares down at her with an innocent joy.

She shakes her head.

"What's so funny?"

"How you do things that hurt. then ones that ease the pain you cause."

"Isn't that what you like?"

"It is. I'm just not used to someone taking such delight in both."

He grins his devil grin. "Poor you." And kisses her fiercely as his hands dance lightly over her skin. "Speaking of pain, I really must get around to tying you like that and whipping your pussy some time."

Ella Jane doesn't answer except by nestling in more snuggly against him. There doesn't seem to be a need. Her body is aglow with the pleasure he has given her. He's spoken, and his voice and the idea have excited her. She has her safe word, and she has no intention of using it unless she needs to. Why speak? He's always been honest with her so far. If they're together long enough he will tie her in the same manner, and instead of or as well as making her cum, he will whip her until he decides she has had enough or until she can bear no more.

Her Fancy and His Fun

T he car waiting to pick them up is a surprise to Ella Jane, "Not your BMW?"

"Afraid not. Johnson's busy this morning, so we're slumming it."

"Slumming it?" The charcoal grey Bentley is even more imposing, even if the driver is of merely human proportions and doesn't address him with the strange blend of over formality and inappropriate familiarity or treat her as if she were some kind of fairytale princess.

He shrugs, "Yea, okay. I'm having a bit of fun." He winks. "Are you complaining?"

"Ha, no." She beams at him as the driver opens the nearside passenger door, and He strides around to the roadside. By the time he gets in, the young American's hands are exploring the texture of the car's luxuriant interior.

"Don't forget to buckle up."

She doesn't take her eyes off him as she fits her seatbelt, doing so with her left hand, while her right continues to stroke the door's intricate inside panelling. Rather than simply click the belt home she repeats her pause, lip nibble, click, sigh routine.

He shakes his head as he fits his own, and reaches across to cup her chin, then leans in to kiss her lips lightly. "Is that going to be your thing?"

Her eyelid batting in response is as conscious as it is lacking in any trace of genuine innocence. "Only as long as it has this effect on you."

His eyebrows go rogue again, and the fingers under her chin stroke as he whispers, "On me?"

"You're making me worse; you know that."

"Oh. Dear. How. Sad." He punctuates each word with a feather light touch of his lips to hers as the car glides away.

They arrive a short while later. The car delivers them to right outside the store. The chauffer opens the door while He holds out his hand to her. She emerges with a this-is-ridiculous smile, but takes his arm with a but-it's-rather-fun squeeze and allows him to guide her across the few feet of sidewalk. He does so as though she were far too delicate for him to have safely or sanely done the many wickedly delightful things he's spent the last few days doing to her.

The store is select. The staff are immaculate and, to Ella Jane's delight and annoyance, the tallest, blondest and cat-walky-est of them all welcomes them. However on the bright side, his eyes spend as much time on her own as he communicates with the statuesque beauty and tell her their needs. The dresses available to hire are both spectacular and seemingly numberless.

He seems to have a clear idea in mind. "We'd like to hire a dress. Blue, dark, form fitting but formal. It should be something that will show her beautiful figure and shoulders without being overly...." he lets his voice fade to convey the message without being indecorous.

Their assistant nods and approves and Ella Jane meekly suggests, "Or black?" half wondering whether she'll be ignored. Two-thirds of her subbornly takes the view that she doesn't want to go to the stupid opera or be bullied into a dress to show off to his friends.

The assistant answers, "You can definitely try black," and touches Ella Jane's hair, "Either would suit your colouring." She turns to him for approval. When he nods, she takes Ella Jane by the arm, "Take a seat while we take a few measurements." She then steers Ella Jane into a smartly appointed dressing room, not speaking until the door is closed behind them.

Once in that private sanctum she asks, "Is there anything you really don't want? Some of them have awful ideas."

A relieved Ella Jane gushes out, "Just nothing pale or baggy, or that makes me look even shorter."

The woman smiles and recites, "You're petite, not short, and I'm elegant not tall. We're both beautiful and deserve to wear lovely things." Her voice says the words as if they're written on a card, but her eyes and the twitching at the corners of her mouth add a warmth that is genuine.

"We're going to the Met tonight if that helps."

"Turandot?"

"Yes!"

She sets about taking Ella Jane's measurements. "You'll love it. A friend of mine's seen the production."

"Really?"

"Yes. Now let's go and have some fun finding things for you to try on."

He's on his feet when they emerge and smiles as they do so before leading the way. The gown he tries to guide her to is an Oscar De La Renta creation in midnight blue, and Ella Jane *doesn't want it to be!* It isn't that she doesn't want to be De La Renta. Until today, she's never heard of the designer, and certainly never had anything against him. It isn't that she doesn't think it's beautiful or that she doesn't like the colour or think it will suit her.

What she doesn't want is for it to be the dress *he's* picked.

Because she wants it to be the one *she has*. She sets her jaw and locks her shoulders.

But it's beautiful.

More so than any garment she owns or has even dreamt of owning.

She looks up at him and sees him looking down with eyes that her imagination pictures see her wearing it to a premiere.

He takes the choice away from her, "The lady will try this one." He doesn't look away from Ella Jane, not to the assistant, not even back to the dress.

And the dress is beautiful.

The assistant shows the discombobulated Ella Jane back into the dressing area and helps her change. Then she adds a few little clips to adjust the way it hangs to fit her better. It isn't quite perfect. But she does a spontaneous twirl anyway. When it finishes, she's facing the mirror, and that's a mistake. This is only a holiday thing, only with him. It isn't real life; it isn't *her* life. She looks at the assistant, and her face makes it worse.

This time he's seated when they return. He looks up from his tablet and his face does the thing Ella Jane had seen her own do in the dressing room's mirrors. He rises and follows as the assistant guides her to a niche with mirrors on three sides and a little pedestal. She steps onto it and looks at herself from every angle, laying down memories in case reality turns this moment into a prank on her.

He speaks, "And it's available until next weekend?"

"Yes, Sir. There aren't any future reservations for it."

"Do you have anything that will look even more perfect on her?"

"We have other dresses that will look *as* beautiful." She looks Ella Jane in the eyes and the two women exchange a wordless word. "Will you need shoes and accessories?"

"I'll leave those up to the two of you."

"It'll need some adjustments."

"Can you deliver it to the St. Regis by seven?"

"I –"

"Thanks, and if you don't mind taking her full measurements, in case we need anything else?"

She looks at Ella Jane for agreement, but Ella Jane is lost in her reflection again. "I've never worn anything like this."

"It's a lovely dress. Now, if you follow me, I can arrange the alterations and find you a bag and shoes."

Ella Jane and the assistant re-enter the public space fifteen minutes later to find someone has supplied him with espresso, and he's buried himself in something on his tablet. He still registers their return though, and he greets her with a wry, "So she managed to pry you out of it then?"

"Just about." Ella Jane bounces with excitement. "Only by promising it would be even prettier once they're done."

"Measurements and accessories all sorted too?"

"Y-es," she answers hesitantly. "What do you have planned for me?"

"Nothing yet," he assures her. But then he leans close and whispers in his deepest rumble, "But a good Dom likes to be prepared." He then straightens, letting his eyes linger on hers for just long enough for them to catch her breath, and turns seamlessly to the assistant, "Could you arrange to send a copy of her measurements with the dress?"

"Of course, Sir."

"Thanks, you've been wonderful." And with those words and a wave of a magic card, he leads Ella Jane outside just in time for the car to slow on the curb. It's Johnson, who usually drives him, not the hotel's Bentley that brought them. If anything, being picked up by a second limousine makes it feel all the more like a scene from a film.

The giant driver doesn't ask where to go, and He doesn't tell him, leaving Ella Jane to suppose that the two have managed everything with the same silent efficiency he seems to manage everything else with.

"Hair?"

"Pardon?"

"Do you want to go the whole nine yards? Hair, makeup?"

"What's wrong with my hair?"

"Nothing, just wondered if you fancied going full pamper. If so, Johnson and I can spend an extra couple of hours at the range and in the gym."

"Is that what you want?"

"I want you to come and play, but most women can only handle a certain amount of ritual male bonding before they start considering lesbianism or abstinence."

She tilts her head. "Are you teasing me?"

"Yes of course. It's your call. There are plenty of places you can try, or we can have the hotel send someone up."

"All just like that?"

"It's your first trip to New York. Your first night at the opera. I'm not enough of a heel to spoil it for you. So long as we're in our seats by 8pm."

"So, you really want to go and not just to be seen?"

"I genuinely love the opera, almost as much as I love Slipknot."

"Slipknot?"

"Love the band, so passionate."

"And Five Finger Death Punch presumably?"

"Two of America's finest. Offspring, too."

"You don't look like a metal head or a punk rocker, but I bet you were one of the people who started listening to Disturbed before they covered The Sound of Silence."

"Yes." He winks. "Appearances can be deceptive."

Ella Jane looks at him and thinks about him. "I suppose you're right. Looking at you, I wouldn't know all the wicked things. Or by listening to you, all the good ones."

On their way to the range, Ella Jane thinks about the dress. She considers how he had decided on it, and how she and the fashionable woman in the shop had gone along with him. Her irritation rises again.

Then she thinks about the dress, and how he may have walked the length of the store's racks and picked out the perfect one for her.

He on the other hand has moved on. "Have you done any handgun training?"

"Yes, my granddaddy taught me to shoot." It's a relief to have something else to think about than whether he is considerate, controlling, or some blend of the two. "And my uncle bought me a personal defence shooting course to piss my dad off when I turned eighteen."

"Anything more recent?"

"Not for a couple of years, no." She looks at the two men; both have been less laid back with the other than usual today. "Can I take it that you two are competitive?"

He grins. "A bit. I always loose at this because Craig here insists on carrying on until I drop a point."

"I recall it was always the other way round Boss. You sulk and quit as soon as you do."

His, *a bit* catches in her mind; he told her he writes a bit too.

Ella Jane is surprised when, rather than dropping them off at the door, Johnson drives the big BMW into the building's underground carpark. He then opens the car's trunk and removes a case before opening her door. For once, she finds herself sandwiched between the giant and her less monstrously proportioned lover, who matches the bigger man's gait, rather than being shown from the car by one into the care of the other. "If I get big headed, it's going to be because you two treat me like a starlet."

In front of her, Johnson rumbles his amusement. When she turns to see how He reacts, His eyes flash warnings of a dozen ways in which her ego might be addressed even as He winks at her.

It turns out that Mr. Johnson is a member; or rather his company has a membership. He rapidly interrogates them as to which brands and types of 9mm ammunition they have in stock and the quantity of each until he finds what he's looking for. He then buys, what Ella Jane considers, an obscenely large quantity.

"Are you really a terminator?" Once she got used to the big man's presence, it hadn't taken Ella Jane long to appreciate his mind and sense of humour.

"More or less. Somebody's got to keep an eye on the boss."

Johnson opens his case to reveal five handsomely engineered Sig handguns. One is smaller than the others. Each has red plastic flags protruding from its muzzle. He removes the guns and lays them out, showing that each is clear of ammunition by half pulling the slides back showing the ends of the red flags extending into their chambers. There are also three pairs of ear defenders, and two of shooting glasses, which he distributes, and magazines. He demonstrates the loading process to her, and Johnson hands her the two smaller magazines and the more compact weapon and checks she can operate the safety. "All good?"

"Yes, right down to knowing which scene this is from the Matrix."

Johnson shakes his head and casts a meaningful glance in His direction. "Lucky for you, I'm used to people who think they're funny." Then he takes two further guns from inside his jacket and places them in empty slots in the case and places it in a locker.

He shows her the safety while Johnson secures his own weapons. Then the three put on their ear defenders and go through to the range.

"Why haven't those two got the ring things?"

He demonstrates the use of the red dot sights. "We practice with and without sights."

Ella Jane finds the compact frame pistol easy to handle, and that it fits her hands as though it had been made for her. It's frighteningly easy to aim and, with the ring sight, the little she knows and the men's coaching, wickedly accurate.

The two men shoot with one pistol and two, left and right-handed. Both even disassemble their weapons, timing themselves as they do so. The guns look like children's toys in Johnson's hands, but he handles them with a swift, efficient dexterity. He does so with a little less ability though after a time. He eventually scores lower on a row of disappearing targets and offers to end their session.

Ella Jane hesitates, but yes, she's done. "Can we come back?"

"Ha! You've found a good one here, Boss."

"Yes, Ella Jane's full of surprises."

She warms at the praise and at being treated as *one of the boys* by these two formidable men, but she can't help looking at Him and asking herself what further surprises this man who writes a bit and a few other things might be filled with.

He puts his arms around her, "Now, would you rather go to the gym with us after lunch, have that pamper session or do your own thing?"

They take a late lunch together at the hotel. Ella Jane eats mindfully of the dress and the evening ahead. The two men devour as though they haven't seen food in a month. The conversation confirms her suspicion that Johnson is a veteran, though not that he was a special kind. However, it reveals little of where and how He learned to shoot as though he were one, just that they met while He was doing research for his Dark books.

Having failed to glean anything further, Ella Jane asks if he'd mind her sticking to just training with Him in the mornings, adding the excuse that she has no desire to get in the way of their boys' playtime.

Thus, it is that two hours later He returns to their suite to find Ella Jane waiting with her hair done and her face made up like a China doll. She greets him naked and kneels, and with a mischievous grin and a sly, "Welcome home master. Does your slave please you?"

He walks around her, stops in front of her, holds out a hand and helps her to her feet as though she were a duchess wearing the fine designer dress that is due to be delivered along with its accessories within the next hour. Once she's standing, he walks around her again. It takes him a time to speak, though his eyes talk to her with an eloquence words would struggle to match throughout that time. "Did you enjoy your afternoon?"

Her already radiant face lights up further. "I did, more than I thought I would. Can I take it you had fun too, Sir?"

"We did, and now I've come home to have a light meal and a little more fun before the opera."

"Why Sir, I'd love to oblige, but the kind ladies you had attend to my hair and make-up were insistent that I do all I can to avoid spoiling their work before we go out."

"Is that so?"

"It is." She bats her eyelids up at him. "Don't you believe me?"

He lifts a hand to her perfectly made-up face as if to cup and then stroke her cheek, but doesn't quite make contact, instead stopping close enough to her that they each feel the other's warmth. "Does your jaw hurt when you set it so to keep yourself from laughing?"

She sucks her lips between her teeth and her body quakes with suppressed amusement. "Maybe, does yours?"

"Frequently." He allows his own smile to spread. "Do you have any idea how frustrated a girl can get when a chap's not allowed to do more than not quite enough to spoil her hair or make-up?"

Her eyes dare him, and then go down to his waist, see his own already visible response and return to his. "No Sir, but I'm a quick study."

So they wait for her gown, and he teases her with words and deeds. She does her best to repay him in kind.

The dress arrives a bare a few minutes before his seven o'clock deadline. It's accompanied by a stern looking a woman from the dress shop, shoes, a bag, and a fine ensemble of lingerie, matching stockings and all.

The woman seeks to take command of Ella Jane from the moment she arrives by demanding a room she can work in. Ella Jane leads her to the suite's second bedroom, and the woman makes it clear that He is not welcome to join them.

Before departing, Ella Jane's eyes linger on his long enough to see the delight, and the fire that follows it. She is caught in her enjoyment of them, and of the realisation that He won't let himself follow through on his obvious wishes yet. That will have to wait until after they've gone out and shown off and shone in front of his friends and the rest of the theatre. They hold long enough that she sees him see her appreciation of his, long enough to read his silent promise *later* and long enough to feel herself give her silent reply.

Ella Jane she rushes to change only stopping and breathing when she hears him call after them, "Breathe, and look at yourself."

Once inside, the woman firmly closes the door and assesses first the room, and then the nervously excited Ella Jane before raising an eyebrow, "Would you prefer to put your underwear on in the bathroom?"

Ella Jane, who, having known that her under things for the evening were being delivered and who is therefore wearing nothing but a robe, immediately answers, "Please!"

The things are in the same black and midnight blue as the gown and are even more delightful to put on and to wear than they had been to look and imagine wearing at in the store. Ella Jane dons her robe over them and returns.

This earns her a tutting, which turns to a gentle laugh when her cheeks flare. "Is this your first time being dressed?"

Ella Jane nods, "Yes, sorry."

"Don't be sorry at all. Just enjoy the experience."

Ella Jane smiles but doesn't move.

"I can hardly finish dressing you over that bathrobe."

"Oh, yes, sorry." She slips out of the robe and stands awkward.

"Here, let me look at you." For the next few minutes the woman inspects Ella Jane and re-arranges her lingerie smoothing and adjusting straps, straightening stockings and even adjusting her bra. "There, is that more comfortable?"

It is, and Ella Jane nods her approval as well as relaxing after the unfamiliar experience of being handled by another woman.

The dress comes next, and although she tries, the woman doesn't allow her to face the room's full-length mirror until she's entirely satisfied.

"Now you can look."

Ella Jane remembers his command to breathe and to look at herself as she turns to the mirror. And then she forgets to breathe again.

Having thus, much to his amusement, found himself banished, he makes his way to the master bedroom. Presuming the women will be some time he dons his evening dress in leisurely fashion without stressing at taking two efforts to knot his bowtie to his satisfaction or worry about anyone seeing his clumsy first effort. Suited and booted to his satisfaction, he takes a minute to select the most suitable place to sit while nonchalantly awaiting their emergence.

When they do return the woman from the store comes first. She presents Ella Jane to him as though she and the gown were her own personal creations.

He rises with a somewhat less than nonchalant *Wow*.

And Ella Jane matches him by gushing, "I'd say I feel like a princess if that weren't such a cliché."

"I think you're entitled. Just this once."

The woman hands them each a printed sheet of quite the most comprehensive list of measurements of a person Ella Jane has ever seen and departs giving them both her best regards and her creation a final look of pride.

Once they're alone, they both spend time admiring Ella Jane and how the dress now holds and elevates every line of her body. Ella Jane spends some admiring him, as well.

"It could have been made for you. It could even have been designed for you."

Her eyes take her reflection in and see his beyond it. "So could your suit." Then she stops herself and clenches her eyes, such a stupid thing to say, of course his suit was made for him.

"I'm glad you like the way I look in it. You should hear my tailor complain! Now, all we need is for you to put your necklace on, and Johnson's bus not to have turned back into a pumpkin."

After allowing himself a little preening time he remembers something, mutters a curse and races to the master bedroom to get it.

Her Musical Pleasure

"**F**or you," he says and holds out a small black velvet bag towards her.

She tilts her head and purses her lips. "You know you don't have to buy me things."

"Don't get excited. It's nothing much."

She hefts the bag in her hand. "It's heavy." She tests it with her fingers to try and guess the contents. "What is it?"

"Depends...," he says and smiles.

Ella Jane's eyes narrow, but he doesn't respond immediately. She opens the drawstring and lifts out the contents, first a gleaming blue stone egg neatly drilled through at the narrow end. "I still don't know what it is."

He drawls, "Keep going."

She tries to frown at him, but the little egg is pretty and she's curious.

"Anyway." he moves to the coffee machine to conceal any possible leak of emotion on his face.

Next come three little plastic bags, one containing a slim silver chain, the others have a narrow raw leather thong, and the third's contents looks like clear nylon cord. "A necklace?" It would certainly match the opera dress.

He smiles as he sips his espresso, then straightens his face to answer. "Could be. Can be even...." Then, turning his carefully composed face towards her, he asks, "Coffee?"

"Ooh! Please."

"Is that please for coffee or a clue?"

She humphs. "Both!"

He turns back to the machine, puts a second cup in place, and presses the button. "It can be worn as a necklace. I think it's pretty enough, but you might want to look up Yoni eggs before you do that."

Ella Jane makes a face behind his back and sharply opines, "Or you could tell me." She then assumes an innocent expression as he turns back to her with the coffees in his hands.

He blinks his mock innocence. "Would that be as much fun?"

The cavalier tone in which he asks brings her irritation back to the surface. "For me? More!"

He hands her an espresso and warns, "That's the sort of attitude that could get you into a lot of trouble, young lady," before sipping his own.

She narrows her eyes and backs away with the cup in front of her. "That might be more fun too."

He looks annoyed, and glances at the time, then crafts a slow, wicked look. "It's your choice. If you want to pay the price of me telling you, then I'm game."

If it were any other man she'd ever been with, she'd flip him the real bird or take her phone and flip him the metaphorical one by just looking up 'Yoni Egg' on the internet. But he isn't. They've taken turns at trying to turn each other on for months. And since they met in real, he's kept her laughing, smiling, cumming and wondering excitedly. What's next? "I'm going to regret this, aren't I?"

"So far you've given every impression of enjoying all of my suggestions even more than you've regretted them."

Ella Jane tightens the line of her mouth as she answers, "There's always a first time."

"There is." He smirks. "But I don't see you googling."

"Very well, tell me."

"You're sure?"

"Yes!"

"And you accept the price?"

She lets out an exasperated, "Yes!"

He tells her.

She blushes. She then licks her lips and asks, "So what's the price?"

"You have to use it during one act of the opera."

"What?"

"Slip out of the box, slip into the washroom, and slip this beautiful thing inside yourself. Watch an act, and then do the reverse."

"What if anyone notices my necklace has disappeared and then reappeared?"

He grins wickedly. "We both act as though they've gone quite insane, of course."

"You would do that, wouldn't you?"

"The music, singing, and costumes are fabulous, but the social side of going to the opera is quite another thing. This will keep us amused with a private joke."

She chews her lip, the something private they both know while in a semi-public setting appeals to her, but there's also a practical side to the escapade. "Can I at least try putting it in and taking it out first?"

He nods. "Of course, the easiest way to do it is to try with the nylon cord attached." When she frowns, he expands. "You shouldn't have any trouble getting it out, but just in case, you can leave the end of the cord outside."

"Like a tampon?"

His lips clamp shut for a few seconds, but he fails to keep the amusement from his voice. "I've been told it's very different by people better equipped than I am to know."

"That's a relief!" She practices threading the silver and nylon through the neatly drilled hole at the narrow end of the egg. The clasp on the nylon cord is more awkward, but she reasons that's not a problem. She has no intention of wearing the egg as a necklace using that cord. Having got accustomed to both, she raises a hand. "Of course, silver – costume jewellery, leather – hippy chic! If I'd thought, I might have got out of doing this."

"Do you want to have got out of doing it?"

"I'm not sure. I'll tell you when I get back." With that she goes to the rest room.

Getting the egg in is easy, and using the cord getting it out is too. She slides it in a second time she takes a couple of experimental steps. It's definitely something she can feel, but it's nothing too much, and it doesn't seem to want to escape with the dainty steps she assays. Satisfied she takes the egg out again washes it in the sink, dries it, straightens her dress and puts it on.

He's lounging in an armchair playing with his phone when she returns but looks up at the sound of her heels. "Did you try it?"

She can't help teasing him back, if only just a little. "That's for me to know."

His eyes narrow, but he doesn't let any annoyance into his voice or the rest of his expression. "I must say you look amazing."

"In the dress *you* chose for me?"

He stands and moves to her. "I was thinking with that glow in your cheeks, and the twinkle in your eyes." And he lets his mouth smile. "Perhaps I should engineer more situations in which I can't muss you or put you over my knee quite yet."

This time it's her turn to give him a narrow-eyed look.

They're running it quite close by the time Johnson collects then from the curb outside, but fortunately it's the shortest of drives to the Met. Johnson parks and opens Ella Jane's car door while he makes his way round. In that time, a paparazzo approaches. Ella Jane makes to shy away, but with a rueful shake of his head, he plays along and persuades her to pose with him. Then he gives the man a card before escorting her inside.

They arrive and make their way to their box. The others are already there. There's a light Sauvignon Blanc and nibbles on hand. A silver haired man wearing a suit that looks as expensive as His, but which he doesn't fill nearly so well plays the host greeting each of them with a glass.

"Ella Jane, I'd like you to meet Wolfgang and Eva van Beek. They run a fund company I'm lucky enough to have a small investment with." With his years of practice, the white lie comes easily to him.

His 'small investment' includes a controlling share interest, not merely the sum he has invested with it.

Eva compliments Ella Jane on her dress and lavishes further praise on Oscar for his love for, and appreciation of, the female form. Her husband asks if she knows Puccinni or if this old scoundrel has dragged her along.

"I've heard the first act, and I liked that. My father loves symphonies, so it's nice to have a chance to connect with classical music."

"That's good. I'd hate to think this rogue was forcing you to come against your will when you could be listening to something more modern."

"He's played me less modern music and more, but nothing I haven't liked yet."

"Inviting Ella Jane is a crafty ploy. If she enjoys the performance, I might be able to persuade her to hop over the pond for Glyndebourne."

"Ha, be warned, he'll abuse the innocent beauty of Mozart and Beethoven to seduce you."

She tightens her grip on His arm and looks up at him. "He's already done that with Audioslave."

Mr van Beek tosses his head back to release a laugh. "I don't go much past the bands of the seventies."

Wolfgang then introduces the others as Brie and Matthais. Their surnames are different, so Ella Jane guesses they aren't a couple, rather than that they're married and have had a fight. Matthais seems the happier of the two to be there. His friends and the other man greet them warmly, and so does the second woman, but when he embraces the woman of the couple, she gives Ella Jane a look laced with pure poison, leans forward and snipes, "That necklace is rather plain."

Ella Jane touches it with her fingertips. "It was a gift from my lover. It matters more to me than mere jewels." She then bites down on her urge to gloat when the other woman's face flashes thunder. After a few minutes more of uncomfortable conversation, she makes her excuses.

When she returns, the necklace is nowhere to be seen.

Sensing that she's scored a point, Brie leans down to Ella Jane again. "Were you so embarrassed by that cheap necklace that you took it off?"

Ella Jane blinks and consciously tenses her muscles around the egg inside her. She enjoys a moment of private triumph as she draws her lower lips slowly between her teeth and smiles winsomely. "What necklace?"

Hearing the word *necklace*, He frowns and looks across. "What's up?"

Ella Jane responds to his question with a knowing smile and explains to him. "Brie here thought I was wearing a necklace."

"Oh, how funny. I wonder if she's a bit psychic?" Eva straightens at hearing that. "Only just this morning Ella Jane refused to let me buy her a sapphire and diamond creation that could have been made to go with her dress."

Brie's eyes flare, but nobody else seems to recall a necklace, and the orchestra begin warming up before she can figure out a way to press further.

Ella Jane is reticent to accept her first top up until He does, commenting, "This is truly excellent," and confides her, "The van Beeks are the perfect hosts."

She'd expected the music, but the atmosphere, the costumes and having dressed up in her borrowed finery add immeasurably to the experience.

She takes a second trip to the powder room before the final act and waits for the lights to dim again before she returns to the box. Her necklace is back around her neck, silver chain, stone egg and all, even if the egg is a little warmer than before.

There's a standing ovation when the performance reaches its triumphal conclusion. The lights rise for the curtain calls. He looks around, smiles to Ella Jane, leans to Eva's ear and whispers. She frowns, reads his wink, shrugs and nods.

Wolfgang announces, "I have a car and a table booked if you'd like."

He responds by nodding to Ella Jane, and with the attention now on the petite redhead, Eva reaches out and almost touches the necklace. "Why, what a lovely little necklace to wear with that dress! I didn't notice it before. So many of you young things add ostentation to ostentation but..." She waves her hand, "Pure classic beauty."

Ella Jane blinks up at him. "He bought it for me. I love it."

Brie stares daggers at her, then looks around the group in confusion, but not one's face betrays a hint of registering what is wrong. She begins, "I th..." then decides that whatever she says is going to make her look ridiculous, and instead opts for. "I think I'll have an early night. The performance has left me quite emotional."

Over dinner Ella Jane learns that Matthais works at the fund and that it was his first time at the opera too. She also learns that the three are very candid with him about their business. "You're so open!"

Wolfgang makes to speak, but He gets there first interjecting, "That's what impressed me enough to persuade me to become one of their first investors. Of course, they *might not choose to tell others the inner workings of the business*, but they've always been frank with me."

Eva reads between his words. "We knew him before we launched the company. He's the most down to earth of men, and he's been invaluable in helping us get to where we are now."

Unlike when eating alone with Him, the van Beeks keep the wine coming over dinner and Per Se clearly has a wine list to match its striking modern decor and exquisite food. Ella Jane doesn't recognise the names, but the dates on the bottles and the reverence with which they are served speak volumes.

At first, she looks to him, but then she asks for water and sips that more than she does her wine.

"Would you care to see the dessert menu?"

"Of course." Mr van Beek turns to Him. "And shall we indulge, my friend?"

"If you wish, then I'd love to. You know our shared vice as well as I do."

"Indeed, could we have a bottle of the Chateaux Y'Quem '62 to accompany dessert."

The waiter does a double take despite the already considerable bill, and He nods his approval, "You are, as always, the most generous of hosts."

He and Mr van Beek effuse on the subject of the wine while Mrs van Beek looks on indulgently. The already slightly tipsy, Ella Jane studies the extensive dessert menu.

Mr van Beek seeks to steer them her towards the apple and pear tarte tatin while He smiles indulgently and suggests crème brulee as an alternative.

Mrs van Beek touches Ella Jane's arm at this and notes, "Of course someone as slim as yourself needn't chose one or the other."

Ella Jane looks at her, flushed with the compliment and wine, then turns to Him to say, "But –"

"He will have both, and a scoop of apple and rosemary ice cream, and so should you."

She eats and drinks and is transported, and despite her efforts, she finds herself having drunk far more than she had intended by the time they leave. She rides back to their hotel in his arms, then leans a little on him when she emerges from the car.

His Question

It's late when Johnson drops them back at the St. Regis. Having been plied with drinks at the opera and over dinner, she's still tipsy despite the food and glasses of water.

They aren't alone again until the elevator doors close, and when they do, he backs her up against the mirrored wall. "Was that fun?" His fingers touch the necklace.

She narrows her eyes. "You want me to say you were right again, don't you?"

"Yes and no. I was asking if that was fun as well."

"I enjoyed the opera, Sir."

He narrows his own in return. "And?" His face grows more serious with her every word, as does her determination to draw this moment out.

"Dinner with your friends was lovely."

He lifts the stone and holds it as far from her as the silver chain allows. "And this?"

"Oh!" she giggles and moves as far away from him as his hold on her necklace allows. "That was okay too."

By now his eyes are at the point of burning holes in the back of her head.

Eventually she twists one foot on the ground and concedes. "Yes, it was fun, and yes, you were right."

"There. That wasn't so hard, was it?" He touches his lips to her cheek. "Did you keep it in for one act or two?"

"Two, Sir." She gives him a half smile.

"Now, I wonder. Is that exactly what I asked you to do?"

She shakes her head with tightened lips. But he gives her a raised eyebrowed frown, so she confesses, "No..." before seeing his eyebrow rise further and adding, "Sir."

"Is it more than I asked you to do?"

This question is more to her liking, and she declares, "Yes, Sir."

"That leaves me at a quandary. By one way of looking at it, you completed your task and more. But by another, you didn't follow your instructions precisely."

Ella Jane opens her mouth. But then she recalls his distaste for being told he could have been a lawyer, so she closes it again. Instead, she thinks about what she wants and what she thinks he wants.

"That leaves me unsure whether to give the reward I had planned and more, or to punish you for not doing exactly as instructed. Then, of course, we haven't set up any actual rules, so there's a possibility that I should do neither. In which case, we should just have a laugh at Brie's rudeness and how well you handled it."

He waits.

She carries on thinking once she's resolved not to let the lawyer jibe spoil the mood for a second time. It doesn't take her long to decide and only a moment longer to come up with an amusing twist. She smiles a smile that gives him her answer as she manages to say, "Both of course, Sir. *And* is a word with far more possibilities than *or* when it comes to this sort of thing."

That wins her a kiss to the back of her hand. "Sometimes I wonder if you memorised our emails and messages." And with that they both fall into one of those silences that happen sometimes in the space between a decision to play and the start of the game for proper. He offers, "And you dismiss the possibility of simply laughing about it?"

"I accepted the task, so it's only fair that I accept the consequences. We can laugh as well though. Her face was priceless! Did you put Mrs van Beek up to complimenting my necklace when it reappeared?"

"I did."

"Was it improvised?" He nods, and she asks, "The sapphire and diamond creation too?"

"Indeed."

"Then you handled her and looked after me very well, even if you were only pretending I'm your lover."

"Pretending or otherwise, we've had a bit much to drink to punish you, so that will have to wait until morning. But I'm sure we can come up with something entertainingly rewardy."

He displays his playfulness with words, the thing that first drew her to him when he was no more than an anonymous source of words on the internet. "Is *rewardy* a real word?"

"It must be. I'm an author."

He says it with the smugness that makes her want to scream! "But you are a slightly tipsy and extremely silly author."

He rolls his lower lip out a little as he nods his agreement. "This is true." Then lets his wickedest grin spread across his face.

"However, that was also rude, so I'm afraid I shall have to increase both your reward and your punishment."

She swishes against him. "Is there anything I can do or say that won't lead to punishments and rewards?"

He furrows his brow and tilts his head. "I'm not sure." He then brightens and strokes the fingers of his right hand together as his smile spreads. "You could always try to say and do everything and find out."

"I may be very brave and just a tiny bit drunk, but I'm not quite that brave or drunk."

"What a good girl. Do you remember me telling you why women don't have cocks?"

"I remember you telling me your theory, yes."

"Well, in the spirit of that theory, your reward will be having an hour to play with my cock, and me having an hour to play with your breasts."

Ella Jane's eyebrows shoot halfway up her forehead in surprise, and she splutters, "And that's my reward, is it?" failing to remember to close her mouth afterwards.

"You can choose who goes first too."

Her eyes send daggers at him.

"What's the matter? Don't you like playing with my cock?"

And that only makes his presumption that this would be a reward worse. It's hardly the praise and orgasms she's grown to expect. She does however icily concede, "Yes."

"Well then, and you always make lovely sounds when I'm playing with your breasts."

"Very well, but I'm playing with your cock first." After the ways he's teased, the idea of spending an hour not quite allowing him to cum and then lying back while he caresses her is appealing no matter how much agreeing will feed his ego.

Her Secret Reveals

He frowns. "I'm glad that's agreed, even if I'm a little less pleased by your lack of gratitude." Then he pauses for effect. "Now I suppose we'd better very carefully undress you so as to spoil neither the moment nor your pretty dress."

It isn't her dress. She knows that, but it feels like her dress. She moves in front of the long mirror, drawing him with her, and hugs his arm to her. Finding a place she can set her phone, she puts its camera on a timer and takes a series of pictures of them together in their finery. At first, he tries to keep from making faces or comments that might spoil her enjoyment. Then he lets himself be swept along by the tide of her Chateaux Y'Quem tinged happiness.

Finally satisfied she picks up her phone and turns face him. "Thank you."

"Don't you want any of just yourself?"

"No thank you. I'd rather do something else. The lady from the dress shop took dozens for me."

And with that, the next moment arrives. She knows what she's wearing under the perfect dress he chose, and she know he doesn't. He hasn't seen the lingerie the elegant woman at the store had persuaded her into by way of accessorising. She's been waiting to show it off for him the whole time he's been admiring her in the gown. It's like the woman in the store had said, there is a feminine joy in knowing her underwear is as lovely in its own way as the g own.

His voice is affected by his efforts to suppress an urge to smile at the return of her eagerness. "Well, if you're quite finished, may I undress you?" Though as he asks, he fails to guess the reason for her dreamy expression and his eyebrows betray a momentary regret that he may not be *addressing her attitude* until the morning before he attunes himself fully to the mood.

"That you may, if I may do the same."

"Ladies first tonight." He takes her hand and leads her to their bedroom where he peels the soft fabric from her with reverential touch, kissing each of her shoulders lightly as he does, and, by so doing, discovers the vapour thin silk and lace ensemble beneath it. "Wow, that's..."

"Is it?" She beams. "It is, isn't it?"

"Ha, yes, and then some. But," he adds with regret, "they'd probably have thrown us out of The Met if you hadn't worn the dress as well."

She looks at herself directly and then in the mirror. "They definitely would! Is it my turn now?"

He hangs her dress and allows her to undress him letting her hands and lips take whatever time and liberties they choose in doing so and lingering on his shoulders and back. She kneels in front of him to undo his belt and trousers. She glances up at him, then forward as his readiness is made clear by the line of his trousers, and back up to him with a sly look in her eyes before taking his shoes and socks off.

Like the other night, she carefully slides his belt from his trousers. She runs it through her fingers and hands it to him, offering herself to him and to it as she does; then finishes taking the rest of his clothes off and folding them.

Once naked, he offers her his hand to help her rise, but she hesitates to accept it. Instead, she leans forward, kisses his shaft, wraps one hand around it, draws it forward, takes the head of his cock into her mouth, and half draws his foreskin back. He tastes of his pre-cum, and she lingers long enough to collect the sweetness.

When she does stand, she twines her arms around his neck, and when he bends to her lips, she kisses the taste of him into his mouth as she welcomes his hunger into her own.

With her lingerie the only covering either of them has, her eyes appreciate the physical signs that he enjoys carefully taking each delicate item of the lacy ensemble from her, even unclipping and removing each of her garter straps singly. He makes a point of kissing her mons and breathing slow heat onto her centre while his eyes taunt upwards when he lowers her panties. Her stocking and heels coming last. Then he rises, takes her in his arms, and crushes her against his hardness, as he growls, "My faith is restored," huskily in her ear.

Ella Jane giggles tipsily at the passion in his voice. "How so?"

"I was beginning to think I liked you more in the dress, and then in your underwear, but it's okay. I still fancy you just as much naked." He races on while her expression is still trying to work out whether he's paid her a compliment or not. "Now, where do you want me?"

"Th-the bed I suppose." So he allows her to lead him there and lay him down.

"Your hour starts now."

Her Reward

Ella Jane puts her hand on his hip, sliding across his warm skin towards his eager appendage as she sidles up to asking the question that rises in her mind, but she stops with her fingertips just short. "Won't this be frustrating for you?"

He shrugs. "If you want it to be. A less self-aware or a less honest man might say *You have no idea,* but I'm pretty sure you do."

She puzzles. "So I can take revenge for your teasing?"

"You *can,* but you *may* wish to consider that I'll be playing with you next, and that you have a punishment coming in the morning."

"That's not f...." She lets her voice fade. "But it is, isn't it?"

"Yes." He takes her hand from his hip and kisses its palm. "It is." His look of triumph is as wicked as the touch of his hand is warm. He places a fingertip on the end of her nose. "Of course, it's all up to you." And he lies back.

She begins slowly, tentatively, more so than has been her habit when touching him, or indeed any previous man. This is different though. She has been told she can play with his cock, and she has an hour, her hour. Although she has no wish to give him cause to make his own play or her punishment more frustrating or painful than she can bear, she has that hour in which to enjoy and to give.

She begins with a microscopic inspection with hands, eyes, and mouth from perineum to tip. Then she draws his foreskin slowly back, watching the opening stretch then circling his emerging glans with the tip of her tongue. Once she has the protective sheath of velvety skin fully retracted, she traces each vein with her lips and takes him into her mouth. She rises, moves forward, and takes him inside herself.

For some time, she experiments with transferring him from her mouth to her opening and back, tensing her muscles around or her tongue against him and seeing which actions make his tip swell with desire.

Having enjoyed herself thus for a time, she takes a leaf from his book. She lays towels across the huge bed and slathers his cock and her body with oil, sliding it between her buttocks and her labia, between her breasts, and into herself. She licks, kisses, and caresses every millimetre of his foreskin and of his root, familiarising her hands, mouth, and body with all of him. She chuckles to herself when she finds ways of touching him that draw sounds from his lips and movements from his body. She's especially fascinated by those touches that make the seemingly independent awareness of his cock itself surge and swell.

Ella Jane's well over halfway through her play time when she gets distracted by the sensations in her own body while sitting astride him and sliding back and forth with his erect shaft between her outer lips, leaning just far enough forwards to put a pleasant pressure on the centre of her pleasure.

"A-hem."

She knows she's been caught but doesn't stop, preferring to open her eyes, smile and answer, "Yes, Sir?"

"You're supposed to be playing with my cock."

"Mmm, so I am." She adds more oil to her hands and rubs her palms across the head of his cock at the end of each rock of her hips, making sure the knuckles of her thumbs run long her mons as she does.

This new variation draws appreciative sounds from his lips, and, with her time running low, she decides to incorporate it into the planned finale she's been slowly developing.

She adds this slow pressure and drawn-out contact between their swollen eager sexes and her hands to her pattern, along with using her mouth, then her hands before taking him inside. She rises up and leans back so the crown of his cock rubs the sensitive places inside her pubic bone. As she continues with this, she experiments with gripping her muscles and her fingers as hard as she is able and driving her full weight down onto his solidity. She then rubs him along her opening and her hands over his tip and her pubic bone. Finally, she draws his foreskin back and presses his cock's tiny lips to the head of her clit and circles.

By varying the time and force she uses, she's able to set herself on the path, and judging from the pulsing and twitching of his cock and the sounds from his lips, she guesses she succeeds in doing the same for him.

His hands half reach up to her breasts, half reach down to her hips. He wants to guide her hands on his cock but each time, he forces himself to lay his arms down and to surrender control of both their pleasure to her, no matter how close he gets or hears and sees her getting.

The minutes tick by and the hour mark passes, and he doesn't tell her, even though by the rules of the game he should.

Ella Jane though is focused. After the hours of teasing and excitement throughout the day, after the days of him controlling each of her many orgasms, she works herself to the edge of the precipice and then concentrates on the pleasure of his cock, rather than her enjoyment of it.

She feels his first convulsion coming as she slides his cock's tiny lips around her pearl. Rather than make him cum in her mouth or inside her, she lets the first wave of his eruption escape against her before taking the second in her mouth and the third and subsequent ones inside herself as her fingertips draw out her own ecstasy.

When they stir, Ella Jane is astride him with her head nestled under his chin and he's still inside her.

"Did you like the first part of your reward?"

"I did." She looks up, moves and discovers they're a little stuck together by a layer of oil and their mingled sweat and essences.

"You do know you overran, don't you."

"Oh, sorry."

He dissolves in laughter, and his hardness twitches inside her as his muscles shake. At first, she doesn't see the funny side, but his laughter is infectious.

Eventually she calms enough to tell him she hates him, which only serves to set them off again. But the second time they stop laughing, she tells him she forgives him. He presses his lips to the top of her head instead of releasing another wave of amusement.

He strokes her back idly until eventually he breaks the silence. "Well?"

The still tingling Ella Jane buries her face in his chest and tries to delay the told-you-so moment. "Well, what?"

"Are you ready for the second half of your reward?"

Ella Jane coos, "That depends...," and snuggles against his warmth.

"On?"

She props herself up so she can look him in the face. "If I say not yet, do I lose it?"

"No...."

"And if I say yes, does that get me out of you saying you told me so?"

"No." He tries and fails to look aghast at the suggestion. "But you just gave the game on that away, so I won't. Not yet anyway."

"Then not yet." And she kisses his chest, then lies back down on top of him contentedly.

She stays there until he softens inside her, and her back starts to feel cool. "Do you get cold after when you're on top?"

"Never yet with you. Why?"

"No reason."

"You could pull the covers over yourself or have the rest of your reward." He reaches out to the bedside and snags a bottle of chilled water, which he drinks from and teases her by holding it over her until a drop of condensation drips onto her skin. "Want some?"

"Yes, please." Ella Jane twists as far round as she can, and he tips the bottle to her lips. Inevitably some spills onto him, and he retaliates by pouring a little onto her skin. She yelps in response and protests, "Are you going to torment me until I let you play with my breasts?"

"What a good idea!" He kisses her lips although they're still a tight line of annoyance. "Or you could be as much the submissive as you claim to be and accept your reward with good grace."

"That's a low blow, Sir." His eyebrows rise, and she concedes, "Except it isn't, is it?" She pecks his cheek and slides off him.

"No, a harsher dominant would cancel your reward, instead of...."

She rushes out, "Instead of adding to my punishment?"

"Precisely." He rolls over her, kisses the end of her nose, then the tips of her breasts, and finally her mouth. "But that can wait until morning. I've been looking forward to rewarding you." With that, he goes to his bedside cabinet and rummages around until he finds a pair of cuffs, some steel spring clips, and a leather strap with steel rings set into its ends.

"Do you strictly have to tie me up in order to play with my breasts?"

"No, but you like being restrained, and I enjoy binding you up."

"By that token, you'd never untie me."

"Don't give me ideas; do give me your wrists."

When she offers her arms up, he shows her how the quick release clips work and attaches the cuffs in such a way that she can reach them and free herself.

Ella Jane watches him demonstrate how she can escape, and, knowing how fastidious he tries to be about ensuring she is utterly at his mercy when he puts her in bondage she asks, "Doesn't this spoil it for you?"

"It changes it. This way you're choosing to stay in bondage you can physically escape from."

"And you aren't worried I'll escape?"

He sidles close to her. "Usually you have to trust me to respect your safe word and limits and to release you at the end of a scene. Tonight, I'll have to trust you to stay in bondage."

"Is that so?"

"It is."

"And why should I do that?"

"Because it would make me happy, and because you like being told you're a good girl."

She allows him to secure her to the bed. He has her escape and binds her again. Then with her stretched out naked, he runs his hands down the lengths of her arms and the sides of her body and takes the lid from the coconut oil. The white waxy oil melts quickly as he works it between his warm hands and spreads silkily as he adds to the residue of her earlier application.

Her lips let out a number of *Oohs* and *Ohs* as he spreads the oil, and when she comments that he's straying from her breasts, they let out some *Ows* as well. In the main though, he remains at his gentlest, stroking to and around her breasts and down to her thighs. He's only straying to more remote parts of her body when, in her need, she arches or rolls to press herself into his hands and forearms, and then returning as she surrenders into powerlessness.

Time passes, and he shows no urgency. Ella Jane voices complaint as his hands move away from her breasts, and though she spreads her legs in invitation, his hands pass by her eager opening. She earns herself a flat-palmed smack to her mons and a low chuckle, but other than that, she makes no impression on his patience.

His lips circle, barely grazing against her aureoles. Then he pulls back breathing hot breath onto her swollen buds. After reaching across into his seemingly bottomless supply of delightfully wicked things, he shows her two bright Wartenberg pinwheels. He roles them over her the swells of her breasts so lightly they give just the barest sense of their needle sharpness and sets them aside as he resumes his tantalisingly slow and infuriatingly peripheral caresses.

His next variation is stroking from her back to the sides of her breasts with his open hands, alternating between one hand on each side of her body and both hands working together on one side. Then he moves to the other side, always moving with a slow, patient power. When he passes over the centres of her breasts, he raises his hands while remaining close enough for her to feel his warmth and yearns towards it. Eventually he does begin to touch the engorged tips of her breasts but at first only with the most feather-light circling of the palms of his hands.

His use of the fiendish little wheels becomes bolder too. He rolls them closer to the tips of her breasts, and she arches to press herself against them. Then, when he lifts them away, she cries out another frustrated complaint in the hope that his chastisement will tip her over the edge into ecstasy. But her cry is to no avail. He seems lost in his enjoyment of her.

On setting the shiny spur like toys aside, his hands return to her breasts, circle and press more boldly, and teasingly stretch their tips. He massages her buds, pinching lightly from their sides and drawing them still further from her body. He abandons each breast in turn to massage, stretch, and caress the other with both hands and then returns, continuing until her body quakes and the rising crescendo is nearly on her. Then he abandons both and slides his palms and forearms down her slick sides to her knees. Lifting her legs, he reaches behind and cups and kneads her buttocks. He then lowers the left leg and massages around her rosebud with the strong base of a thumb, strokes up the length of her outter labia, and presses heavy power down onto her pubic bone.

For a seeming age, he repeats this caress, swapping which of her legs he holds up and which side he caresses whenever the pace or catch of her breathing hints that she is getting too close.

Eventually he tires of this game, and she is able to rouse no more than a whimper of regret as he lays both her legs down and glides his hands back up her body to resume his earlier teasing.

It takes him a time to rekindle the sweet, congested warmth and sense of over-fullness in her breasts, but he seems to pay no heed to time. He's regrasped the pinwheel and focuses on her as his hands and his gleaming spiked wheel rolls over and press into her sensitive flesh. She cries out her frustration as the timer on his phone starts chiming, but his motion doesn't stop. With each cycle of teasing, the sense builds in her that her breasts are close to eruption, and with each flicker of his gaze from his work to her eyes, the sense that a fire in him is reaching for the one growing within her becomes stronger.

His breathing deepens. A sheen of sweat forms on his chest, matching that she feels on her own skin and multiplying the oil's slickness. Her heat rises still further and burns away the sense of pain as he runs the little wheels over the swollen tips of her breasts, pressing their sharp spikes deep into her flesh, and replaces that pain with the feeling of a final rise towards the heights of passions. Then he takes a hold of her breasts, squeezes, draws the buds away from her, forcing her to arch as far as she is able, and rolls them between his forefingers and thumbs.

The shockwaves that rise and run through her reach down and up and then return to their unfamiliar starting points and echo there only to spread again as his now once again gentle hands continue their ministrations.

When Ella Jane moves again, she finds her wrists are no longer linked. "You freed me!"

"I did."

She snuggles against him. "You overran too."

"Was that a complaint?"

"No, Sir. More of a thank you." She takes one of his hands and kisses its palm, then takes the tips of each finger into her mouth and sucks the coconutty sweetness of his skin. "So long as you aren't going to be even more insufferably smug."

He lets out a sudden burst of laughter. "Could I be?" He rolls on top of her, taking a hold of her cuffs in one hand, pinning her wrists together, and stretching her arms above her, and enters her.

As they lie together afterwards in the small hours, he enquires, "You didn't mind going to the range today?"

"No, it was interesting."

"Interesting but not fun, or...?"

"And fun. It was fun shooting and learning more about it. That gun was amazing and scarily easy to aim. It felt like a part of my body. And watching the two of you was mad too. Are you sure you were never in the army?"

"Johnson? Very! Me? I wasn't even a cadet." He squeezes her to his side and touches his lips to her. "How was it interesting?"

"Going to an indoor shooting school and...."

"Yes?"

"It was interesting seeing you not being in charge."

"I wasn't in charge at the conference."

"You were in charge when you wanted to be. I think that's why that awful woman got so upset."

"And when I didn't want to be?"

"You were flirting with me or ordering the parts to build your own private dungeon in your suite." She narrows one eye unconsciously as gauges his reaction and continues only when his smirk and shrug let her know he's accepted her point. "Other than that, everyone was fawning all over you or ignoring you so studiously anyone could tell you were the centre of their thoughts."

He shrugs again. "And at the range?"

"You let Johnson take over."

"Ah." He nods. "Can I let you in on a little secret?"

Ella Jane leans forwards. "Is it about your mysterious past or his?"

His *Neither*, is quite final. "For one thing, I don't have a mysterious past."

"Oh."

"So you don't want to know?"

"I do...I just hoped."

"Well, I'd wind up looking pretty stupid if I tried to pretend I know more about guns or shooting than he does. As much as I hate not being in charge, I hate looking stupid more."

Her Sweet Punishment

Ella Jane groans when she registers movement, then smiles when the scent of fresh coffee percolates through to her consciousness and blinks her eyelids open. What she sees makes her groan again. He's standing by the bed wearing gym kit. "Are you going to make me train before you punish me?" His spreading smile answers her. "You are, aren't you?"

He passes her coffee and sips his own. "I'm going to let you drink your coffee first. After that, shall we say, how hard you work may have a significant impact on how much you enjoy your punishment?"

"It's only supposed to be for doing more than you said!"

"I did, didn't I?" His face assumes its usual unrepentant expression. "If you think about it, then it should have the potential to be very funishmenty indeed. If you don't mess it up by slacking-off on your training."

Ella Jane grumbles "You are such a slave driver!" but smiles into her coffee cup as soon as she's said it.

He doesn't give her a moment to lie and prepare herself. As soon as she finishes her coffee, he whips the covers from the bed and, when she doesn't jump, the flat of his hand lands soundly on her thigh.

This morning he changes things around so they face each other for the more complex exercises, and that, together with her greater familiarity enables her to get them right faster. Thus, she receive more smiles and strokes from his hands and fewer of those from his whip make her yelp with pain rather than gasp at forbidden thrills.

She basks in his praise for her improvements, but misses the frequent sharp, bright sensations of impact on her skin and the firm, calm way in which he coaches her on how to do better that often follows being so frequent as during her first sessions.

Despite her improvements, she's weary when he brings the session to a close and her focus quickly melts into the soothing way he towels the perspiration from her skin and the pleasant heat that it kindles.

When she's reciprocated and he's stopped her progressing from towelling to canoodling, he takes her back to the bed and secures her ankles to the wide spreader bar again. This time though, he doesn't bring her to orgasm, he just edges her and then raises the subject of her pending chastisement. He speaks while she's still kneeling, having cleaned the sweat from his thighs. "I think it would be sensible to address your failure last night, don't you?" The voice he uses is his deepest and softest, the one that touches through to her bones with a solicitous gentleness.

It instantly affects her breathing and heart rate. "As you wish, Sir."

He squats down in front of her and strokes her cheek. "Do you accept that you kept the yoni egg inside you for two acts rather than one?"

"Yes, Sir."

"Good girl, and do you agree with me that there was no malice in your disobedience?"

There's a temptation to disagree, to see how harsh he might be, but there's also the plain truth that there had been none. "Yes, Sir."

He leads her into the suite's dining room where his long, heavy suede flogger has been arranged artfully on the table and asks her to adopt inspection pose while he prepares. She positions herself to one side of the doors and faces the room with her legs spread and fingers interlaced behind her neck. Though she watches, rather than keeping her eyes downcast, as he takes four of the chairs from around the table and places them carefully. The arrangement, two touching side by side facing the other two just less than her body's length away and a little over a foot apart facing inwards, is sufficiently obvious to her that when he signals for her to move, she knows his intention and is able to kneel in place with her knees on the separated pair and her elbows on the touching ones without further instruction.

She sets her elbows on the side-by-side chairs and her knees on the other pair. The position is as comfortable as it is lewd. Her hands are just over shoulder width apart and her knees a little wider, leaving her openings and her breasts free for whatever *funishmenty punishment* he might have in mind.

He continues to use his bedroom voice. "Well done. Now, you agree that the punishment should fit the crime?"

"Yes, Sir."

"And the crime was a lack of attention to detail and having something in one of your sexual openings for longer than instructed?" As he interrogates her, his hands run over her skin with long, firm strokes and light caresses.

Ella Jane sighs under his touch and the hypnosis of his voice but manages another ritual. "Yes, Sir."

"So something to chastise and something to remind you...." He leans over her, wraps one arm under her breasts, and reaches around her with the other to lightly cup her open vulva. "That your body belongs to me, and not to you."

It isn't something they've agreed, but she had asked him to act as though he had the right, and it's hard to have willingly placed herself in this position and be held so and not let her submissive soul take over. "If you please, Sir."

He kisses the top of her head and breathes, "Good girl." He strokes her back one last time. "Now hold still, and this will soon be over.

He doesn't speak further as he kneels, teases the tips of her breasts to even greater hardness and applies a clover clamp to each.

Ella Jane tenses against the pain as he lets her breasts take the weight of the clamps and looks down as she surrenders herself to it. The clamps are linked by a chain, and the chain has three sections, each ending in a clamp. It doesn't take a woman of her intelligence to know where the third is going, and it doesn't take him long to attach it over her hooded clit.

The tension, the weight of the clamp, and that of the connecting chains apply when he releases this third clamp is less familiar and more intense, but he isn't finished. He carefully tests that each of the three has a firm grip on her by applying steady pulls to them that stretch her trapped buds and hooded clit further than the clamp's weight alone before resuming his caresses and praising her for holding pose. Satisfied, he moves away, and she closes her eyes in expectation of either the sound of the flogger moving through the air or that of his voice instructing her to count.

With her eyes closed, she doesn't see what he's really doing. Only when she feels his warmth close to her nakedness does she open her eyes and see the wand. She watches with puzzlement as he attaches it to the chains, winces as he lets her body's most sensitive parts take its weight, and gasps as he turns it on. Its vibrations travel along the taut lengths of chain and into her stretched buds.

Her world shrinks down to her immediate existence: the four chairs, her body above them, raised, open, offered, the pain of the clamps and stretching, the erotic tension they apply, and above these the vibrations and the liquid fire they send through her.

She registers his hand on the small of her back and hears his voice, though she doesn't hear him say, "Do your best to hold still." She sees the hardness of desire that his workout shorts fail to hide, looks up for a moment, and half registers or half imagines the lust in his face.

And then the flogger falls across her back and across her buttocks and across her thighs. Its falls wrap and bite tender flesh intimately and with sweet force.

He doesn't whip her hard.

Doesn't make her count.

Doesn't rush.

Doesn't speak.

He just whips her long and slow. He whips her until the warmth and thud and bite of the falls on her skin and the tension and vibrations are more than her shrunken world can contain, and then whips on as her world explodes.

Ella Jane registers him removing the clamps and lifting her, his warmth against her, him enfolding her, but nothing more than those things until his, "Hey, wake up. Breakfast's getting cold," and the rich aromas of coffee, bacon, toast, and pastries.

His Forgiveness

S he accepts the cup and his kiss. Then she nearly spits some of the coffee out when she sees the time. "I really zonked out!"

He chuckles. "You were dead to the world, but you have had a busy few days."

"I'm so sorry. What did you do while I was gone?"

"This morning? I ignored my emails and did some writing." His lips find hers. "You should do some while New York is fresh in your mind. Try to set down a few notes about the place."

Ella Jane, whose first book had been about a young woman far more innocent than herself and certainly far more innocent than her last several days and nights, answers with a curt, "I'm not sure Abigail is quite the sort for this kind of coming of age!"

He folds the covers back in a hint to get up now. "She would still have her first experience of a big city, and you could always pen the beginnings of something with a more worldly central character."

When she rises, Ella Jane goes to the robes, reaches out to hers, smiles over her shoulder, and then scoots to the door, managing to do so just fast enough that her bum escapes the pursuing palm of his right hand.

Over her first and second what are clearly at least his second and third helpings he steers their conversation to experiences of New York, and those of its sights they have yet to experience together. She mutters at first, but he brings her laptop in and makes a point of opening his while he continues to talk.

He goes to the kitchen, and when he returns with fresh coffees, Ella Jane's computer screen remains dark. The firmness with which he sets her cup down suggests he isn't impressed, but the way he slides his warmed hand into her robe and uses it to cup a breast, flooding it with heat while he bends and kisses her beneath her ear sets her body humming. He keeps up the kiss and caress until she leans back against him before taking a firmer hold of the tip of her captive breast and growling, "It's a good job for you we're only playing at this little one, or your failure to do as I suggested would have resulted in a rather less enjoyable punishment."

"Do I have to?"

"No, but I'm going to do a little, and if we were in a dynamic, I'd expect you to." He then repeats his neck kiss and resumes his tender ministrations inside her robe.

It isn't as if she hasn't seen and done things she wants to write down, and his touch and that voice he uses are kind of persuasive. "Not all day though?"

His hand's movement on her skin suggests that he has other plans for much of the day ahead. "I certainly don't intend to write all day."

Credits

My thanks to Kate, Allie, Maria, Mira and others for their years of encouragement, and to those who have told me I'm the naughtiest man they've ever met.

I'd also like to thank Maria, Erin and Leanne at All Write Well without whom Ella Jane's may well have remained an ever-growing but never-heard story.

Also By

Continue to follow Ella Jane's explorations in **Ella Jane Book Two: Exploring with Him**

Having moved into his hotel suite, Ella Jane stays with him for the holiday part of his time in New York, and begins to appreciate the implications of his wealth and power. She encounters more of the people in his world, and they each discover more of the other's deliciously wicked ways.

While they get to know one another, and begin to face the possibility of a longer dalliance, others manoeuvre to push them together or apart for their own ends. Be sure to pick up your copy now.

Get it here: https://mybook.to/ExploringWithHim

If you enjoyed reading about Ella Jane, you may enjoy **Meredith's Journey Begins**

Meredith Webb has built herself a pleasant, though unchallenging life, with a decent job she doesn't strive too hard at. Oh, and she has two cats she loves very much.

William Farrow on the other hand, knows there's something missing from his.

Reader Comments:

"A richly crafted journey into passion"

"Tantalisingly teasing"

"Stylish, smart and captivating! Sprinkled with moments of spine tingling awkwardness and evocativeness."

Get it here: https://mybook.to/MeredithsJourneyBegins

About Author

Edward has written technical papers and articles that have been read by millions. Now he turns his writing talents to the world of erotic romance by applying his thirty years of experience in massage therapy, fine dining, and as a bdsm practitioner to create stories with a uniquely rich sensuality.

In **Meredith's Journey**, he creates a relatable world with characters you might meet in the street. Meanwhile, in **Him and Her, the Ella Jane Stories** he tells a tale of exotic, high-living beauty, and in the **Black Choker Diaries** he investigates the pleasures and pitfalls of a three person love story.

Each is crafted in a way that will leave you begging for more.

Ingram Content Group UK Ltd.
Milton Keynes UK
UKHW020343300523
422450UK00009B/92